Edward of the designer suits,
Gabe Stone of the Stone's book dynasty
and boy next door C. D. Valentine
are in for the shock of their lives.
In fact, life as they know it is about to end,
and a whole new precious one will begin,
once each meets their

Valentine
Babies

Anne Stuart has, in her twenty-five years as a published author, won every major award in the business, appeared on various bestseller lists, been quoted by *People*, *USA Today* and *Vogue*, appeared on *Entertainment Tonight* and warmed the hearts of readers worldwide. She has written more than thirty novels for Harlequin and Silhouette, plus another thirty or more suspense and historical titles for other publishers. When asked to describe herself, she has said, "Anne Stuart has written lots of books in lots of genres for lots of publishers. She lives with her splendid husband and two magnificent children in the hills of Northern Vermont, where it snows so much, she hasn't much else to do but write."

Tara Taylor Quinn's love affair with Harlequin Books began when she was fourteen years old and picked up a free promotional copy of a Harlequin Romance novel in her hometown grocery store. Shortly thereafter, she was suspended from her high school typing class for hiding a Harlequin Romance book behind the keys of her electric typewriter! Ten years later, she was hired as a stringer for the *Dayton Daily News*, and taught high school English before turning to writing full-time. Her first novel, *Yesterday's Secrets*, was published as a Superromance title in 1993, and was a finalist for the Romance Writers of America RITA Award. She is now busily working on her thirteenth novel, and will be featured in the Maitland Maternity continuity series later this year.

Jule McBride received the *Romantic Times* Reviewer's Choice Award in 1993 for Best First Series romance, and ever since has continued to pen heartwarming love stories that have met with rave reviews, been nominated for awards and made repeated appearances on romance bestseller lists. A native of West Virginia, she is a two-time Reviewer's Choice nominee for Best American Romance, and has also been nominated for a Lifetime Achievement Award in the category of Love and Laughter. With more than twenty novels to her credit in six short years, she is definitely a star on the rise!

Valentine Babies

ANNE STUART

TARA TAYLOR QUINN

JULE McBRIDE

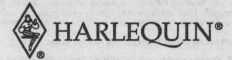

HARLEQUIN®

TORONTO • NEW YORK • LONDON
AMSTERDAM • PARIS • SYDNEY • HAMBURG
STOCKHOLM • ATHENS • TOKYO • MILAN • MADRID
PRAGUE • WARSAW • BUDAPEST • AUCKLAND

ISBN 0-373-83429-2

VALENTINE BABIES

Copyright © 2000 by Harlequin Books S.A.

The publisher acknowledges the copyright holders
of the individual works as follows:

GODDESS IN WAITING
Copyright © 2000 by Anne Kristine Stuart Ohlrogge

GABE'S SPECIAL DELIVERY
Copyright © 2000 by Tara Lee Reames

MY MAN VALENTINE
Copyright © 2000 by Julianne Randolph Moore

This edition published by arrangement with Harlequin Books S.A.

® and TM are trademarks of the publisher. Trademarks indicated with
® are registered in the United States Patent and Trademark Office, the
Canadian Trade Marks Office and in other countries.

Visit us at www.romance.net

Printed in U.S.A.

CONTENTS

GODDESS IN WAITING
Anne Stuart

For my cousin, Ginny Doroshuk,
and the wonderful women (and men)
of the Sew Abundant on-line sewing list,
and most of all, for Vladimir, the Bulgarian Serger.

Prologue

MARY WAS IN A VERY BAD mood. Jordan had already left, eons ago, but then, time meant little in the strange, cloudlike limbo where she waited. It might have been a century, it might have been a heartbeat since her best friend and cousin had vanished—leaving her alone, waiting for the summons that never came.

She knew where she belonged. She'd been clear and certain about it since she'd first begun to formulate thoughts. Known, too, that Jordan would always be her best friend and companion, an annoyance and a treasure.

What she hadn't known was that he'd go first. Or that she'd be so terribly alone.

Oh, they said it was a good place, and she supposed it was. A safe, warm cocoon where she could while away the immeasurable hours until she was called.

One thing was for sure, she wasn't going to be happy about having to wait so long. She intended to let everyone know how irritable she was about the whole situation. Loudly, noisily, endlessly, until she made their lives as miserable as they'd made hers.

And then she'd forgive them. That was all she wanted. A chance to breathe the air, to feel arms wrapped safely around her. She was willing to endure anything for that, anything at all.

She just wished they'd hurry up with it. She was getting very tired of waiting.

Chapter One

IT WAS CHAOS AS USUAL at Goddess in Waiting. Tanya was in tears over a botched seam, Ellie was in the bathroom throwing up, still dealing with morning sickness in her sixth month of pregnancy, and Pam was nowhere to be seen. There were two customers in the parlor of the old Victorian house that served as living quarters, storefront, factory and shelter for unwed mothers. The telephone was ringing, and Marike could see the truck from the electric company heading their way. She'd probably forgotten to pay the bill, she thought with an air of calm desperation. That would just top off the day beautifully.

She couldn't stop Ellie from throwing up, nothing but time would take care of that little problem, and Tanya, another pregnant teen, was emotional enough to weep over a dog food commercial, and God only knew where Pam was. Whoever was on the phone would call back, and it would take at least five minutes for the electric company to get to her door. She could deal with the customers first.

She identified them immediately as first-timers, a serene, newly pregnant woman and her panicked husband. Odd, but most of the husbands seemed absolutely terrified no matter how often they'd been through this. But it was the first-timers who were particularly pathetic.

"We've come for maternity clothes," the young man blurted as she approached them. He took a good look at her and turned slightly green around the gills.

"She knows that, Edward," the wife said patiently. "Why else would we be here?"

"Let me take care of this, sweetie," he said to his wife, turning back to Marike. "She needs something…pretty," Edward continued, his voice high-pitched with strain. "Maybe little flowers?"

Marike had a great dislike of tiny flowers adorning pregnant bodies, and an even greater dislike of husbands managing their wives' pregnancies. "For you or your wife?" she murmured sweetly.

Edward subsided into a choked silence, and Sweetie patted him soothingly on the arm. She was going to be a very good, patient mother,

Marike decided approvingly. Sweetie met her gaze with a conspiratorial smile. "What do you suggest? We only just found out, but Edward was determined that we needed to spring into action, and he's a little rattled."

Marike felt a brief pang of sympathy for the poor man. As long as he allowed Sweetie to handle things then Marike could be generous. She looked down at the two of them from her impressive height. "If you've only just discovered you're pregnant then you should have plenty of time to think about clothes. Why don't the two of you come into the tearoom and one of the girls will make you some nice herbal tea with honey while you look at some of the designs."

Edward still looked rattled. He stared up at her with a faintly hunted expression, and she could smell tobacco smoke on him. She arranged her mobile face into a frown. "And no smoking," she said to him.

"I never smoke in other people's houses without asking," he replied, affronted.

She shook her head. Her hair was magenta this week, a startling sight for the poor man. "You don't understand. No smoking anywhere. You don't want your baby breathing secondhand smoke."

"For God's sake, we've only just come from the doctor!" he cried.

"Good. Now's the time to quit." She held out her palm to him, waiting patiently.

It took less time than it usually did. The pack of cigarettes was placed in her strong, well-shaped hand, and she crushed it effortlessly. "Your life is about to change, Edward," she said in a soothing voice. "Might as well begin now."

Sweetie was looking at the two of them in absolute astonishment. Edward had already wandered into the tearoom, a glazed expression in his eyes. "How did you do that?" Sweetie whispered. "I thought I was going to have to make a major battle of it."

Marike smiled down at her. "It's a gift," she said in her deep, slow voice. "You just have to show them who's boss."

The electric company was almost as easy. They'd gotten used to her by now—whenever they showed up to turn the power off she'd charm them with cups of tea and rueful promises to behave herself. After all, it wasn't as if she couldn't pay the electric bill, even for her expensive monstrosity of a Victorian house. She just wasn't very good about attending to details.

By the time that crisis was dealt with, and Mrs. Peterson—whose name was Grace, not Sweetie—had chosen three striking outfits over her husband's mumbled objections, it was nearly lunchtime. After Marike carefully steered Grace away from an inappropriate Gypsy-style dress better suited for an Amazon such as herself, she shooed the couple out the door. The next thing she knew, Pam had shown up, looking only slightly guilty, Tanya had ripped out the botched hem and begun working with newfound cheer, and Ellie had managed to eat a few crackers and wanly answer the phone.

Marike shoved a hand through her thick, wavy hair. Maybe she'd just go upstairs during lunch and shave it all off. She felt restless, edgy, when she usually prided herself on her calm. Her horoscope had said that great changes lay in store for her, but she only tended to believe in horoscopes when it suited her, and she wasn't sure if she was ready for any changes. Her life was quite pleasant now that Daniel was completely out of it. He and his new wife had moved to the east coast, and if the skinny bitch got pregnant, Marike wouldn't have to know about it. She could get on with her life.

She was usually better than this when dealing

with crisis-strewn days. So an entire bolt of hand-painted batik had been ruined—it wasn't the end of the world. So her water heater had given out for the third time this week, the roof was leaking, Tanya had almost fallen through the back stairs, and it cost a fortune to heat the old mausoleum. Things could be worse, had been worse, more times than Marike cared to remember.

She had the huge old house, part sanctuary, part albatross, around her neck. She had the girls for company, and when one was ready to leave the nest and make it on her own, there'd be others to take her place. In truth, none of the young girls ever left her life completely. They always came back, bringing their babies and their woes and their triumphs.

She had enough money to house the girls and pay them. She had enough money to meet her bills. She was healthy, creative, independent. So what was wrong with her today?

It's true, her life could be unpredictable and a bit crazy, but her childhood had been far from conventional. As the only child of an eccentric single mother she'd lived a solitary, rootless life, and she'd always thought it was what suited her best.

Which didn't explain why she'd married the first, totally unsuitable man she'd met.

And didn't explain why, in a desperate need to give herself roots, she'd spent her entire nest egg on a falling-down house.

Well, she had roots now. A home, even a family in the girls who came to stay and learn and work. There was no husband, of course. He was gone, thank heavens.

So why did her life feel so damned empty all of a sudden? And why did she want to run away?

The phone rang again, and this time Pam picked it up, chipper and upbeat as she nibbled on a chocolate bar. "Marike?" she said into the phone. "I'll see if she's available." She put her hand over the receiver and caught Marike's eye. "It's someone named William Lambert."

Marike shook her head violently. She wasn't in the mood to deal with bill collectors or officious husbands at the moment. "Tell him I've gone out."

"I thought you said lying only got you into trouble," Tanya said, looking up from the computerized sewing machine she was trying to outsmart.

"I'm not lying," Marike said, grabbing her

orchid-hued ruana and tossing it around her shoulders. "Hold the fort," she said. And a moment later she was out in the frosty winter air, temporarily, blissfully free.

WILLIAM LAMBERT slammed down the phone, glaring at it. The day had gone from bad to worse, and he saw no signs of imminent improvement. The sky was leaden outside his Chicago office building, the vast expanse of windows letting in nothing but the murky light of a gloomy winter's day. And nothing was going as he'd planned.

He'd been at work since 6:00 a.m. this morning, his usual time. He'd gotten out of the habit of sleeping in, and besides, he didn't like sleeping alone. He wasn't crazy about sleeping with other people, either, for that matter. Maybe it all boiled down to the fact that he didn't like sleeping, period. It was a waste of time, when there were already too many things to fill what time there was.

Thelma must have sensed his frustration. His always-dependable executive assistant was trying to duck out of his way when he stormed out of his office. "I told you I'm not doing it," she said flatly.

"Thelma, you're a woman. You understand about these things." He tried to make his voice sound conciliatory. Thelma, the young woman who'd worked for him for the past five years, wasn't fooled.

"I don't know nothin' 'bout birthing babies, Mr. Lambert," she shot back, paraphrasing the line from *Gone With the Wind* in an exaggerated Southern accent. "And I'm not about to go shopping for maternity clothes for your sister. Rick and I haven't been dating for that long, and word would get back to him, I know it would. Besides, pregnancy gives me hives."

"I'm not asking you to get pregnant, Thelma. I'm asking you to go to this designer and pick out some clothes for Lindsay. Is that so much to ask?"

"Yup," Thelma said, pushing her tawny mane of hair back from her gorgeous face. "And if you're so worried about Lindsay then you can go yourself. I found the woman's name for you—what more do you want? Don't answer that—I'm not going."

Will stared at her in frustration, knowing he was trapped. Thelma was smart, beautiful and as tough as he was in negotiations. There were times when he thought she was better suited to

run Lambert Publications and its stable of upscale magazines than he was. He certainly
couldn't do it without her.

"Thelma…" he began again in a more plain-
tive voice, hoping to soften her up.

Thelma didn't have a soft bone in her perfectly proportioned body. "No. And don't
bother asking Susan, either—she won't do it."

"Who's Susan?" he demanded, diverted by
another prospect for the task of saving him.

"She's the editor of *Sew Abundant*. She's the
one who found Marike and Goddess in Waiting.
But she's not going out there for you."

"Why not?"

"Because I told her not to. Time to grow up,
Lambert. Lindsay is your sister, and there are
times when simply writing a check won't do it.
I've canceled all your appointments for this afternoon, there are no imminent crises, and the
storm is supposed to miss us. You can drive out
to Derbyfield in half an hour, order a ridiculous
amount of clothing and be safely back in the city
before you get contaminated by the horrors of
the real world."

"Very funny," he grumbled. "Any particular
reason why you enjoy making me suffer?"

Thelma's smile would have turned a lesser

man into a doting slave. Will had known her for too long to be bewitched. "Time to grow up and face your responsibilities."

"I've been facing my responsibilities for the past ten years, ever since I inherited this company. You think I've been enjoying myself?"

"Probably as much as you would have been enjoying your law degree."

"What's that supposed to mean?" he snapped.

"When you figure it out, let me know," Thelma said sweetly.

"You're fired."

"You wish. You couldn't survive without me, Lambert," she said. "Go on out to Derbyfield and I'll keep things running properly. Don't I always?"

She did, in fact. She had better instincts about the magazine business than anyone he'd ever met in the ten years since he'd reluctantly inherited his father's mega corporation. She should have been old Wilhelm Lambert's child and heir.

"I'll go," he said finally, knowing when he'd lost the battle. "But I won't go happily."

Thelma's response was a smug, elegant smile.

HE LIKED DRIVING, and he sped along the high-way at a good clip, dividing his attention as he'd learned to do. While one part of his brain was cognizant of the traffic and the road, another part remembered his sister's teary conversation of last night. Remembered his frustration and horror at being asked to deal with emotions rather than facts. Lindsay was ten years younger than he was, happily married to a college professor at Northwestern, blissfully pregnant after three years of trying. Except that the bliss seemed to have faded. She was feeling huge, ugly, unlovable, ungainly and wretched. She had no one to talk to about it—even her husband Phil seemed impatient and distracted—and she needed her big brother to fix everything as he had when she was ten and he was twenty.

Even though she was twenty-five now, and had a life of her own, she had three months to go and he needed to do something to make it better. Just as he had when she was fifteen and their father had died of a sudden, massive stroke.

As Thelma had so wickedly put it, this time he couldn't write a check. He couldn't throw himself into work, propping up the corporation his father had founded, pushing and slaving and devoting his life to something he didn't really give a damn about. Of the dozen magazines Lambert Publications was responsible for, he barely glanced at any of them, other than *Historic Renovations.* For some reason the glossy pictures of old wood paneling and shiny power tools soothed him as nothing else could.

But his sister had depended on him, the countless employees of Lambert Publications had depended on him, so he'd kept it going, made it stronger through grit and sheer will. And managed to survive every empty minute of it.

He had to admit, though, as Thelma had also pointed out, he wouldn't have been any happier as a lawyer. At the age of thirty-five he was sick and tired of pushing paper and money around, and watching it grow. He was too young for midlife crises—those weren't supposed to happen for at least another five years. But his work gave him no pleasure. Very little did. He'd always enjoyed working with his hands, but where would that get him?

Making his sister happy was probably a step in the right direction. Otherwise why the hell was he driving his Lexus too fast on a February day when he should be stuck in the office making decisions he didn't care about?

He let his foot off the accelerator slightly.

Getting a ticket would make a bad day worse. He needed to find Goddess in Waiting, order some nice, sedate maternity clothes that would make his admittedly huge sister feel less conspicuous, and then get back to work before the entire day was shot. If he skipped lunch he wouldn't be that far behind.

He'd only had coffee for breakfast, but that wasn't unusual—he quite often forgot to eat. Food was usually an afterthought, and most nights he was too tired to do more than nuke a frozen dinner. Fortunately his housekeeper came three days a week and kept his freezer well stocked.

He got lost. Derbyfield was a small, determinedly cute town on the far outskirts of Chicago. Urban sprawl had turned most of it into a bedroom community, but the Victorian feel remained in the town, and the narrow, poorly marked streets changed his mood from bleak to furious. It was after one by the time he pulled up in front of the bizarre monstrosity that housed Goddess in Waiting. A light snow had begun to fall. And he was ready to kick something.

He stared up at the building in dismay. It was a Victorian gingerbread, four stories high, painted lavender, for pity's sake, with white and aqua and pink on the ornate trim. The soft colors were an abomination to the architecture. A house wasn't supposed to have a sense of humor, he thought grouchily.

The roof needed redoing, he could see that immediately. And some of the gingerbread trim on a third-floor balcony needed replacing. The owner should have put money into repairs instead of that absurd paint job.

However, it was none of his business. His job was to step inside that nightmare, order half a dozen maternity suits and dresses, and then get the hell out of there.

The front door was sky-blue, and there were white, fleecy clouds painted on it. In his current foul mood, he was half tempted to punch one of the clouds, but he settled for leaning on the old buzzer with a bit too much emphasis. In curlicued letters a sign on the door read Ring The Bell And Enter. For some reason he felt like Alice in Wonderland about to tumble down the rabbit hole. And he'd never been fond of steep drops.

He should have known that the inside of the building would be just as bizarre as the outside. Colors assaulted him, giving him a headache. To the left he could hear the sound of some kind of machinery, a low, rattling whir of noise. To the right was a parlor, a room that looked like a cross between a Victorian boudoir and a pasha's harem. There was a rack of clothes at one corner, and various dressmaker dummies adorned with exotic prints draped over their swollen tummies. And not a shred of sedate navy blue in sight.

"May we help you?" The teenager was small, shy, and heavily pregnant, with pale hair and pink cheeks.

The white rabbit, he thought dazedly. "M-maternity clothes," he stammered.

"Marike!" she shouted in an unrabbit-like screech. She smiled at him then with cheerful enthusiasm. "The boss will be down in a minute," she told him. "She's in a bad mood, so watch your step. Go on into the parlor and I'll bring you some herb tea."

"No, thanks."

"Marike insists," the girl said with a touch of anxiety. Marike must be a tyrant, he thought dazedly. The Queen of Hearts, perhaps?

"Then make it coffee."

The girl shook her head. "No caffeine. It's not good for pregnant women."

"I'm not pregnant."

She seemed to find that hysterically funny. "I'll see what I can find," she said, and he had no choice but to wander into the parlor, feeling gloomier than ever at the vibrant colors that surrounded him.

The windows of the parlor looked out over the winter-dead garden. The remains of a gazebo sat in the midst of it, a beautiful old structure that cried out for repair. Marike would probably paint it turquoise, he thought grumpily.

He needed to get the hell out of here. He sat on one of the hard sofas, shoving a tapestry pillow behind him. He glanced down at his Rolex, trying to stifle his impatience, when he realized he was no longer alone.

He looked up—way, way up—and it was only by sheer force of will that he kept his mouth from dropping open.

She had to be well over six feet tall. She had spiky hair the color of God knows what, and she was draped in a flowing blouse of some celestial fabric full of moons and stars. Beneath her jeans her long, narrow feet were bare.

She had an exotic face, with faintly slanted eyes, arched brows, a wide mouth and high cheekbones. She looked huge and magnificent and terrifying, and Will simply stared up at her, half expecting her to say, "Off with his head."

The Queen of Hearts had arrived and, now more than ever, he wished he'd never set foot into Goddess in Waiting.

Chapter Two

THE MAN UNFOLDED himself from her over-stuffed sofa, and Marike noted with some surprise that he was taller than she was. She should have worn shoes, but she tended to tower over all the husbands who came to see her, anyway, so she didn't always bother. This time she'd made a bit of a tactical error, but it wasn't crucial.

He had to be about six foot three, she guessed. A little too thin, but strong. The suit was Armani. She hated men in suits, especially after her short-lived marriage to Daniel, but this Armani was undeniably flattering. She checked out the suit and the body with professional dispassion, then made the mistake of looking into his face.

A thin, narrow, clever face, with hair too long and shaggy. The hair didn't go with the Armani or the Rolex she'd recognized, but it went with the face. There was an artistic streak in the bones, a yearning in his winter-gray eyes, which he tried to make flinty. She looked at him and for the first time in years she suddenly felt vulnerable.

"I'm Marike," she said abruptly, thrusting out her hand. She had big, strong, beautifully shaped hands. His were bigger. Stronger. More beautiful. She didn't like it.

He'd been in a bad mood when she arrived, she could read his body language as clear as day, but his mood seemed to have shifted, almost against his will, and a faint smile curved his mouth. Sexy mouth, she thought. Sexy hands, sexy body in an Armani suit. Thank God he was married.

"Where's your wife?" she inquired abruptly.

"I'm not married."

Bummer. Marike did her best to not pass judgment, but she was looking for a reason to dislike this man, even desperate to find an excuse to despise him. "Then your significant other," she said breezily. "Your partner, your girlfriend, the mother of your unborn child?"

"My sister," he said.

"Your sister's the mother of your unborn child? Do the police know?"

He blinked. At least she'd managed to startle him. His faint smile disappeared. "My sister and her husband are expecting their first child," he said with only a trace of irritation. "Her birthday is on Valentine's Day and I thought I'd get her some new clothes to cheer her up, make her feel, er, prettier. Something to make her feel smaller, maybe dark colors," he added helplessly as she continued to watch him. "A navy blue, perhaps?"

"With a little white collar?" she said sweetly.

He was too smart to be fooled by her dulcet tone. "No?" he said in an inquiring voice.

"No. This isn't Victorian England. Women don't hide their pregnancies and pretend children arrive by the stork. They grow them in their wombs, and the sight of a pregnant body is a miracle to be decorated and celebrated..."

"'Decorated'?" he echoed, clearly horrified at the notion.

"Would you prefer pregnant women went into seclusion, Mr....?"

He managed to look sheepish. "Lambert."

"So let me get this straight, Mr. Lambert. You were thinking a discreet navy blue for your sister. Any other thoughts?" She was setting him up, and he knew it, but it was clear he couldn't find a way to avoid it.

"Er...maybe something easy to take care of? Polyester? That's a material, isn't it?"

She took pity on him. "Sit down, Mr. Lambert, and I'll give you a crash course in women's clothing."

He didn't move. "I don't need a crash course in women's clothing. I have people who do that sort of thing. I just want to get my sister something to make her happy, and then get back to work."

She couldn't fault him there. He really did seem to care about his sister; despite the suit, he might not be past saving.

"Sit down, Mr. Lambert," she said again, adding a note of steel to her husky drawl.

Most men sat, and quickly, when she used that tone. Then again, she was taller than most men. Lambert simply cocked his head to one side and watched her with just the same sort of dispassionate interest she'd used on him. And then he stretched out on the sofa, crossing his legs, oddly at ease.

"Then instruct me," he said, reaching for the cup of espresso one of the girls had brought him. "This day's been shot to hell, anyway. And the name's Will."

"Will?" A little piece of the puzzle clicked into place. "William Lambert of Lambert Publications?"

"How did you know?"

"One of your magazines did a story on me last year. The piece was fine but I tend to be wary of what publicity I get, so I checked out Lambert Publications. The article I found said you were one of Chicago's most eligible bachelors. I didn't even realize they used the term bachelor anymore."

His gray eyes narrowed. "You don't like me much, do you? Is it just me, or do you always try to run off your customers?"

She should have frozen him out, but she couldn't help it. He was the worst possible man at the worst possible time, but even at her most threatened, Marike was scrupulously fair. "I try to intimidate most of my male clients," she said with a fair amount of cheer, taking the seat opsite him. "They have a bad habit of trying to ntrol their wives' pregnancies, and it irritates ᵊ. And I don't like men in suits, even when ᵉy're Armani."

He glanced down at his beautifully cut suit. ʼou've got a good eye."

"It's my business."

"I can take it off."

She blinked, but his smile was so innocent she decided it was nothing more than a joke. "I'll put up with it," she said. "Tell me about your sister. How tall is she? What's her coloring? How far along in her pregnancy? What does she love, what does she hate?"

"I want clothes for her, not a psychoanalysis."

She waited, showing only a trace of her impatience, and he gave in. "She's short. About five-seven."

"That's not short."

"It is in our family. She's got dark hair and pale skin. She's very sweet but she's also emotional and irrational and impetuous, even when she's not pregnant. Pregnancy makes it worse."

"It usually does. How far along is she?"

"Farther than you. I think she's about six months, but she's absolutely gigantic."

It wasn't the first time someone had made that mistake, Marike thought calmly, but it might very well be the last. "'Farther than me'?" she echoed in a deceptively calm voice.

"You're not pregnant," he said flatly, realizing his faux pas.

He was fast, she had to grant him that. "No."

"It's a logical assumption. All the women in your office are..."

"I train young women in a career so they can

support themselves and their children. I've been doing this for five years, Mr. Lambert. I could hardly be pregnant that long. It's not like we're cows that need to be freshened."

"You really don't like me, do you?"

Oh, but she did. That was the danger, Marike thought, wishing she could have bitten her tongue. "Sorry," she said in a deliberately breezy voice. "I've had a bad day. I don't suppose there's any way you can find out what size your sister usually wears, short of sneaking through her closets..."

"My assistant has that information. Along with her measurements, color preferences."

"I presume you usually have your assistant buy your presents," she said in a neutral voice. "Why didn't she take care of it this time?" *Because you're making a mess of it,* she wanted to add. But for the first time that afternoon Marike kept her tongue still.

"She refused," he said gloomily. "She was afraid everyone would think she was pregnant."

"You run a tight ship," she said sarcastically. The words were out before she could stop them, and this time she slapped her hand over her mouth, horrified. "I really am sorry," she said.

"I don't know what's gotten into me." A lie, but a nice, social lie.

He stared at her, irritation and reluctant interest at war in his expression. "Do you want my business or not?"

It was a simple question, and she should have given him the answer she longed to. Told him to go away. So what if Lambert Publications never did another article on Goddess in Waiting? So what if Will Lambert and his upper-class family sat on the boards of various charities that could prove incredibly helpful to the girls who passed through her studio? She could do it all herself, couldn't she? She always had.

"I'd be happy to provide some clothes for your sister," she said in what she hoped was a meek voice. Since she hadn't used it often in her twenty-nine years, she wasn't sure how it worked, and indeed, Will Lambert didn't look fooled. "Why don't you have your assistant call me and give me some details about your sister? Maybe even send over a picture? I could come up with some ideas, run them past her, and she'll get final approval from you." *And I'll never have to see you again*, she added silently, having no idea why it mattered so much.

For some odd reason he didn't look pleased

at the prospect. "Sounds sensible," he said, rising. "I'll have Thelma—"

To Marike's utter astonishment, all color left his face, turning him a pale ivory. He swayed. If she hadn't reached out and caught him, he would have crashed to the floor.

Fortunately she was a strong woman, not easily overpowered, or she would have been on the floor beneath him, definitely the last place in the world she wanted to be. She pushed him back onto the sofa, shoved his head down between his knees, and tried to ignore the muscle and bone beneath the elegant Armani.

"Are you sick?" she demanded. To herself, she sounded anxious, but that was only natural. Any business owner would worry about a prospective client nearly passing out. Another nasty thought came to her. "Are you drunk? On drugs?"

Sitting up, despite her effort to keep his head down, he managed a rough laugh. His face was still pale, but there was an endearing stain of color on his high cheekbones, which, she realized, was embarrassment. "Sorry," he muttered. "Just a little too much caffeine and not enough sleep."

"When did you last eat?"

"I don't remember," he said. "I don't usually bother with breakfast."

"What about lunch?"

"I came here instead. Don't worry, I'm fine now. I'll get something to eat when I get back to the city."

"No, you won't. I'm not letting you drive anywhere until you've had something to eat. Are you able to walk to the kitchen or should I bring something in here?"

"Look, I'm fine. I don't need anything," he protested.

She rose, not bothering to argue. "I'll bring something back."

She realized he was at her heels when she reached the swinging door to the old kitchen, and she almost turned and ordered him back to the parlor, then thought better of it. She'd been enough of a witch already, and it was hardly the poor man's fault. He wasn't to blame if he was utterly, dangerously gorgeous. And, really, there was nothing wrong with a suit.

"Sit," she said, pointing to the well-scrubbed kitchen table. She hadn't spent a penny on updating the kitchen—it was well enough equipped to provide decent meals for her and the young women who lived here. She found washing dishes to be a soothing experience. Tanya didn't agree, but most of the other girls had been more than amenable.

The cabinets were glass-fronted and tall. She had no trouble reaching them, pulling out a Depression glass plate that had come with the house, and searching for the loaf of bread from this morning.

"You allergic to peanuts?" she asked as she sawed two generous slices off a thick loaf of oatmeal bread.

"Nope." He'd taken his seat with a meekness she found highly suspect.

"What about milk?"

He made a face. "I'm not allergic to it, but I don't like it."

"Tough," she said. "You need calcium, and with the way the young women who live here go through milk, I make sure we always have plenty on hand." She set a peanut butter and jelly sandwich and a glass of milk in front of him, her expression daring him to make a comment.

He looked down at it dubiously. "I haven't had peanut butter in twenty years."

"Then you've spent twenty years without one

of nature's great pleasures,'' she said, seating herself at the table. ''Drink the milk.''

He ate, slowly and obediently, and she was relieved to see the color come back to his face. His eyes no longer looked so bleak; instead they looked both sheepish and faintly amused. She didn't know what he found so damned funny about her—her ill-advised hostility, her magenta hair, her oversize presence, or something else entirely. But she didn't like it.

''What are you looking at?'' she demanded, knowing exactly what he was staring at. Her face.

''You mother everyone you can get your hands on, don't you?'' he said, draining the milk with a faint shudder. ''Do you have any kids of your own?''

''No.''

''Why not?''

''No husband at the moment. I'm a conventional woman at heart—I think children do better with a mother and a father.''

Before she realized what he planned to do, he reached over and ruffled her short-cropped hair. ''Conventional, are you?'' he murmured. His hand rested on her curly magenta hair for a brief, almost caressing moment. ''I would have thought your hair would be stiff and spiky." He smiled at her. "Like your personality."

He was good, she had to admit. She'd managed to throw him off balance in the beginning, but he'd already adjusted, meeting her on her own terms.

She moved out of reach, keeping her face expressionless. "I think you've recovered," she said dryly. "I'm sure Lambert Publications has access to a messenger service. Have someone bring out some photos and details about your sister and I'll see what I can come up with. It's quite a short amount of time, though. Valentine's Day is less than two weeks away, you know."

"I suppose I'm asking too much," he said, charmingly rueful.

She didn't want to be charmed. "You are," she said. "But for Lambert Publications we'll make the effort."

"It's not for Lambert Publications. It's a personal favor."

She knew exactly what she was going to say. *In that case, find someone else.* She opened her mouth to tell him that, but the wrong words came out. "All right." At least it sounded sulky, but that was small consolation when he smiled at her. Men shouldn't look that devastatingly beautiful when they smiled. Especially suit-wearing men such as Will Lambert, who doubtless had a tiny, skinny, perfect girlfriend somewhere. He'd tell her about the bad-tempered giantess he'd run into, and they'd both laugh. Marike should have told him to take the Lexus she'd seen parked outside her house and drive it into Lake Michigan.

As she led him back to the entryway, she silently acknowledged that her heart was acting in a strange manner. Probably, she concluded, from stress. There was no question that Will Lambert was a very disturbing influence, and she'd had more than enough to last her. "Tanya!" she called. "See Mr. Lambert out." She started to disappear back into the kitchen, almost desperate to get away from him, when he reached out and caught her hand. There was nothing the slightest bit controlling—his hand was strong, the skin cool and surprisingly callused, and she was so startled she didn't yank free.

Instead she shook it—a firm, brisk, professional shake—and backed away, and there was no way he could stop her, no way he could say what he seemed to be about to say. While part of her was curious as to what he wanted to tell her, she figured she was much better off not knowing. "Thank you for coming, Mr. Lambert," she said in her most professional voice. "And get that information to me as soon as possible. I wouldn't want to disappoint you."

He stared down at her. "I'm not sure if you could," he said softly.

Before she could think of anything to say, he left. All she could do was stare after him in bemused dismay—still feeling the strong, warm touch of his hand on hers.

Chapter Three

FOR THE FIRST TIME in more years than he could remember, Will Lambert didn't go straight back to work. As a matter of fact, he was strongly tempted to not show up at Lambert Publications again that day.

A light snow was falling, but hadn't begun to accumulate on the roads leading into the city. He usually drove like a bat out of hell, determined to reach his destination in the least amount of time, and he'd bought exactly the right kind of car to do just that. His Lexus could cruise at prodigious speeds, hold corners, detect speed traps, plow through fresh snow and race through heavy rains. He had the tickets to prove it.

But for some reason he didn't feel like speeding to his destination. He wasn't even sure where he was going. He only knew he needed time to think, and driving too fast in the light snow wasn't going to accomplish anything.

It wasn't as if he didn't know perfectly well

what he should be doing. He could call Thelma, have her send Lindsay's picture and measurements over, and leave everything in Marike's large, capable hands. Taylor Hotchkiss was back in town, fresh from her divorce, and she'd called him several times. For the sake of friendship, if nothing else, he should call her, see if she was busy tonight. Then maybe he'd get the thought of Marike's hands out of his mind. Stop wondering how they'd feel against his skin.

The snow was turning into nothing more than random flurries. Thelma was right—the storm would miss them. She was usually right about such things. This was only a brief squall that would soon blow over. And maybe the odd, restless feeling in his soul was the same—a small, torrid blip on the radar that would soon settle down.

It would settle a lot faster if he passed this particular blip back into Thelma's hands. Hell, he'd driven all the way out here in questionable weather, ignoring his business responsibilities. Surely that would qualify as doing his fraternal duty.

He'd spent the past ten years of his life being wise, making the smart decisions. He'd probably behaved that way even longer, ever since he'd been in law school. Maybe today he'd do what he damned well pleased.

Then again, maybe he wouldn't. He'd call Thelma, have her to finish up with Marike. Then he'd call Taylor, see what she was doing tonight. For some reason he didn't want to be alone. He could take her to dinner, let her cry on his shoulder. Maybe they'd even sleep together. It had been good in the past, and he'd been uninvolved for a long time now.

He was almost home when he realized he was hungry again. Absolutely starving. He had two choices: head for the French restaurant where he ate most of his meals, or stop in at the tiny hole-in-the-wall grocery store near his apartment.

For some reason he didn't think L'Arbre d'Or would have peanut butter and jelly sandwiches. And he had a sudden inexplicable craving for them.

MARIKE SET THE RECEIVER back in its cradle very carefully, staring at the phone as if it were a rare piece of Japanese silk. She sat motionless, prodding her feelings, looking for pain, rather like one touched a sore tooth to see if it still hurt.

But there was no pain. She wondered if she

was numb, so she reached out and pinched herself. "Ouch!"

"What's up?" Tanya inquired lazily. Marike turned to look at her. Poor Tanya didn't have much choice other than to lounge around. She was getting very close to delivery, and while she wasn't as huge as some of the girls had gotten, she was understandably exhausted. Marike usually insisted the girls spend their ninth month taking care of themselves, away from the various tasks involved with Goddess in Waiting, but Tanya preferred to be in the heart of the action.

Marike looked down at her strong, well-shaped arm and the mark she'd made. She'd pinched herself hard enough that she might even end up with a bruise. And her heart still didn't ache.

"That was my ex-husband," she said casually.

"The Rat." Tanya identified him.

"The Rat," Marike agreed, not the slightest bit interested in defending him. "His new wife's pregnant and he wants me to make a maternity wardrobe for her."

Tanya's eyes widened. "Super Rat!"

Marike shrugged, still looking for even a trace

of pain. "It's what I do. The only problem is, he wants a discount."

"Supreme Rat," Tanya said flatly. "What did you tell him? I mean, the guy left you flat and refused to pay alimony, after all."

"I didn't want alimony," Marike protested.

"He still should have paid for cheating on you and then dumping you."

Marike wasn't sure how thrilled she was to have her situation summed up so neatly, but that was the thing about teenagers—they viewed things head-on, without rationalizations. At least, in everyone else's life. "It's been two years since the divorce," she said. "Time enough to move on."

"And have you?"

"Of course," she said. "I just don't like men in suits."

"Even the gorgeous creature who was here today?"

Marike had been doing her absolute best not to think about Will Lambert, and she'd been far from successful. "You mean, Grace's husband...Edward?"

"Don't try that garbage on me. You know exactly who I'm talking about. That tall, beautiful man with the dreamy eyes. He was a major hottie, if you ask me. Tell me you didn't notice his eyes.''

"They were nice eyes," Marike affirmed. "But right now I'm not interested in men. I've got a business to get established.''

"Sure," Tanya muttered. "And I'm gonna be crowned Miss America tomorrow, pregnant belly and all."

"In my clothes it could happen," Marike said archly.

For a moment Tanya said nothing. Of the dozen or so young women who'd made their way through Marike's house, Tanya was both the most grounded and the wisest. Far wiser than her sixteen years. She would make it, Marike thought. Despite Marike's best efforts, she couldn't be sure that all of them would.

"So you're not in love with the Rat anymore?" she asked.

Poke, prod. Not even a twinge. "Not anymore," Marike said truthfully, astonished at the sense of relief that washed over her.

Tanya nodded, satisfied. "Then I think you ought to consider the gorgeous hunk who was here today."

"I'm not going to see him again. The stuff I

needed came by messenger this afternoon, and I'll be dealing with his assistant from now on.''

"Drove him away, did you?" Tanya said wisely.

"You can only drive away those who are willing to be driven," Marike said.

"Maybe. But you gotta admit, he sure was cute, even in that suit."

Marike thought back to Will Lambert, but it wasn't the suit she saw. It was those deep, disturbing gray eyes, hinting at the soul of an artist.

But artists didn't wear Armani and run multimillion-dollar corporations, she reminded herself for the twentieth time. And he wasn't the only tall man in Chicago. There were at least a dozen Chicago Bulls who could easily top him. He wasn't the only man in the world.

He was just the only man she'd reacted to in more than three long years, ever since she'd found out Daniel had been cheating on her.

Maybe she should simply take it as a sign, a good omen. She'd noticed one man, maybe she was ready to notice another, more available one. Someone not as handsome, not as rich, with the soul of an artist and the hands of a craftsman.

If she could just stop thinking about Will Lambert—and his strong callused hands. A surprise, but they'd probably come from an upscale rowing machine.

Still, he had those wonderful eyes....

WILL WOKE UP at 5:00 a.m., alone. Alone by choice, in the big bed with its Egyptian cotton sheets, the murky light of a midwinter, Midwest day pouring in the uncurtained windows in his high-rise condo.

Taylor had made it abundantly clear that she would have been more than willing to share his bed as she had for a time several years ago, but he'd tenderly and tactfully declined the offer. She'd gone from being a lover to a friend, and he couldn't bring himself to think of her any other way.

And besides, the lean, elegant form of her body, the slender delicacy he'd always admired, was suddenly looking seriously undernourished. He'd watched her toy with her salad—she'd requested them to hold the dressing—and he'd had the sudden urge to force-feed her peanut butter.

He'd kissed her gently on the cheek when he'd taken her home, and almost broken his teeth on her cheekbones. He'd left her with her pride intact, and he could only hope she'd go into her kitchen and eat an entire pint of Ben &

Jerry's Cookie Dough ice cream straight from the carton. Maybe he should send her a case of the stuff, along with a huge box of Godiva chocolates. There were some things even the strongest woman couldn't resist.

But for some reason he'd rather watch Marike eat Godiva chocolates. He wondered whether she'd take a tiny bite out of one to see if she'd like it. Or whether she'd toss the whole thing into her mouth and let the experience take her wherever it led her. He was already reaching for the phone, ready to order some, when he stopped. Even if he sent Marike chocolates he wouldn't be there to watch her eat them. He'd done his duty, put things into motion, and he had absolutely no reason ever to see her again.

He had bagels with peanut butter for breakfast, and for the first time arrived at the office after nine o'clock in the morning. He had peach conserve on thin slices of semolina bread for lunch. With peanut butter slathered in between. By midafternoon he'd given up all pretense of working, simply sitting in his office, staring at the falling snow.

"I'm letting everyone go home early today," Thelma announced, rousing Will from his abstraction. "This storm is supposed to hit hard."

His reply was a muttered monosyllable. He'd done absolutely nothing the entire day, and it hadn't mattered. Thelma had simply, efficiently, seen to everything, and he'd sat in his leather chair staring out at the wintry Chicago skyline with his mind in a fog.

"Did you talk with Marike today?" he asked suddenly.

"Who's Marike?"

He sat up abruptly. "The clothing designer. You were going to send Lindsay's picture and measurements out to her. You must have forgotten. Now I'm going to have to go out there myself in this storm," he said happily.

"I took care of it," Thelma said. "I just didn't realize that was the designer's name. I thought it was Goddess in Waiting."

His momentary sense of elation vanished. "Did she get the stuff? Maybe it got lost on the way..."

"I had a courier take it, and someone signed for it. It's all under control."

"But how does she know what to make? I haven't placed an order..."

"I told her to use her judgment and gave her a price range. That's what you usually tell me to do." Thelma was looking at him strangely, but he wasn't about to explain. His abstraction had vanished, along with his lethargy.

"Not good enough this time," he said, shaking his head. "I'd better go out there myself. After all, Lindsay's my only sister, and this is important to her. I shouldn't just leave it up to strangers."

A tiny smile curved Thelma's mouth. "Absolutely," she said. "But what about the storm?"

"I've lived in the Chicago area for most of my life. I know how to drive in snow," Will said in a lordly voice that never managed to impress Thelma. "Besides, this is too important to ignore. Valentine's Day will be here before we know it."

"That reminds me...did you want me to send flowers or chocolates to the usual suspects? Not that you've been seeing anyone recently, but I wondered if you and Taylor were getting back together."

"No!" he said with a bit too much emphasis. "No," he repeated in a calmer voice. "She's an old friend, but she's not my type."

"She always has been. Skinny and elegant and sophisticated. When did your type change?"

"Yesterday." He hadn't meant to say it out

loud, hadn't even wanted to admit it to himself. But it didn't matter—Thelma knew him better than he knew himself.

"This have something to do with your sudden craving for peanut butter?"

"It might," he allowed.

"And a certain shop in Derbyfield?"

"It might."

"Then I suggest you get going before the snow gets any worse."

MIDLIFE CRISIS, he decided two hours later, driving into the thickening snow. The headlights bounced off the flakes, making visibility almost impossible, and what traffic there was had slowed to a crawl. Most people had left work early, and once they got home, they wisely stayed. Not Will Lambert.

He glanced at his reflection in the rearview mirror, wondering if he'd suddenly turned into a complete stranger. He'd gone home and changed his clothes, not quite sure why he'd done it. If he'd left straight from the office he'd have been in Derbyfield by now, eating peanut butter in her big warm kitchen, drinking espresso, or even damned herb tea, if she made him. She'd insult him and mock him as she had before, and he wouldn't mind. He'd given up resisting the pull she had.

It wasn't that verbal abuse was a turn-on. He had Thelma around to tell him off, and despite her cover girl perfection, he'd never had even a stray lustful thought. Marike filled him with the most unlikely desire, and after twenty-four hours, he was tired of fighting it.

He made it to within a couple of streets of her old Victorian house. The Lexus was fast and sleek but unfortunately low-slung, and the rapidly deepening snow proved something even the killer tires couldn't deal with. He ended up stuck on the side of the road, the tires spinning, the lights staring crazily into the swirling snow.

What the hell was he doing here? He had his cell phone—he should call a tow truck and get his sorry tail back home. He was nuts to have come out on a night such as this.

He was frozen, covered with the blowing snow, by the time he trudged up to Marike's front porch. He looked around and the world was a silent blur of white. Everyone was safely tucked into their houses. The only sound came from the Victorian—the faint strain of music and a shriek of girlish laughter, cut off abruptly when he pushed the doorbell.

He waited, shivering, impatient, for a full two minutes. Then he pushed the bell again.

The door opened a crack, a guard chain firmly in place, and through it he could just see Marike's spiky magenta hair as she peered out at him. "Can I help you?" she asked. "Did you go off the road? We'll call a tow truck but I'm afraid I can't let you in."

"I'm freezing to death," he said, no longer having doubts that this was the worst idea he'd had in his entire life. "And I have no intention of waiting out here on the porch. Valentine's Day is less than two weeks away, and you said you couldn't wait."

"Couldn't wait for what?" she asked blankly, not making any move to unchain the front door.

Clearly she'd forgotten all about him, while he'd been mooning over her. Just the sort of thing to put him in his place, he thought with his last ounce of humor before the wet cold took over.

"My sister," he said patiently. "Lindsay? Her birthday's coming up."

"Will Lambert," she said, and there was an odd note of absolute horror in her husky voice that didn't make things any better. "I didn't recognize you covered in snow. What in God's name are you doing here?''

''I told you. I came to talk to you about my sister's present. My assistant told me I was a rotten brother for not arranging it myself.'' It was only partly a lie—Thelma had told him that early on, but he'd already done his duty.

Marike was still peering at him through the chained crack in the door. ''Oh,'' she said.

''Are you going to let me in, or are you going to slip fabric samples through the crack in the door?'' he drawled, getting tired of this.

She closed the door, and for a moment he wondered whether she'd bother to open it again. He heard the slide of the chain, and a moment later the door opened wide, though Marike appeared to be hiding behind it. ''Shake off some of that snow, would you? You look like an Abominable Snowman.''

''I feel like one.'' He did his best to brush the snow off, then trudged inside. She made no effort to close the door, still hiding behind it, and the snow swirled into the hallway around them. ''Don't you think you should close the door?''

She sighed, sounding like a prisoner heading for her execution, and pushed it shut. ''Come into the parlor once you've taken off your wet things.''

He was wet to the skin, but he figured she didn't mean that, so he simply took off his outer clothes and boots and followed her into the room. Then he stopped, staring at her.

As before, her long, narrow feet were bare, and wet from the snow he'd tracked in. She was wearing a kimono style dressing gown, the material similar to a Georgia O'Keefe painting, all vivid, colorful, exotic flowers. She'd pulled it up tight to her neck and was staring at him with acute suspicion.

''Where are the girls?'' he asked innocently. ''I thought I heard their voices when I first came to the door.''

''They abandoned me, the little wretches,'' she said bitterly. ''They must have known it was you.''

He found the notion fascinating. ''Why would they abandon you to me?''

''They have their reasons. They've gone up to bed and the little beasts know I can't come after them.''

''You can't go upstairs? Why?''

She shook her head. ''Never mind. What did you want, Mr. Lambert? When I talked with your assistant she told me to go ahead and use my judgment. I hate to tell you, but I did just that, and the order is almost finished. You made the trip for nothing.''

He wanted peanut butter. He wanted her to stop looking like a Victorian matron with unlikely hair. ''But since I have, couldn't we sit and talk about this?'' he asked, using his most beguiling smile.

She shut her eyes for a desperate moment, leaving him even more confused. ''No.''

''No, we can't sit?''

''No, *I* can't sit. I can't climb the stairs. I can't do anything until you leave.''

''Why?'' he demanded, totally bewildered.

''Because,'' she said in a desperate tone of voice, as she flung open the bright silk kimono, exposing what was underneath.

Chapter Four

HIS EXPRESSION was comical enough that under other circumstances Marike would have laughed. Should have laughed. But Will Lambert had a habit of throwing her off balance.

"What," he said faintly, "is that? Some kind of disco-bondage Halloween costume? Discount store armor? What?"

"It's a duct tape dummy," she said, glancing down at her silver-taped body. "It's an inexpensive way to make a personalized dress form."

"I always heard there were a million uses for duct tape, but this one defies imagination. Are you wearing anything underneath that or did they simply tape it to your skin?"

She threw him an irritated look. "You wear a long T-shirt and then wrap the tape around it."

"And how are you supposed to get out of it? Assuming you ever want to sit, climb the stairs, or use the bathroom again."

He was enjoying himself, Marike thought with only a trace of rancor. In fact, she couldn't blame him. She was standing there like some bizarre, anachronistic Valkyrie swathed in silver tape armor from neck to mid-thigh. It was utterly ridiculous.

"They were supposed to cut me out of it when we finished," she said.

He glanced around, spied an unfinished roll of duct tape and reached for it. "I don't mind doing another layer or two," he said in a dulcet tone.

Just what she wanted—Will Lambert wrapping duct tape around her breasts and hips. He looked suspiciously eager to help out, but there was a limit to Marike's newfound determination to be pleasant. It wasn't his fault that she found him threatening.

"We were finished," she said hastily. "If you could just go find one of the girls to cut me out of this—"

"Why bother them? I can do it."

She was good at keeping her face absolutely blank—the very idea was vaguely horrifying and disturbingly erotic. The problem was, she couldn't really think of another way out of the situation. The girls had vanished, and she could only suspect some misguided notion of matchmaking. He wouldn't be able to find them if they didn't want to be found.

"All right," she said wearily. "The scissors are over on the table." She turned and presented her back to him, unwilling to look at his expression.

"Where do I cut?" He was closer than she'd realized and she jumped slightly as she felt his breath on her neck. She shivered, a strange thing, since the room was warm and the duct tape stiflingly hot.

"Up the center of the back, in a zigzag pattern. Through the T-shirt but preferably not through my underwear or my skin," she said dryly.

The touch of his hands, even through the layers of tape, was astonishingly erotic. She stood very still, holding her breath as the scissors slowly cut through the thick wrapping. "Reminds me of a space-age mummy," he muttered under his breath.

"Wait till you see what's underneath. Just bones and desiccated flesh," she said cheerfully.

"Doesn't look desiccated to me," he murmured. "Okay, it's done. What next?"

"Next we pry it off me very carefully so we don't mess up the proportions, or the clothes will end up looking like something out of a Picasso portrait. And you keep your eyes averted. I don't relish the idea of prancing around in my underwear in front of you.''

''I didn't know prancing was an option.''

The soft air of the room was a definite improvement over the smothering duct tape as he pulled it apart and she slid out of it with one swift movement, leaving it in his capable hands while she dived for her kimono. She still remembered his hands from the previous visit—elegant, beautiful hands.

They matched his beautiful eyes, which were watching her quite steadily.

''Did you design that underwear?'' he asked as she quickly wrapped herself in the thin silk kimono.

She was wearing fuchsia and lavender silk, adorned with ribbon embroidery, and she had indeed designed and made it. She had a weakness for decoration.

''Why do you ask?'' she said suspiciously, feeling only marginally better now that she was properly covered. He was still holding the shell of the duct tape dummy, and for some reason the sight of his hands against the silver tape seemed oddly arousing. As if he were touching her.

''Just professional curiosity. You could make

some like that for my sister after she has her baby.''

"I could," Marike allowed.

"On second thought, I don't know if I want to picture my sister wearing something like that. A little too...stimulating.''

"Then you can order some for your girlfriends.''

"I don't have any girlfriends at the moment. Or women friends, either. Not that I'd buy underwear like that for. I guess I'm just going to have to make do with thinking of you wearing it.''

With another man that line might be obnoxious. With Will Lambert it was oddly endearing.

And she was oddly out of her mind, Marike thought, tying the belt tightly around her waist and advancing on him. "I'll take Brunhilda." When he looked perplexed, she added, "The duct tape dummy.''

"Brunhilda? She's a Valkyrie, after all.''

"Just like me. I'm half Danish and I have Viking blood. Don't mess with me.''

He set the dummy down on the table with obvious reluctance. "Don't mess with you?'' he murmured.

He had the most damnably sexy voice, too,

she thought. Just her luck, a gorgeous package of manhood had to show up at her doorstep when she was totally unable to deal with it. She was too vulnerable at the moment. It had only been two years since the divorce; she wasn't ready for this. Wasn't ready for the big leagues. She needed to start out with someone a little less gorgeous, a little less seductive, a little less…everything.

Suddenly she was too close to him, when she needed to be halfway across the room. She couldn't remember why she'd moved so close— something about taking Brunhilda from him, but it was already discarded. And even as she was backing away from him he was following her, calm, determined, not the slightest bit threatening. So why was she feeling so threatened?

She came up against a wall and halted, staring up at him. He reached out and touched her face, his long fingers sliding into her hair. "You've got something in your hair," he said calmly.

"What?"

"My hand." And he kissed her.

For a brief glorious moment she let him, closing her eyes as she leaned into the caress of his fingers on her scalp, his mouth against hers, gentle, tasting, softly teasing.

She let out a soft, compliant moan, barely a whisper, and he foolishly took it for encouragement, sliding his other arm around her waist and pulling her up against his hard, lean body. She went, melting against him, opening her mouth for him, needing him.

Suddenly she went into panic mode. She jerked away from him, and he let her go immediately, but unfortunately she was too close to the door and she slammed her head against the wooden trim. She slipped out of his reach, almost faint with relief and disappointment that he let her go so easily, and didn't turn to look at him until the entire breadth of the room separated them.

"No," she said. Her voice came out shaky and breathless, and the man might be forgiven if he thought she sounded aroused. The man would be right.

"No, what?" he said calmly. "No, you didn't like it? No, don't ever do it again? No, you hate men in Armani? I'm not wearing Armani right now."

Indeed he wasn't. He was wearing faded jeans that had earned their well-worn condition, and a flannel shirt that was old and soft, as well. Everything else about him was deliciously hard—

she'd discovered that in the few short seconds he'd held her. He was a far cry from being on the elite list of Chicago's most eligible bachelors. He looked like a man, a real man, one you could touch, one you could taste, one you could have.

But she was having none of it. "I didn't say I didn't like it," she said defensively, honest to a fault. "I just said no."

A very faint smile curved his mouth. "You didn't say not to do it again, either," he said.

She was safely by the door to the hall, and the stairs were just behind her. "I can't imagine why you'd want to," she said frankly.

"It doesn't require imagination, Marike. Just common sense."

She stared at him for a long moment. "My name is Mary," she said suddenly. "Mary Jensen. Marike's my professional name."

"Your Valkyrie name. Mary suits you."

"No one calls me that anymore. I'm Marike now," she said defensively.

"Maybe. To everyone else. Are you going to run away, Mary? Or are you going to come back here and let me kiss you properly? I need to kiss you. And you need to be kissed."

It had to be someone else walking back across

the room to him. It couldn't be the wise and wary Marike, who'd taught the pregnant teenage girls to think with their heads, not their hearts or their hormones.

No, it was Mary Jensen, inexplicably lovelorn, who walked straight up to Will Lambert, slid her arms around his neck and kissed him full on the mouth, her heart pounding in panic.

She didn't quite know what she expected. Surely not the strength yet tenderness of his arms around her, not the slow, enchanting deliberation of his mouth as he met her kiss, deepened it, kissed her with an utter completeness that stole her breath and her heart.

The soft silk of the kimono had somehow become unfastened, his flannel shirt was unbuttoned and halfway off his shoulders, exposing a black T-shirt that caressed his body and danced beneath her hands, and he didn't need to pull her hips against his for her to feel his erection, and she didn't care that she was out of her mind. All that mattered was that after three long years she finally wanted someone. Wanted him so badly she was willing to risk everything, even her heart...

The crash was loud enough to shake the house, and the scream that followed was louder still. Marike tore herself out of Will's arms and took off up the stairs without a second glance, too frightened to think straight.

It wasn't as bad as she thought it was, and it was far worse. Sure enough, the three girls had been hiding out in the upstairs living room watching MTV and eating the disgustingly healthy food Marike insisted on. Tanya was lying on the floor, groaning, with the other two clustered around her. One of the windows was broken, letting in swirling drifts of white snow, and all three girls were crying.

It took only a moment for Marike to calm them down enough to figure out what the real problem was. Tanya's water had broken, and she was in labor.

"She started to fall, Marike, and she caught the curtain and the rod smashed the window..." Pam was saying excitedly. "And I was afraid she was cut, but I think she's okay, but what are we going to do? Do you want me to boil some water?"

"I'll call 9-1-1." Will had followed her up the stairs, and she only allowed herself a brief glance at him. He looked calm and unruffled. "Unless you were prepared for a home birth?"

"Nine-one-one," Marike said dazedly.

"Come on, girls, let's get Tanya out of the cold and cleaned up a bit while we wait for the paramedics."

"You make the phone call," Will said. "I'll move her." He knelt and scooped Tanya's ungainly, shivering body up into his arms with surprising effortlessness. Tanya was alternating between sobs and screeches of pain, and the two other girls were on the edge of hysteria, as well.

"Show Will where to take her while I call the ambulance," Marike said sharply. "And calm down. Everyone needs to remain calm. If worse comes to worst I can deliver the baby, but I think we'd all be happier in the hospital. Go on now. Pam, you find some clean dry clothes for her. Ellie, you make sure she's got everything packed in her suitcase for the delivery. Will, you be careful with her. Take her down to the salon and put her on the sofa and the girls can clean her up there."

"Yes, ma'am," he said with deceptive meekness, but Marike was too busy to do more than notice.

By the time the ambulance made it through the snow-clogged streets of Derbyfield, Tanya's contractions were three minutes apart and Marike was close to tears herself. By the time they reached the hospital, the contractions had stopped entirely and Tanya was being wheeled into an emergency room, leaving the other three women to sit in the abandoned waiting room, staring at each other, feeling faintly let down in their state of aftershock.

"What happened to the hottie?" Pam roused herself enough to ask. "Bad night for match-making, eh?"

"I didn't see him when we left. He'll have gone back to where he belongs," Marike said listlessly.

"And where's that?"

"In a high-rise in Chicago, wearing suits and dating models," she said. "He doesn't belong out in Derbyfield with the likes of us. We're too disorganized. I can't imagine what made him come out in a storm like this."

"Can't you?" Pam said. "I thought you were smarter than that. He's got the hots for you, big-time."

"Don't be ridiculous. He just met me yester-day. You may be young enough to believe in love at first sight but I've lived long enough to know that's a bunch of crap."

"So how come you're acting like you believe in it, too?"

"Pam!" Her warning voice trailed off as a subdued-looking doctor appeared in the door of the waiting room. "Ms. Jensen? I'm afraid there've been some complications in Miss Smith's condition. It looks like it's going to be a long night. If you and the young ladies would like to go back home, we'll be in touch when the situation changes."

Marike shook her head. "We'll stay," she said firmly.

The doctor nodded. "That's fine. You'd probably have a hard time getting home in the storm. There's a cafeteria open all night long if any of you want something to eat or drink." He cast a professional eye over the other two pregnant teenagers. "But if this goes on for much longer then I think these two young ladies should get home and get some sleep once the roads are cleared."

"I'm not leaving Tanya," Pam declared mutinously.

"Me neither," said Ellie, glaring at the doctor.

"They'll be fine," Marike assured him. "They're both very healthy."

He nodded. "I'll let you know how things are coming."

They looked at each other once they were alone again. "Don't you think you should at least call him and tell him what's happening?" Pam demanded.

"Call who?" Marike demanded, stalling. "Tanya's boyfriend hasn't been heard from in seven months. I wouldn't have the first idea where to look for him."

"I'm talking about the hottie, Will Lambert. When we were leaving he asked us to call as soon as we had word," Ellie said.

"Why would he care?" Marike said. "Besides, I haven't the faintest idea where to call him."

"Why don't you try the house in Derbyfield?"

"I told you, once we left he would have called a tow truck."

"I'll bet you a banana split with real ice cream that he's still there," Pam said with the assurance of someone who has all the answers. The problem was, she usually did.

"No way. You're so determined to get ice cream you'd probably hitchhike into Chicago, kidnap him and drag him back just to win the bet," said Marike.

"It'd be a lot easier to hitchhike into Chicago

and buy my own banana split," Pam drawled.
"He's there, waiting for you. I bet you."

The very thought sent a cold chill down Marike's spine and a warm ache in the pit of her stomach. She could still taste his mouth on hers, still feel the solid warmth of his body. If fate hadn't intervened then God knows what she would have done with a perfect stranger.

And he was perfect. Utterly gorgeous and divinely perfect, and she wasn't made for perfection.

But Tanya, after a textbook-perfect pregnancy, had gone into premature labor, and Marike had been saved from making one of the worst mistakes of her life. If she weren't so worried about Tanya and her baby she'd be counting her blessings.

But first things first. They had to get this baby safely born. And then Marike could figure out what to do with her empty house, the broken window and the hole in her heart caused by a man she knew she couldn't have.

Chapter Five

IT TOOK WILL LONGER than he expected to cover the window with heavy plastic. Marike might have the finest sewing machines in her workroom, but the rest of her tools were strewn all over the house and downright pitiful. By the time he found a sheet of plastic large enough to cover the smashed window, the snow was piled inches deep on the old Oriental carpet. At least she had a staple gun, albeit an ancient, rusty one, and by the time he'd finished covering the window and shoveling out the snow, it was past midnight.

He made a pot of decaf coffee and three peanut butter sandwiches and set to work on the wobbling banister leading upstairs. It was a good thing one of the girls hadn't taken a tumble on the stairs and clutched the railing for support—it would have torn away from the wall.

By 2:00 a.m. he'd finished securing the banister, repaired the dripping hot water faucet in the old-fashioned bathroom at the top of the stairs, and replaced one of the rotting steps on the back stairs up from the kitchen. That problem had been one of the easiest to find, since Marike had taped a big sign to it saying Dangerous—Do Not Step On This! The new step was cut from a piece of old pine, but it was a hell of a lot sturdier, and at least the stringers hadn't suffered any damage.

The roof was leaking in one corner, but there was nothing he could do about that for now in the midst of a blizzard. He'd have to wait until the snow melted to see whether it needed a patch or a whole new roofing job. The sticking doors and cracked windows needed better tools. When he came back he'd bring his plane and enough of his stuff to get the work done. He might as well leave them here—it wasn't as if he had anything to do in his brand-new, spotless condo. He wasn't even sure why he'd bought the tools, except that his soul had longed for them.

Almost as much as his body longed for Marike. Mary. Marike was the Amazon with the spiky hair and the chip on her shoulder. Mary lurked in the wary eyes and the soft mouth and the body that seemed to melt against his while she argued. He wasn't sure whom he wanted more.

He ought to go home, he told himself, wan-

dering through the deserted house, half an ear
cocked for the sound of the telephone. Even in
the midst of a blizzard, a man with Will Lambert's connections could get anywhere he
wanted to go. There was just one little problem
with that.

He was exactly where he wanted to be.

He finished his second cup of decaf and pol-
ished off the third peanut butter sandwich.
Funny, but her peanut butter tasted better than
the stuff he bought. Funny, because he'd been
careful to buy the same brand. Maybe it was a
bad vintage, he thought wryly, knowing perfectly well what made the difference. Everything
in Marike's house looked better, smelled better,
tasted better. It was if in the rest of his life he
was only half alive, the world covered with a
gray, enveloping veil. Here the veil was ripped
away, and everything was in blazing, glorious
color.

He tried stretching out on her Victorian sofa,
but the Victorians hadn't been much for comfort,
and he gave up. He wandered through the house,
looking for a place big enough to accommodate
his long frame, but the only thing that came
close was the shabby, overstuffed sofa in the TV

room, and it was too damned cold there, even with the plastic over the broken window.

He settled for Marike's bed, feeling like nothing so much as a modern-day Goldilocks. He knew it had to be her bed—it was huge, rumpled, covered with vibrant sheets and a down comforter encased in some sort of swirly flannel that was as soft as a cloud. He climbed into the high, huge bed, and lay there, wondering whom she had shared it with. If she would willingly share it with him. He lay there, listening to the sound of the wind howling and rattling the old windows, alone in the huge, empty house. He closed his eyes and fell asleep.

IT WAS DAWN when Marike arrived home, or at least she assumed so by the time on her watch. The light in the sky was a murky gray, the taxi could only get her to within a few blocks of her house and she had to trudge the rest of the way on foot. She'd left the two girls behind, almost as exhausted as the happy new mother. Tanya's contractions had started again with a bang, and Amy had been born a little more than two hours ago, mother and daughter both doing fine.

The nurses had set up a recliner and an extra cot in Tanya's room—there was no way they were letting two pregnant teenagers out into the worst blizzard Chicago had seen in the past few weeks. So Marike had struck out on her own, exhausted and grateful that her three charges were being taken care of, desperate for a few hours of solitude so that she could come to terms with what had almost happened earlier that night.

The house was pitch-black when she let herself in, and for a moment she thought they'd been foolish enough to turn everything off when they'd left. It took only a few useless flicks of the light switch to realize the power was out.

It couldn't have been off for long—the house was still warm, and considering there was a broken window letting in half the night air, the ancient furnace must have been working on overtime. Marike shut the door behind her, locking and double locking it. It was hardly the time or the weather for prowlers to be out and about, but it didn't hurt to be careful.

She kicked off her boots, feeling her way toward the stairs in the inky darkness. Not a ray of light penetrated the place, but she knew it well enough to find her way without too much difficulty, being careful not to put too much weight on the shaky banister as she climbed slowly up the stairs. She felt tired and cold and achy, restless in ways she wasn't even going to think about. All she wanted was to find her way to her bedroom, strip off her snow-damp clothes and climb up into her big high bed, pulling the duvet around her and shutting out everything.

Her room was marginally lighter than the staircase. It had huge floor-to-ceiling windows, and she'd draped them with a filmy gauze, enough to let faint trickles of gray misty light into the dark room. She stepped out of her jeans and tossed her cotton sweater onto the floor beside them as she reached for the bed.

She saw him before she had time to scream, and she bit back her shriek at the last minute, coming out with a strangled kind of mumble. He stirred, then settled back in her bed, wrapped in her duvet, his shaggy head on her pillow. She tried to summon up some sort of outrage, but in truth, he looked both exhausted and angelic lying there, dead to the world. He was Goldilocks, and she was the grumpy Papa Bear, demanding to know who'd been sleeping in her bed.

The man she wanted there.

She backed away from him, silent, though her earlier, noisier entrance hadn't disturbed him. She peeked into the TV room, but the window had been neatly covered, the broken glass and wet snow cleaned up. She eyed the overstuffed sofa questioningly for a moment. She'd dozed off there before—she could easily catch a few hours' sleep and be awake in time to get back to the hospital once the roads were clear. It was only a little chilly in the room, though if the power stayed off it would undoubtedly get colder, but she could borrow a duvet from one of the girls' beds and be just fine.

She headed back into the darkness, and this time when she came up against a solid, breathing form in the pitch-black she did scream, a small, breathless sound.

"How's Tanya?" Will asked.

It was almost more intimate than having him lying in her bed. Yet they were in darkness—he wouldn't be able to see she was wearing only her flimsy underwear. Even if he could, it wouldn't be that exciting—he'd already had plenty of chance to observe it. Except for some reason she knew that wouldn't matter. A man as passionate as Will Lambert would not be unaffected by the sight of her in a piece of lingerie he'd already admired.

"She's fine," Marike said breathlessly. She'd lost her sense of equilibrium. Was the staircase directly behind her, or over to her left? Was the door to her bedroom ahead of her or behind her? "She had a little baby girl. Mother and daughter are doing fine, and the other girls are staying with her until the roads are passable. What are you doing here, besides sleeping in my bed?"

She hadn't meant to say that, or at least, not have it come out so provocatively.

"Waiting for you," he said, and in the velvet darkness his voice was low. There was something about his calm stillness that seduced her far more effectively than intensity or force. She wanted a calm, still man to take her to bed. Daniel had always been so dramatic about it, and yet the act had never quite lived up to the fireworks and the foreplay.

And what the hell was she doing, thinking about foreplay?

"In my bed?" she said, as caustic as she could be.

"In your bed," he agreed. He took her hand in both of his, cradling it beneath his warm, strong skin. "You're cold. Let me warm you."

It had been a long day, and a longer night. She could question, she could argue, she could fight, or she could do what she was longing to do.

"Yes," she said. And he pulled her through the darkness to her bed.

She could see him now in the misty gray light. He was barefoot, wearing the faded jeans and a dark T-shirt that fit him perfectly. She always had a weakness for men in dark T-shirts, she told herself. Hell, she just plain had a weakness for this man.

"Well?" he said, dropping her hand, standing by the bed, waiting. She wasn't quite sure what he was waiting for—an engraved invitation?

"Well?" she echoed, struggling for irritation and feeling only nervous.

"Well," he said, and put her hands on his waist, on the hem of his soft cotton T-shirt. She couldn't help herself. She slid her hands underneath it, to his sleek, smooth skin, and her fingers trembled.

"This is crazy," she muttered. "I don't know you, I'm not ready for this, I don't even know if I like you..." She was pulling his T-shirt up, over his chest, and he obligingly lifted his arms so she could pull it over his head.

"Do you want me to go away?" he asked, sliding his hand up her stomach to the front clasp of her bra, unfastening it with one deft flick of his fingers.

"Yes," she said, reaching for the waistband of his jeans, fumbling with the snap. When she reached the zipper she stopped, but he covered her hand with his, pressing it against his hard, straining flesh. She didn't pull away, she let herself feel him through the layer of denim and metal zipper.

"Do you want me to go away?" he asked again.

"Yes," she said, and sinking to her knees in front of him, she kissed him through the thick layer of cloth.

She felt the shiver that raced through his body. His hands were in her hair, fingers threading through the short, soft strands. "When?"

"What?" she muttered dazedly.

"When do you want me to go away?" His voice was tight with strain, but his hands were slow, gentle, and she rubbed her face against him, against the bulge in his jeans.

"Not now," she said. "Later." And she reached for the zipper.

He hauled her up against his body with more strength than she'd ever felt in a man, and when he kissed her she kissed him back, her breasts naked against his chest. She wrapped her legs around his hips, and he turned and set her down across the high bed.

He kissed her mouth and her eyelids, slow, lingering kisses. He kissed the base of her throat and the hollow between her breasts, he kissed her belly and the mound covered by her silk panties. And then he stripped them off and kissed her between her legs.

She climaxed immediately, hard and fast, finished almost before she'd begun, and she wanted to cry, when she'd swore she'd never let a man make her cry again.

But she hadn't taken a man such as Will Lambert into account. He was far from finished with her, even if she thought she was done.

She tried to move away from him, but he wasn't about to let her go. His hands were strong, inexorable, gentle but insistent, and he made love to her slowly, silently, in the magic, silvery-gray light of a winter's dawn.

She was afraid to touch him, and he didn't force her, content to simply explore her body with his mouth and his fingers, building her slowly to a new peak, and when he spread her legs and slid deep inside her she climaxed again, another short, sweet spasm of pleasure she'd never experienced.

"Hold on," he whispered in her ear, his hands wrapped tight in hers as he began to move, a slow, endless sensation of hips and thighs, wet and clinging, tight and deep, again and again. She wanted to tell him she couldn't come this way, that he needed to touch her again, when all the slow, relentless power of him suddenly culminated and he felt so rigid, so deep inside her, she could almost taste him. The explosion came from nowhere, everywhere, around her and inside her, a vast storm that made her cry out like a lost soul.

But she wasn't lost, she was found, filled with him, consumed by him, one with him. For the first time in her life, she was no longer alone.

She was holding him, she realized. He had collapsed in her arms, shivering, his heart racing against hers, his breath raw and raspy, and she was cradling him against her, holding him tightly. She needed this to last forever, she thought as the last stray shudders of completion drained away from her body. She wanted time and space to freeze, so they would always be this way.

And then he lifted his head and kissed her, and it was even better. He cradled her face with his big hands, and she had no notion why she was crying, but it didn't matter. All that mattered was his mouth against her skin, her eyelids, her cheekbones, her lips, his fingers stroking her face.

All that mattered was him.

And that she had made the worst mistake in her mistake-strewn life.

MARIKE WAS LIKE A LIVING furnace, Will thought lazily as he lay beneath the duvet, wrapped around her luscious body. She was divinely warm, her smooth, beautiful skin heating his everywhere she touched him. He had no idea when the snow had finally stopped. He'd been listening to the plows out in the streets for more than an hour now, and the room was filled with a dreamy half light, touching everything with silver, including Marike's soft shoulder. And there was nowhere else he'd rather be.

He'd spent thirty-five years of his life being sensible. He'd known his share of women, even thought he'd been in love once or twice. But this was different. To hell with logic, to hell with being practical, sensible. He'd been waiting for Marike his whole life, and it took finding her to realize it. He was in love, completely, irrationally, totally in love. He might have added blindly, but that wasn't particularly true. She was a prickly sort, despite her soft, lush elegance. She was also surprisingly shy in bed, at least the first time they'd made love. By the third time she'd gotten delightfully bolder, and it was no wonder she was sleeping like the dead. If he weren't feeling so disgustingly happy he'd be sleeping, too, but he didn't want to miss a moment of this amazing new feeling.

He wondered how she'd react if he asked her to marry him so soon. Probably hit him, he thought with a lazy grin. If he had any sense he'd wait a few days, a few weeks before hitting her with it. Give her time to get used to it, used to him.

Should he at least tell her he loved her? She'd probably think he was lying, but the more he thought about it the more he knew he had to do it. He'd never told a woman he loved her. He'd never told Taylor, and it was just as well, since the moment she left he'd moved on without a qualm. And he could barely remember the name of his first love, the nineteen-year-old who'd cheerfully deprived him of his seventeen-year-old virginity.

He didn't want to wait this time. He didn't want to be careful, safe, patient. He wanted to wake her up, roll her over into his arms and kiss her into sleepy compliance, and when he was deep inside her he wanted to tell her that he was ready to give everything, risk everything...

The cold was sudden, shocking in the light-filled room. She'd pulled away from him, slid across the bed when he thought she'd been sound asleep, the duvet falling from her body.

Unfortunately she had to pull it from him to cover herself. She turned to look at him, then jerked her head back around. Not before he could see the color staining her face, as if they hadn't shared a lot more than the sight of his nude body just an hour before.

"You said you'd leave," she said in a hushed voice. "Now would be a good time."

The chill that filled him was beyond physical. "Just like that?" he said.

"Just like that." She kept her back to him, refusing to look at him, and for a moment he stared at the gorgeous curve of her back, the rich, creamy skin that had felt like silk beneath his hands.

He didn't bother arguing. He pulled on his discarded jeans, pulled the T-shirt over his head. And then he walked around to the other side of the bed, deliberately, so she couldn't avoid him.

He stood directly in front of her, but she kept her face lowered, refusing to look at him. He put his hand under her stubborn chin and forced her to look at him. Her eyes almost broke his heart.

"It won't work," she said flatly. "It was very nice, but you belong in Chicago and I belong out here. You wear suits, I wear duct tape and clothes with astrological symbols on them."

"For pity's sake, I'm wearing a T-shirt!"

"It's Armani."

Unfortunately he couldn't deny it. "You're going to kick me out because of the kind of T-shirts I wear?"

"I'm sending you back home where you belong because the kind of T-shirt you wear tells me where you belong."

"And it doesn't matter that I'm in love with you?"

It was hardly the reaction he was hoping for. She shuddered, closing her eyes, and the shake of her head was barely perceptible, yet unavoidable. "Go back to your condo, and don't come back," she said in a low, miserable voice.

He squatted in front of her, pain warring with the patience he was trying to summon. She wouldn't look at him, and he couldn't force her. "I'll go," he said. "But I'll be waiting for you.

You're going to have to come to me, though. I'm not used to being shot down."

She lifted her eyes for a moment and he thought he could see the glint of tears. "I am," she said.

Chapter Six

MARIKE HAD HAD BETTER weeks in her life. As a matter of fact, she couldn't really think of a worse time, including when Daniel had left her for his skinny new wife. At least in Daniel's case she'd had some inkling, some warning, and she'd had every right to feel miserable and abandoned.

She had absolutely no right to feel miserable and abandoned this time. She had sent Will Lambert away, and it was about the only smart move she'd made since he'd walked into her life. So why was she feeling so completely wretched?

Tanya was back home, with little Amy a delightful addition to their motley family. With so many eager, surrogate mothers, not to mention her own, the baby had no time to be fussy, cranky or colicky, and she should have been enough to distract Marike from her endless, useless brooding.

Except that when she looked down into Amy's little eyes and crooned to her, her heart ached, anyway, and she refused to consider why.

She jumped every time the phone rang, but apart from business, it was never for her. The three girls were whispering among themselves, obviously suspecting something had gone on, but she refused to say anything, and nothing short of torture would make her. She could easily go to her room, lock the door and crawl into the big bed, wrap the duvet around her and try to forget she'd shared it with Will Lambert. Or even better, close her eyes and pretend he was still there, holding her.

She was so absorbed in her own misery that it took her far too long to realize what was happening in her ramshackle house. By the time she thought about getting the broken window repaired she was astonished to see it was already fixed. The banister was suddenly sturdy, and on impulse she raced to the back stairs to find the broken step replaced.

He hadn't found the crumbling sill in the back bathroom, but he'd fixed the leaky faucet. Or sent someone else to do it, when she wasn't around. Someone like Will Lambert couldn't actually do such practical things himself, could he? Where would he have learned skills like that in the rarefied atmosphere he survived in?

She walked down the back steps, testing each

one. There were two others that were iffy, but the worst had been repaired. Pam and Ellie were in the kitchen, and whatever they'd been discussing came to an abrupt halt when she appeared.

"Someone fixed the back stairs," she said.

They both looked suspiciously innocent. "It wasn't us. I'm hopeless when it comes to carpentry," Pam said. "And Tanya's been too busy with the baby to tackle anything else."

"Well, there are two other steps that aren't quite secure, so be careful if you use them," she said evenly. "Who fixed the broken window in the television room?"

"Beats me," Ellie said. "It was done when we got back from the clinic on Monday. I thought you must have arranged to have a carpenter come in while we were out."

"No," she said. "And no one has keys but the four of us."

"Maybe it's a good fairy," Pam suggested cheerfully.

"Maybe it's a housebreaker," Marike said sourly.

"Who comes in and fixes broken windows? We should all be so lucky."

They weren't going to tell her, and nothing

she said would get it out of them. Besides, she didn't need them to confirm her worst fears. He told her he'd be waiting for her. Obviously he needed to hear "no" once more.

"Are the clothes for Lambert's sister finished?" she asked in a neutral voice.

"Yup. But I was thinking you shouldn't use a delivery service. After all, it's a substantial order, and it might be nice if you delivered them yourself. As a gesture of good faith. After all, we haven't seen the hottie since the baby was born, and it would be only polite of you to thank him for his help. You've been trying to drill manners into us."

"Parenting skills and a way to earn a living are slightly more important," Marike said wryly, not fooled for a moment. "So you think I should take the clothes to his sister myself?"

Pam thought fast. "Well, he's the one who ordered them and he's the one giving them. Shouldn't you deliver them to Will?"

When had he become Will? Probably one of the times he'd come to her home when she'd been conveniently absent. "You're absolutely right," she said grimly. "I'll deliver them to him personally and thank him for his help. All his help," she added meaningfully. "And that'll be the end of it. Do you understand?"

She'd never been able to quell Pam, even in the best of times, and Pam simply blinked at her, unconvinced. "Sure," she said. "But we all think you're out of your mind."

"Thanks for sharing," Marike said. Not certain she didn't agree with them.

It hadn't snowed in ten days, not since the night they'd spent together. The air was clear and cold and crisp, a bright winter day with a bleak heart. Odd, since it was the day before Valentine's Day.

She found herself hoping that her aging Volvo station wagon wouldn't start, but it was reliable as always, and there was nothing to keep her from making the trek into the city, not even traffic. All she had to do was ignore her heart, her nerves and her better judgment, and concentrate on midtown parking.

She'd had no trouble finding Lambert Publications. The idea of facing him at his office didn't appeal to her. But it was just as well. In truth, she supposed there was unfinished business between them, and if she had to see him one more time, to make it entirely clear that she'd meant what she said, then on neutral territory, in public, was the best away to accomplish it. Maybe then she could get on with her life.

The one time she looked forward to the usual nightmare of midtown parking, there turned out to be a spot only yards away from the front entrance of the Lambert building. She parked, switched off the car and sat there, trying to calm the beating of her heart.

You're just here to tell him goodbye, she reminded herself. *There's no way you can be so completely stupid again, not when you're in the middle of someone's office. It's safe, it's smart and it'll be over.*

Either the Lambert building had the world's most lax security standards or someone was expecting her. Within minutes she was on the thirty-seventh floor, face-to-face with the kind of woman who belonged with William Lambert. Reed-thin, ruthlessly well-dressed, stunningly beautiful, and staring up at Marike with... interest, not the condescension she was expecting.

She held out her perfectly manicured hand. "Hi, I'm Thelma Ryerson, Will's former executive assistant. You must be Marike."

"He told you about me?" she asked warily.

"Not a word. But we've all been dying of curiosity around here, so someone dug up that copy of *Sew Abundant* and we read all about you," she said cheerfully.

"Why?"

"We wanted to see why the mighty Will Lambert had finally fallen. Now that I meet you, I'm not the slightest bit surprised. You're not at all like the women he used to date."

Not skinny, not sophisticated, not part of his world, Marike thought flatly, but she didn't say it out loud. "No, we have nothing in common. And I'm afraid you're mistaken—there's absolutely nothing going on between us. I'm just here to deliver the clothes for his sister and say hi."

"Too late," she said, clearly unconvinced. "He's already left."

"Well, I can just leave the stuff here..."

Thelma was shaking her head. "No, I mean he's really left. As of today he isn't working here anymore, or at least, he's only working on an occasional basis. He's the CEO emeritus, which means all he has to do is let me run things and he'll collect the money."

"You're the new CEO? He retired?"

"Actually, he quit. He's starting a new career.

Though why someone who's got a law degree and a company to run would prefer to renovate tumbled-down houses is beyond my comprehension. I told him that, and he said that's why I'm perfect to run the company and he's perfect to run away.''

Marike was filled with an inexplicable dread. "Run away? He's going somewhere?"

"I don't really know. He's home now, and I think he was wanting to get those clothes to Lindsay by tomorrow. Why don't you head over there and I'll give him a ring and let him know you're coming?"

She'd rather chew ground glass, but there seemed no way around it. He was leaving, when he told her he'd wait for her. It should have been a relief, to have that kind of assurance that she'd made the right decision. "I don't know where he lives."

"I'll write it down for you. It's one of those huge new condos on Lake Shore Drive, though I gather he's got it on the market. He's offered me first crack at it."

"I really don't think I have time..."

"Sure you do. You wouldn't want him leaving Chicago without paying you for all your hard work, would you?"

"I could just bill him."

"You aren't afraid of seeing him, are you? I thought you said there was nothing between you?"

Marike plastered a determined smile on her face. "Very little frightens me. Give me the address and I'll see if I have time to stop off there on my way home. I could probably leave the clothes with the doorman."

"The building's so hi-tech there's no doorman, though I suppose there's a super somewhere on the premises. Don't worry, Will doesn't bite."

Actually, he does, Marike thought with a faint blush. Small, erotic little nibbles timed just right to be astonishingly effective. She could feel the color rise in her face, and only hoped Thelma Ryerson was too short to notice. Though she suspected that there wasn't much that Thelma missed.

"I'll see what I can do," she said vaguely. "Thanks for your help."

"Glad to be of assistance," Thelma said with indecent cheer. "See you soon."

"I don't think so," Marike said.

"I do," Thelma said cheerfully.

"DELIVERY FOR YOU, Mr. Lambert." He heard Joe's voice on the other side of the front door, but he was too busy trying to placate a weeping Lindsay over the telephone. It was some new pregnancy-induced, imaginary trauma, but he'd become adept at soothing her when she wouldn't listen to anyone else.

"Just set it inside the door!" he shouted, knowing the super would have the key to his and everybody else's apartment. Fortunately he trusted Joe implicitly, and he didn't even bother to turn around when he heard the key turn in the lock and the front door swing open. Instead, as he listened to his sister, he concentrated on the Chicago skyline that he was more than happy to be leaving.

"Listen, darling, stop crying. You know I love you, and I wouldn't let anything bad happen to you. I'll be out there by this evening, as soon as I get the rest of my things packed, and it'll be just like old times. In the meantime just stop worrying. You know you're my best girl and always will be."

She wept noisily on the other end.

"That's right. I love you, sweetie. See you tonight." He hung up the phone, suddenly aware of an odd tension in the atmosphere. Even before he turned around he knew whom he'd see.

But he'd underestimated how he'd react. Marike stood in his doorway, dressed in something soft, pale and flowing over her tall, gorgeous body. She had a wrapped bundle of brilliant-colored material over her arm. In contrast, her expression was cold, frozen.

He took a step toward her, but she backed up, so quickly she knocked the door shut behind her, closing herself in with him, and he halted, not wanting to scare her into running. He couldn't understand the pale, stricken look on her face, and then he realized she'd overheard his telephone call.

"That was my sister," he said hurriedly. "The one you made the clothes for. She's gained another ten pounds and she thinks her husband hates her, which is ridiculous but she's not being reasonable…"

The frost in the air lessened only slightly. "Women can get unreasonable when they're pregnant," she said. "It's the man's job to soothe and support her."

"I don't think it's pregnancy that makes women unreasonable," he said when she made no effort to come closer, and he didn't dare move. "You're not pregnant and you're being entirely unreasonable. Why are you here?"

"Didn't Thelma call you and tell you I was coming?"

"No. And I'm guessing from the look on your face that you haven't changed your mind."

"I don't see why it would matter. You're leaving."

"I'm leaving the apartment. Helluva place, isn't it?" He gestured to the buffed gray walls, the steel-framed windows, the angular furniture and cool, heartless sophistication of it.

She set the clothes on a Danish modern side table. "Where are you going?" she asked.

"Do you care?"

"Just curious," she said with a toss of her head. "It doesn't matter..."

"I thought I'd find a place in Derbyfield. Maybe an old Victorian monstrosity I could fix up, maybe sell when I'm finished. You see, there's a woman out there I'm in love with, and I find that all the determination in the world won't change my mind. So I figure I could move near her and be patient. Sooner or later she'll come to her senses."

"What if she knows what she's doing? What if you're the one who needs to come to his senses? What if you don't mean anything to her and never will?''

''Why don't you come over here and prove it? Or are you afraid you'll be tempted?''

She was easy to play, just hard to convince. She walked across the room to stand directly in front of him, her shoulders back, a steely glint in her gorgeous eyes. She was close enough that he could see the tension in her body, practically feel it thrumming through her. Close enough to touch, close enough to kiss.

''No regrets?'' he asked softly.

''I've lived with nothing but regrets since I was idiot enough to spend the night with you...''

''I don't mean that. And it wasn't a night, it was three short hours. Very short. I mean no regrets about sending me on my way?''

''Not a one,'' she said, and he knew she was lying through her teeth. She knew it, as well, but she wasn't about to back down.

''All right,'' he said. ''Will you let me kiss you goodbye? Since it won't mean anything.''

There was no way she could say no. And if she tried, he was going to kiss her, anyway, and to hell with good intentions.

''Of course,'' she said calmly, bridging the gap between them, putting her arms around his neck and pressing her cool, firm mouth against his.

Two seconds later her hands were under his shirt, against his bare skin. Ten seconds later he'd managed to strip off her shirt and bra.

A minute later they were on the thick carpeting, their clothes scattered around them, and he was deep inside her, and she was climaxing, her body clamping down so tightly on his that he was afraid he'd follow her, too soon, too soon, when this might be the very last time. He had to make it good for her, perfect for her, so perfect that she couldn't leave him, couldn't send him away again, but the wave after wave of pleasure rippling through her body proved too much for him, and with a strangled cry he pushed deep inside her, filling her with rapid pulses of white heat.

He didn't try to hold her when she pulled away this time. Holding her wasn't the way to keep her. She had to come to him on her own, and there was no way he could make her. She dressed quickly, and he made no move to stop her, simply lay on the thick carpeting and watched her. It wasn't until she was halfway out the door that he spoke.

"I want to marry you," he said.

She paused, looking back at him, and this time she didn't avert her gaze from his naked body. "Are you out of your mind?" she demanded in a voice thick with unshed tears.

"Probably. Love does that. You seem pretty unbalanced yourself right now." He sat up. "Are you sure you aren't in love with me?"

She slammed the door behind her when she left, and Will didn't know whether to laugh or hit something. At least he'd managed to get her clothes off again, proof that she wasn't immune to him. If only she wasn't so damned scared, and so damned stubborn. If only he'd handled it better, been more tactful. Maybe if he hadn't put his arms around her waist when she'd kissed him, hadn't opened his mouth and used his tongue, maybe if he hadn't reached for her full, gorgeous breasts...

Maybe he'd still be sitting here in a tight knot of frustration. At least his body was relaxed after the most tense ten days he'd ever spent.

Now if he could only get his heart, soul and mind in order, as well.

Chapter Seven

IT WAS A GOOD THING the afternoon was clear. She managed to hit rush hour on the way home, and all the traffic that had gone her way now seemed determined to make her crazy. It didn't help that she couldn't stop crying.

She kept wiping her face with one hand as she tried to deal with the kamikaze drivers that surrounded her. At least three-quarters of them were talking on cell phones as they snaked in and out of the traffic at death-defying speeds. She clutched her steering wheel with its ratty leather cover even harder. If she were ever fool enough to think things might work with someone like Will Lambert the first thing she'd do was throw out his cell phone.

A horn blared in her ear, and she jerked the wheel, just missing a car. The driver sped past her, shaking a fist at her with one hand while he used the other to hold his cell phone. She had no idea how he was managing to steer, and she didn't want to think about it.

There was no sign of the girls when she finally dragged herself into the old house at half past seven. A drive that usually took her thirty-five minutes had wound up lasting two and a half hours, and her face was stiff from tears, her throat ached from choking back her sobs, and her body felt sticky, achy, hot and empty.

She headed straight for the shower, determined to wash every last trace of Will Lambert from her body, from her mind. The hot water vanished the moment she got the shampoo in her hair, and she stood under the icy stream of water just long enough to rinse off.

By the time she grabbed a towel and staggered out of the bathroom she was shivering and cursing, past tears and into despair. The door was off her bedroom, leaning against the wall. The railing had come loose from the stairway, two windows were stuck open, letting in a blast of frigid air, and by the time she got down to the deserted kitchen she was ready to scream.

There was no answer to her cries—the house was empty, the girls long gone. The faucet had been taken off the kitchen sink, and water was gushing out, sending a fine spray over the room.

She waded through the water on the floor to

the kitchen table. There was a note waiting for her, signed with the girls' names.

"'Dear Marike,'" she read. "'The house is falling apart. We've taken the baby and gone over to Pam's mom's house for the night. You need a plumber. You need an electrician. You need a carpenter. You need a man. Dial-A-Hottie will help. Call 555-5078 and stop fighting it.'"

The portable phone was sitting beside the note, waiting for her. At least they hadn't sabotaged the electricity, which showed more sense than she would have given them credit for. She shuddered to think what else they had done to the rest of the house.

She picked up the phone and dialed.

She'd never heard his voice on the telephone. It was slow, deep, infinitely soothing, and she wondered why she'd even hesitated.

"The house is falling apart," she said.

He didn't need to ask who it was. "That's nothing new."

"I'm falling apart."

Silence at the other end of the line. He wasn't going to make it easy on her. In for a penny, in for a pound. "The house needs you. I need you. Get your butt out here before I freeze to death."

"Do you have peanut butter?"

"Yes."

"Will you make coffee?"

"Yes."

"Will you sleep with me?"

"Yes."

"Will you marry me?"

She took a deep breath. "Yes," she said. And suddenly all the anxiety that had been eating her soul dropped away, and she was at peace, and blissfully, astonishingly happy. "I do love you, you know."

"I know," he said. "I know."

Epilogue

One year later

THE ROOF at Goddess in Waiting had been repaired, the windows reglazed in time for the next winter, the electricity updated and the plumbing redone. Pam and her young son were still in residence, but Tanya and Ellie had moved on. Ellie had married the father of her baby, a surprisingly steady young man who seemed determined to do the best by his young wife and baby, and Tanya had started her own sewing and alteration business in between doing contract work for Goddess in Waiting. There were three new girls in residence, as well, and Pam had done an excellent job riding herd on them while Marike had been busy giving birth to a baby girl on Valentine's Day.

Will was sitting in the salon, where the uncomfortable Victorian sofa had been replaced by a shabby chic chesterfield, holding his tiny daughter in his arms, his doting expression not the slightest bit marred by baby Mary's bad-tempered howls. She'd graced her mother with a nineteen-hour labor and expressed her irritation with the world in general for the past three days since she'd come home.

"Lindsay and Philip are here," Marike said. Her hair was no longer magenta—at the moment she was favoring a kind of mottled stripe that made her look faintly tigerish, and she moved carefully, still a bit battered from Mary's tempestuous entry into the world. "Come and meet your new little cousin, Jordan."

Ten-month-old Jordan perked up at the sound of his name, turning around in Lindsay's arms to crane his neck toward the baby. He made a babbling sound, and Mary's howls stopped instantly as she stared up at her cousin with pale eyes that seemed to focus.

"That's your cousin Mary, Jordan," Lindsay cooed. "She's a little tiny baby, isn't she? You have to be very gentle with her."

Her husband Phil snorted with laughter. "I don't think he's going to want to get anywhere near her, darling. Do you see that expression on his face? He looks disgruntled. Doesn't want to share the limelight."

"I wouldn't say that," Will said slowly. "It's

more like he's saying, 'What took you so long to get here?'"

"I was thinking the same thing myself after nineteen hours," Marike said as she slowly lowered herself into a comfortable chair.

"He can't keep his eyes off her, Marike," Lindsay said. "They're going to be best friends, I just know."

"They're going to be utter hellions," Marike said cheerfully.

"That, too," Lindsay agreed. "You think they'll even like each other?" She'd knelt by the new baby, holding Jordan out to examine his new cousin.

Jordan reached out his chubby little hand, and a moment later Mary had grasped it tightly. The four adults shared mystified looks.

"They must have known each other in another lifetime," Lindsay said.

"Not that New Age crap," Will complained good-temperedly.

"I don't know," Marike said. "It looks like these two have been waiting a long time for each other."

And Mary turned toward Jordan and gave her first smile.

GABE'S
SPECIAL DELIVERY

Tara Taylor Quinn

Chapter One

Valentine's Day, 2000

BAILEY COOPER STONE gently lifted the infant carrier from the seat beside her and slowly stood as the Chicago Transit Authority's Red Line came to a complete stop. Less than a month old, her baby daughter weighed only seven and a half pounds. Despite that, Bailey's movements were slow as she trudged off the train and out of the station to the street, but the heaviness she carried was in her heart.

She forged ahead anyway, because she was doing the right thing. She and Eve had talked about this day a million times over these past months. Even her father would've had to agree on this one—had he been consulted. He hadn't been to see the baby yet. Not even when Bailey had broken down and begged him to come as she'd lain in her hospital room, waiting for the next wave of pain. He'd only stayed on the phone long enough to find out it was Bailey at the other end before he'd had a more pressing matter to attend to.

Colonel Evan Cooper was an important man. A respected man. A powerful man. In charge of a weapons unit, he held the safety of millions of Americans in his hands. Bailey was proud of him, and she understood that many crucial issues required his attention. She'd just never learned how to gain any of that attention for herself. His love she'd had. But not his time.

Her father had liked Gabe.

There'd only been two times in her life when Bailey had really pleased her father. When she'd chosen to teach art instead of practice it—and landed herself a job at one of the nation's premier art academies. And when she'd introduced her father to Gabe.

Of course, Bailey thought as she walked up the tree-lined Lincoln Park street with the bundled baby asleep in her carrier, Gabe and her father had been two of a kind. More than she'd realized. Until it was too late.

Shaking her head, she held the baby closer to her body. She couldn't think about that now. She pulled the open edge of her long army jacket around the side of the infant carrier—almost as though she could somehow keep the child to herself forever. As though it could somehow be just the two of them again. But she knew it wasn't possible. Her solitary idyll with Mignon had been little more than stolen moments; she'd known that from the beginning.

"He'll love you, Mignon," she whispered to the baby who slept peacefully in spite of the bumpy ride in her mother's arms. In spite of the biting February cold.

Please, dear God, let him love her, Bailey silently prayed. Let him not blame the child for the sins of her mother. Let him be capable of all the love little Mignon deserved.

"He'll love you," she said again, more loudly—with certainty this time. How could a man who knew James Baldwin's *Stories Retold* by heart, who read the classics and favored fairy tales over spy thrillers, not be capable of a deep and abiding love? As long as the person needing that love wasn't Bailey...

Rounding the corner, Bailey stopped when she saw the house she'd lived in, happily, for such a short while. She'd expected to make this trip much later in the day. She'd called the store, pretending to be a publisher's sales rep, to find out how late Gabe would be working. She learned that he'd taken the day off. So she'd set out immediately. It was time for Gabe to meet Mignon. She wondered if Gabe would understand the significance of Mignon's name. If he'd remember the story, "Mignon," the one about the little girl who won a stranger's heart with her light steps, her entrancing eyes and lively spirit. Surely Gabe would be like Wilhelm in that story. Surely he wouldn't be able to turn away from the child. *His* child.

"I'm an idiot, you know," she murmured to the sleeping baby as she approached the house—and the moment when all things would change yet again. "If he rejects you, I get to keep you to myself forever. No guilt attached."

She couldn't think of anything she'd like more. For herself.

As she gazed at the soft cheeks, at the long lashes lying innocently upon them, Bailey knew she didn't really want that. Her heart ached so hard it brought tears to her eyes as she envisioned her own baby growing up as she had, starved for her father's affection, always striving for an approval that was impossible to win. She wanted *everything* for Mignon—the world at her feet, her dreams within reach, the security of a father's adoring protection.

And she wanted to know that Gabe forgave her—Bailey—for this last omission, at least.

Approaching the house stealthily, Bailey slid behind the wall of bushes covering the front window. She stopped briefly, listened carefully for sounds from inside. She watched her breath rise like steam in the frigid air, and glanced around the impeccably groomed winter yard. Afraid, lonely, weak from months of turmoil, Bailey checked once more to make sure the note she'd so carefully written was still securely in place—and visible.

With an ear cocked toward the living room window, she proceeded slowly to the front door, set down her bundle, and rang the bell. Then she quickly fled back behind the bushes, just as she'd told herself she'd do when she'd run the plan through her mind for the millionth time that morning. As soon as she knew Mignon was safe, Bailey would disappear—alone—into the cold gray February morning. A fitting plan, she figured, for this painful Valentine's Day.

Gabe wouldn't approve; that was to be expected. But he'd love Mignon.

Bailey was strong. She'd survived eight of the most agonizing months of her life. But she wasn't strong enough to see Gabe again without falling apart. Today was for Mignon, for Mignon and Gabe. Father and daughter. They deserved it to be beautiful, special, not tainted with Bailey's pain. Or Gabe's recriminations.

Those would have to wait. Her breath caught in her throat, practically choking her as she heard the front door finally click open. And then saw Gabe's hand reach toward the bundle she'd left him...

"What the—"

Bailey shrank farther down in the bushes, her trembling knees giving way until she felt the cold hard ground beneath her. She couldn't believe, after the passage of so many months, that just seeing the man's hand could be so excruciating. She'd thought herself better prepared. Tears dribbling down her cheeks, she forgot, for the moment, the next phase of her plan. The part where she faded away into the sunset.

Instead Bailey was engulfed by memories, by emotions she couldn't fight. Or control. That hand—a scholar's hand—had touched her, tenderly and with passion. Those fingers had played her body as though it were a perfectly tuned instrument. Brought to life feelings she'd been certain, until Gabe, she'd always live without. Gabe's gentleness had warmed her, had won her heart. And his cold logic had chilled it, crushed it, flung it away.

The pain, even after all this time, was debilitating....

Chapter Two

Eleven months earlier

"EXCUSE ME. I don't mean to bother you, but I was just wondering if you'd like to have a cup of coffee with me?"

Startled, Gabe Stone looked up at the glorious vision in front of him.

He was tempted to pinch himself to make sure he wasn't dreaming. A second ago, he'd been alone in the Medieval Literature section of the bookstore he'd grown up in. And now...

"You're talking to me?" He forced out the words.

"Uh-huh." Long golden-brown curls fell haphazardly to the woman's shoulders. Gabe was fascinated by her hair, the way it bounced and rippled as she nodded. He was fascinated by the materials draped around her body, as well. He wondered what you'd call whatever she was wearing. A layered dress, maybe? A sarong?

"You want me to have coffee with you?" He

got a whole sentence out this time. She made him think of Titania, the spirit queen from Shakespeare's *A Midsummer Night's Dream.*

"Well, you could have juice or something, if you'd rather. If you don't drink coffee, I mean. Or we could just sit at a table and order nothing." She frowned, her brows puckering. Gabe opened his mouth, figuring it was his turn to speak, but as usual, he couldn't think of a single witty, sophisticated thing to say. All he could think about was how much he'd love to sit at a table, or anywhere else, with this unusual woman. She even tinkled when she moved.

On his regular morning tour of the store, he'd stopped for only a few stolen minutes when he'd spotted the volume of Chaucer's *The Canterbury Tales.* It had been so long since he'd read it he'd suddenly found himself craving a refresher. He'd never dreamed history would come to life right in front of his eyes.

"It's always a bit awkward when you're first getting to know someone, don't you think?" She spoke before he could fumble his way through the uncomfortable situation. And continued without seeming to notice his lack of response. "I mean, it's happened a million times. You see someone you think is interesting, but you don't know for sure...."

She thought *he* was interesting?

"So you have to go through this social thing where you get a little peek into that person's life, his head. But what if you don't like what you see and there you are, peeking in...." She shrugged and that beautiful hair rippled again. "It could be awkward—or worse, you could even hurt the other person when you try to back off. Do you know what I mean?"

Gabe nodded. Unbelievably enough, he did.

"Or," she continued, still frowning as she looked up at him, "you like the peek so much you want to charge right in, but you don't know if he liked what *he* saw or if he wants you to come in. Or if someone else is already in there and it really doesn't matter if you liked what you saw because it's not available, anyway."

"No one's in there." *Dumb.* What an incredibly asinine thing to say.

The woman's face lit up. "Really?"

"Really." Gabe didn't see what the big surprise was. She had to know by now that he wasn't a sparkling conversationalist.

"No one's in here, either," she said, still grinning up at him.

Silence fell. He was supposed to come up with light sexual banter here. And this was where it fell apart. His thoughts tended to be of a more serious nature. Banter, no matter how hard he tried to learn it, escaped him. He waited for her to excuse herself.

"So, was that yes or no to coffee?"

Over the spirit queen's shoulder, Gabe saw Marie approaching. One of his more capable employees, his store manager also tended to think she had to run every little problem by him whenever he was on the floor. Problems Marie handled quite capably by herself during the hours he spent in his office on the third floor of the massive bookstore.

"Uh..."

"It's okay, you don't have to." The enchantress had obviously misinterpreted his distraction. "You've probably had enough of a peek already—"

"No!" Gabe couldn't remember ever replying so quickly in his life. Marie had been momentarily detained by a customer in Psychology and Self-help. "Coffee..." He paused. "Or whatever, would be fine."

"Oh." He'd actually brought the grin back to her face. "Good." She turned as if to head toward the café on the second floor of Stone's Bookstore, and stopped when he didn't follow. "Now's not a good time?"

Marie was going to be through with her customer soon. And he had twenty other employees milling around, serving in the café, finding reasons to need him. "Let's go somewhere else. More private."

"How about the coffee shop across the street?"

"Fine." Placing the book carefully back on the shelf, Gabe followed her to the escalator, down to the first floor and out of the building. As if he did this kind of thing every day.

As if he'd ever done this kind of thing before in his life.

PRACTICALLY FREE of tension for the first time in months, Bailey skipped across Chicago's Michigan Avenue, dodging traffic, jaywalking her way to the coffee shop. It was a beautiful March day, warm enough to be out without a coat.

She wasn't used to men like Gabriel Stone so readily agreeing to spend time with her for no reason at all. He was so logical, so responsible and respectable; she knew that, even though she didn't know *him* yet.

She knew it because she'd observed him at work, because she'd learned of his reputation...and because Eve said so. Bailey was the opposite of this obviously methodical man. She ran through life skittering from one emotion to the next, so filled with intensity that it often spilled out and...and ruined things. But maybe not this time. Maybe she wasn't making another huge mistake. Maybe there was some actual truth to Eve's "vision" nonsense. Maybe she wasn't an idiot to act out of desperation—and deep trust for her oldest and truest friend.

"So, Gabe." She shot him a quick glance over her shoulder as he held the door of the restaurant open for her. "Do you like coffee?"

He nodded.

"Where do you want to sit?"

"Here's fine." Stopping at the first table he came to, Gabe held out a chair for her.

Bailey sat. His manners reminded her of her father. As a child she'd taken great comfort from his habitual politeness. As a woman she wasn't much of a queen or a princess or the kind of sedate, helpless female who inspired people to want to take care of her. But, she had to confess, it was nice to be coddled, just for a change.

"They do latte divinely here," she said without looking at the menu he was studying. She studied him, instead. Tall. Dark hair in a refined, dignified cut. Shoulders broad enough to lean on. He looked up from the menu, but said nothing. "It's Colombian espresso with just the right amount of steamed milk. I get a touch of cinnamon sprinkled on top," she blurted.

"You come here a lot?"

"Every time I'm in Stone's—which, if I have my way, happens at least once a week."

"I've never seen you there."

She grinned. "I'm usually hiding out in a corner reading."

Gabe nodded, his brown eyes watching her for another second before he stood and went to the counter, where he ordered—and paid—for both of them.

Reaching into the pocket of her ankle-length cotton skirt, Bailey slid a five-dollar bill across the table as he brought the coffee. "I don't expect you to buy," she said. She hadn't intended this experiment of hers to cost him anything.

"My pleasure." He completely ignored the money.

Remembering too late the millions of lectures her father had delivered on ladylike behavior, Bailey tried to tactfully slide the money back into her pocket. And continued to watch her companion.

Eve had insisted that Gabe was the man for Bailey. The answer to Bailey's prayers. The solution to her problem. Personally, Bailey suspected that Eve had finally let all her otherworldly claptrap rid her of what common sense she still possessed. But Eve hadn't seemed the least bit out of this world when she'd told Bailey to approach Gabe. She'd seemed completely, uncompromisingly certain that Gabe Stone was the man for her.

The man was an enigma. Solid. Respectable. Gorgeous. And about as talkative as Gladys, Bailey's pet turtle. Which normally would have suited Bailey just fine. She rather liked holding the floor at home with Gladys. But she needed to get to know this man. If there was no chemistry between them, she was going to have to come up with Plan B in a hurry.

"I love books," she murmured. He *had* to have something to say about books—he owned millions of them. "Especially fairy tales. I'll bet you think that's silly, huh, for a thirty-year-old woman to still love fairy tales?''

"Not at all." Gabe smiled at her. A smile that warmed her insides more than the latte she'd been sipping.

"I just can't leave 'em behind," she said to cover up her unexpected reaction. The triple rings in her ears jingled as she shook her head, but they only complemented the clinking of her bracelets as she raised her cup to her mouth. Bailey loved her little symphony. And hoped Gabe, unlike her father, wouldn't be irritated by the sounds. "I've got this little green hardcover book that must be fifty years old called *Fifty Famous Stories Retold....*"

"James Baldwin," Gabe said, nodding as he sipped slowly from the cup he held.

"You know it?" She couldn't believe it. The book was a rare one.

"The original copyright is 1896."

"You have an original?"

"Two."

"Oh, my gosh! I'd love to see one! I've read that book a million times. Have you ever read it?"

"Yeah."

"Then you know the story of Androcles and the lion?"

With a single slow nod, Gabe confirmed that he did.

"It's my absolute favorite, you know?" Carried away by her excitement, Bailey continued. "I remember when I was a little girl and my father—he was a lieutenant colonel then—would yell at me for spilling paint on my carpet or getting so caught up in a project I'd forget to come down to dinner. Or he'd be mad if I came down with smears of glue or something on my dress or with my hair falling out of its ponytail because I'd been dancing, or just about anything I did that..." Her voice trailed off.

Gabe was staring at her.

"What?" she asked, rubbing her mouth in case an unknown dollop of whipped cream was hanging there.

"Don't you ever stop for breath?"

"I'm sorry." Bailey looked down, then back up again. She was blowing it already and this was only the first date. Hadn't she been reminded a million times that she spoke too fast when she got excited? Her father had certainly told her often enough when she was young. And most of her friends had teased her about it over the years. "I do tend to go on," she said, apologizing again for good measure—just in case he hadn't already made up his mind to leave as soon as he could decently excuse himself.

"No, really, it's okay," he surprised her by saying. And he meant it, too. His eyes gave him away. "Go on."

Because Bailey was Bailey, she did. "Anyway, when Dad used to yell, I'd get all choked up and tense and I'd really hate it. A lot." Bailey couldn't remember her mother, but she sure remembered missing her. "Then I found Androcles, and Dad's yelling never bothered me so much anymore. I'd found courage, you know? I'd read that story again and again, and know that if I was a good girl and had courage, I'd be okay. No one could ask any more of me than that. And no one really had the right to make me feel bad, either, just for being myself. Not even my dad."

"He was mean to you?"

"Not really. He's just military all the way to his bones and used to giving orders. Can you imagine a logical man like that raising a child who thought—and acted—with her emotions rather than her intellect most of the time?"

"I imagine the experience brought his life new dimensions."

Bailey thought about that. And decided she liked his answer. Of course, there was no saying that the new dimensions were a *positive* addition....

"He didn't understand me, that's for sure," she continued, allowing Gabe the opportunity to identify with her father if he needed to. "I think I'm more like my mother. She named me, you know."

He blinked. "I don't know your name."

"It's Bailey. Bailey Cooper."

"And your mother...she understood you?"

Bailey shook her head. "She died when I was three months old. She had bad kidneys and had taken a risk having me. She made it through my birth, but went into kidney failure a couple of months later. I take after her, though."

"How so?" Elbows on the table, he leaned forward.

Bailey practically glowed under his attention. He was really listening to her.

This was dangerous. Definitely dangerous.

"She loved art."

"You're an artist?"

"The clothes give it away, right?" She

shrugged again, lightly. Her choice of dress had probably started out as a rebellion against all the things she was not, but as she'd gotten older, Bailey had recognized that her clothes were also an expression of the spirit inside her that refused to be quelled. Every time she looked in a mirror and saw glorious colors swirling around her, every time she felt the cool glide of silk or cotton against her calves, her unencumbered breasts, her shoulders and arms, she felt a spurt of wonderful.

"I like them."

Shocked enough to still her coffee cup in midair, Bailey looked at Gabe—and smiled. "You do?"

She was well aware that respectable, straight-laced, nonartistic people such as her dad thought she was a little on the weird side.

He nodded. "What do you call something like that?"

Still smiling, Bailey said, "It's really just a skirt and tank top. I simply add scarves or jewelry or a shawl—whatever else feels good on any particular day. Today it's a bunch of scarves."

"How do you get them to stay on?"

She tied them of course. But he looked so

damn cute with that frown furrowing his brow, and he was studying her so intently, Bailey couldn't bear to stem his interest with prosaic fact. "Magic," she said solemnly.

Nodding, Gabe sat back and folded his arms across his chest. Bailey, who'd posed nude on more than one occasion during her college art class years, actually started to feel a little self-conscious.

"So, how'd you get such broad shoulders?" she asked him when the silence started to make her feel downright uncomfortable. "Been lifting boxes of books your whole life?"

"Yeah."

"Really?" She leaned forward, her forearms resting on the table. "Stone's was a family business, then?"

"I was practically born there."

She had to ask. "Practically?"

"My mother went into labor while she was working at the store."

"Wow." She had a whole new respect for her favorite bookstore, being the site of something so momentous as the almost-birth of this man, the man Eve insisted Bailey was searching for. "Was it Stone's then?"

Another nod. "My paternal grandfather opened the store."

"So your family was the original owner?"

He nodded again. "They contracted the architect who built the place."

"Oh, my gosh, they knew John Mead Howells?" You couldn't be an artist in Chicago and not be aware of the architecture for which the city was famous, or the many important architects whose work was showcased both on the Loop and, like Stone's, on the Magnificent Mile. Bailey knew them all, taught them all to her students, but Howells's work spoke to her in ways no one else's did.

"My grandfather knew him in New York."

"I can't believe it! Did you know he designed the Tribune Tower?" She barely waited for Gabe's nod before she continued. "But did you also know that he won the opportunity to see his structure built by entering the design in a contest?"

"No."

"He inspires me, you know?" she said, excited by Gabe's interest in something she found fascinating, something that seemed lost on most people. "The man had a dream and the courage to take a chance, the daring to open himself up to ridicule. And he won!''

Gabe smiled.

"Stone's was one of the first buildings to go up after the opening of the Michigan Avenue Bridge, wasn't it?''

"You know your stuff.'' His words might be sparse, but his admiration, clearly, was not. Bailey's whole body tingled beneath that warm stare. She wondered if for once she'd actually made the right decision when she'd made up her mind to approach Mr. Gabriel Stone.

Chapter Three

BAILEY HADN'T INTENDED to move so fast, but the very next morning she was back at Stone's, looking for Gabe. Being with him had felt so right. Their time together had left her invigorated for the rest of the day. She had to find out if it had been simply her imagination. Or an overreaction to the unseasonably beautiful spring weather. Or the unreasonably handsome Gabe Stone...

She'd been thinking about him nonstop since yesterday. About the way he'd looked at her. The way he'd made her feel. The way he'd seemed engrossed by her conversation. Though she could hardly believe it herself, she was actually starting to give credence to the possibility that Eve might have been right. Gabe could be the answer to Bailey's prayers.

Much to her dismay, strolling every inch of the bookstore turned up absolutely nothing. She'd been so certain she'd find him here. Had counted on being able to run into him again, to offer a casual invitation to lunch. Disappointed, she wondered if maybe he was purposely avoiding her; the thought made her cringe. Then she told herself not to be ridiculous. The man had to work, didn't he? He couldn't do bookstore-owner stuff walking around reading from the shelves.

What should she do now? Just leave? After having boarded the Howard Red Line to get over here, specifically to see him? She headed toward the stairs that would take her down to the first floor, reminding herself that she always rushed everything. She could come back the next day, and the next, if need be. She bought a thirty-day pass every month for unlimited use of the city's various forms of public transportation. Eventually, he'd be in the store again. She'd found him so easily the day before, it shouldn't be that hard to do it again.

The problem was, she didn't have a lot of time. Lonnie's ultimatum, ignored for many months, was looming too close for comfort. After a lifetime of being out of balance, Bailey had finally found, at Lonnie's boarding school, something that fulfilled her soul. As a troubled teenager at the institute, Bailey had first discovered the passion that drove her, the thirst for beauty and color that prompted every decision she'd ever made. And now, back as a teacher, her work gave her an outlet for that passion. But Lonnie Winston's ultimatum threatened to take all of that away. Not only from her, but from the couple of hundred kids like her who attended the institute every year.

Back on the first floor, she scanned the aisles again, just in case.

She could easily have become a teenage suicide or drug abuse statistic if it hadn't been for the institute. Lonnie's art school had given her a place to fit in. For the first time in her life, she'd felt as if she were home, as though she belonged. She'd been in sync with herself, and the feeling had been heady enough to carry her through the next fifteen years of her life. The institute had given her the confidence and the inner strength to accept that her own talent was small—and to recognize that her real gift lay in her ability to recognize talent in others, the intrinsic beauty and power in an artist's beginning attempts. She had the ability to somehow get out of others what she could never quite bring out of herself. The institute had once again become her home.

Almost at the store's entrance, her feet took a

slight turn and brought her up to the counter with its registers and computer terminals.

"Is Mr. Stone in this morning?" she asked the official-looking woman behind the desk.

The woman picked up a phone. "Who should I say is calling on him?"

Bailey glanced toward the door. She should just leave. Play it cool. She was going to blow this before there even *was* a "this."

"Bailey Cooper."

"SO TELL ME ABOUT your parents, your family. Do you have brothers and sisters?" Bailey asked, sitting across a table from Gabe Stone for the fourth time in four days, this time at Bennigan's, one of her favorite restaurants.

"No." He dug into his sandwich with gusto. Bailey knew all that meat and cheese wasn't good for him, but she sure liked the passion with which he attacked it. Though she'd seen him each of the past three days, it had just been for coffee, until now. This lunch had been at his invitation.

"No brothers and sisters? Or no, you won't tell me about them?"

"I have no family."

"Your parents are both gone?" she asked,

feeling instantly sorry for him. As much of a pain in the ass as her father was most of the time, she couldn't imagine life without him.

Gabe shrugged. "They were older."

"How much older?" She toyed with her avocado salad, wishing she dared snitch one of the fries from his plate.

"My father was fifty-one when I was born. Mom was forty-four."

"Wow." She thought about that for a minute. And then, "You didn't have any older brothers or sisters?"

"Nope."

"What about school? I'll bet you had a million friends."

"You use that word a lot."

"What word?"

"Million."

"Oh." Bailey smiled. "Yeah, I guess I think big." She noticed he hadn't answered her question about school. "I hated school," she confessed.

Gabe looked up from his lunch. "Why?"

"I just never really felt like I belonged. One reason was probably that we moved around so much."

"And the other reason?" His gaze seemed to

penetrate all the layers she'd wrapped around herself.

"My mind had a tendency to wander, which meant that when the teacher asked me a question, I usually didn't have a clue what was going on."

Smiling his understanding, Gabe's eyes encouraged her to continue.

"And I was interested in different things from most of the other kids." She forked up a hunk of avocado. "I'd much rather draw than play kick ball or jump rope during recess. And I used to tap-dance in line." Giving in, she snitched one of his fries. He didn't seem to notice.

"What about friends?"

Bailey's earrings jingled as she shook her head. "I didn't have many. Being in the military, we were transferred every two or three years. Sometimes more." A sip of water cooled her dry throat. "And somehow I never got infected with the need to be cool. I wore the clothes I wanted to, in spite of the fact that the colors didn't always match and they weren't at all fashionable." She grinned at him under her lashes. "Maybe that was partly because it bugged my dad so much. But I also didn't listen to the right music or hang out in the right places.

So, no, I didn't have a lot of friends." Not until her father, washing his hands of her, had shipped her off to live at the institute and she'd met Eve.

"Me neither."

Shocked, Bailey studied him. "You weren't the most popular guy in school?" She'd just assumed he had been. He looked the part perfectly. The clothes. The hair. The quiet confidence. The body.

Gabe gave her an ironic grin. "Hardly."

"And here I had you pegged as quarterback of the football team."

"I was."

"I knew it!" she said, trying to ignore her instinctive disappointment at this revelation. For the first time in four days, she'd found something about him that wasn't perfect. All the football heroes she'd ever known had been stuck on themselves. Her talkative nature only irritated them because she left them so little time to talk about themselves. Which had made her the target of more than a couple of their cruel pranks.

Except that Gabe didn't appear to be stuck on himself. And she'd never met anyone who talked less than he did. Except Gladys, of course.

Still, there was her competition. He'd had cheerleaders, groupies. Prom queens, no doubt.

Cute girls. Women with predictably perfect looks and perfectly predictable attitudes. How could she ever hope he'd be attracted for any length of time to a zany art teacher like her?

"You probably dated every girl in your senior class, right?" she asked. And then, because she wasn't eager to hear his confirmation, she went on. "You never spent a Saturday night at home, never had to do your own homework, always had someone to sit with at the pizza place after school, and the only problem you had in the lunchroom was finding enough room at your table for all your admirers."

"You were right about your creativity."

"You're telling me it wasn't like that?"

He shook his head. "I did my own homework."

Bailey laughed, though she was still envious of those other girls. And disappointed, too. "But the rest of it was right—wasn't it?"

He studied her for a long moment, his eyes serious. "No," he finally said as if coming to some kind of decision. "I was okay on the field..." He started and then stopped. "Better than okay, actually, I made all-American my junior and senior years."

"I knew it," she said again, slumping in her seat.

"But off the field—" he cast his eyes down "—I wasn't anything spectacular."

She found that extremely hard to believe. "With your looks?" She snorted.

"I was too reserved," he admitted. "Still am."

She couldn't argue with him there. "So?"

"Women expect to be entertained."

"In high school, maybe, but what about when you got into college? University women are not as likely to be scared off by a reserved manner. And with your looks…"

His eyes shone with pure male satisfaction and, realizing what she was saying, Bailey shut up.

"I saw a different woman practically every night during my junior year," he admitted frankly. He didn't seem the least embarrassed by the confession, but Bailey sure felt her own cheeks turn red. Maybe because she was envisioning, a bit too clearly, just what those women had had the luck to experience. The man's body was perfection.

"Just your junior year?" If she was smart,

she'd get off the subject. But she'd never been smart enough for her own good.

Shrugging, as though bored with the topic, Gabe picked up his glass and took a long swallow of cola. She watched the muscles in his throat move as he drank. At the moment, even that was arousing....

"What I had to say didn't interest them."

"Why not?" She leaned forward, eager to know as much about him as she possibly could.

"I found that most college girls aren't big on Emerson's epistles or medieval history or fairy tales or the acquisition of language or—"

"What about body language?"

"One subject I could handle adeptly..."

That had to be an understatement.

"I never quite knew what to do with them before or after bed."

"You must have picked some amazingly stupid girls."

"Maybe." His lips curved into a half smile. "All I know is that by my senior year I was worn out on meaningless one-nighters with girls whose last names I never even knew."

"I'd have made sure you knew my last name." Bailey heard herself say the words and wished immediately that she could shut her stupid mouth. It was far too soon to be coming on to a man like Gabe. Yet here she was, speaking before she thought—speaking from instinct and emotion rather than intellect. Her father had tried his damnedest to break her of the habit.

Gabe pushed his plate away. Picked up the bill. Looked anywhere but at her. She applied herself to her salad. No matter how disastrous the occasion, she couldn't let the food go to waste when there were so many people starving in the world.

"You said yesterday that you sketched instead of doing your math in school?" Gabe asked. He was leaning back in his chair, his glass between his hands as he watched her eat.

"Yeah."

"So, drawing's your specialty?"

Chomping her lettuce, relieved he was still speaking to her, Bailey wondered how to answer him. She wanted to impress him—but she couldn't lie.

"I'm not very good at it."

"But you're an artist."

"An art teacher, actually," she reminded him. "I'm on staff at the Winston Art Institute down on the Loop."

Gabe whistled softly. "You must be good."

"I have vision." Shrugging, Bailey tried to explain what she didn't really understand. "I can see things, beautiful, amazing things. I just can't seem to express them the way they appear inside.

"But I can recognize them in other people's work, and from other people I seem to be able to extract them just fine."

He was still watching her closely, contemplating, and she couldn't tell what he was thinking.

"I was a dancer, too," she added, though nothing, not even dance, had completed her the way her teaching did. "That was the one area where I did succeed at expressing the visions I saw inside. I was accepted at the Bradford Dance Company in New York."

"They were just in Chicago a few months ago," Gabe said, looking impressed. "The show was fabulous. It was also sold out."

Her mouth fell open. No one she currently knew, other than students at the institute, was familiar with the modern-dance world. Not even Eve was going to believe *this* coincidence. "You like modern dance?"

"I do." He inclined his head.

Shivers ran up and down Bailey's spine at

those two words. She couldn't believe how badly she wanted to hear them again...in front of a preacher. And not just to appease Lonnie Winston, as she knew Lonnie would assume. Not just to retain her job, her life's work. And not to take over the institute when Lonnie retired, either. Although all of those things would happen if she met her boss's ultimatum and got married to an acceptable man. But they weren't the force moving her forward.

GABE WAS ASTONISHED WHEN he heard himself embark on a two-minute discourse about the artistic significance he found in good modern dance. Seemed that being with Bailey Cooper was freeing his tongue.

"...and the physical stamina, the strength those dancers have is amazing," he rattled on.

Plus, they were sexy as hell. Just like her.

"They train for hours every day," she interjected. "Ballet, conditioning, technique classes, rehearsals. By the end of the day, you're aching and sure you'll never be able to get out of bed once you finally get in. But you do and there's an incredible high in those moments when your body does exactly what you want it to, when you feel something inside of you burst forth and fly free.''

She was so beautiful, so passionate. Blood flowed quickly to his nether region as he entertained another vision of her passion bursting free...and in his direction. "So why aren't you in New York dancing?"

"I was in a car accident," she said as though it had been no big deal. "My knee was crushed under the dash."

"Damn!"

"It's okay." Bailey smiled and Gabe couldn't breathe. He'd known the woman four days and was already addicted to her smile.

"I recovered," she continued. "But not quite well enough to withstand the pressure of a million grand pliés a day. Or a million grand jetés, either. I probably would never have survived in the big city, anyway. I didn't like the crowds. And I wasn't ruthless enough. Besides, the accident allowed me to discover what I was really meant to do."

"Which is?"

"Teach." She grinned at him.

Gabe wondered if he was dreaming. In his entire life he'd never felt as alive as he felt right now, sitting across from her.

He just couldn't figure out what in hell was making *her* stay.

AT HOME in his Lincoln Park residence that night, Gabe slid into the oven the casserole Mrs. Ingall, his five-day-a-week housekeeper, had left him. He poured a glass of wine, set silverware and a napkin on the dining room table, and then headed for the computer he had set up in his family room.

It only took him a couple of seconds to access the ticket line on the Internet. And another couple of minutes to come up with a list of modern dance shows that would be coming to the Chicago area in the near future. Pulling his credit card out of his wallet, he bought two tickets to every single performance. Just in case.

THE NEXT MORNING Gabe was engrossed in a conversation with the woman who handled publicity for a well-known New York publisher. They were working out the logistics of a book signing he was going to be hosting later that month. The author, Talia Nelson, a multiple *New York Times*'s list prima donna, had some requests. She didn't sit when she signed, so he'd have to bring down a lectern or a tall table at which she could stand. She would only remain in the store for half-hour intervals—though she agreed to do several of them. She refused to sign used copies of her books. And she had to have a particular brand of bottled water provided on a continual basis.

Wonder how many times she'll need to use the toilet during her half-hour stints, Gabe was musing when Marie poked her head inside his office door.

Motioning her inside, he spoke into the phone. "No problem. We'll be happy to accommodate her." He rolled his eyes at Marie and mouthed Talia's name.

He didn't notice the bag Marie was carrying until he'd ended the call.

"Bailey Cooper left this for you."

Gabe was out of his seat and at the door before Marie had a chance to make it to his desk. "Where is she?" he asked, barging into the hall.

"She's gone." Marie was staring after him.

Gabe, realizing what an idiot he must look, came back into the office, took his seat and jotted down a few more notes regarding the signing. Marie had left the bag on his desk.

"Talia's still on?" Marie asked. Talia's publisher refused to deal with any local bookseller except Gabe, and they gave him an exclusive appearance whenever the author's tours brought her to Chicago.

Unlike many of the hourly employees in the book superstores, Gabe's people knew books. They sold books. And Talia's publisher knew that.

"She's still on," he confirmed. "End of the month."

Marie nodded, briefly discussed the number of books they'd order for the signing, and then, with one last, curious look at the brightly colored gift bag on his desk, she left.

Gabe waited only long enough to hear her footsteps on the stairs before digging into the bag.

His questing fingers encountered several little packages. Too impatient to take them out one at a time, he dumped everything on his desk. Unwrapping the first, he discovered a ceramic ring-shaped thing with an indentation on top and a bottom that would fit over a tennis ball. He frowned. What in hell could that be for?

There was a little terra-cotta football about the size of a key chain hanging from a loop of string. Upon further inspection he discovered that it opened.

Next in the pile was a little pot with a plug attached. Mini fondue?

And last, he discovered a small vial of fluid. Neroli, the label read. That was all. There wasn't room for any more information. Such as directions. Definitions. Anything that would give him a clue as to what he should do with the stuff.

The woman was a nutcase. And he couldn't remember a time he'd had so much fun. Couldn't ever remember receiving a gift for no reason. Taking a whiff from the vial he decided the scent might grow on him. Perhaps it was special cologne. He'd heard of places where you could have scents created just for you.

Dabbing some on, he kidded himself that Bailey was interested enough to buy him cologne. Maybe she was, and maybe that meant it was only sex she was after. Even if that was the case, he'd take what he could get.

Now that he was on a roll, he picked up the football and turned it over and over in his hand, determined to figure it out, too. He finally decided it was a male version of a pill holder, simply because he couldn't think of anything else small enough to fit inside it, except earrings—which he certainly didn't have. Emerging from his private bathroom with a bottle of aspirin so old the expiry date was long past, he shook out a couple of tablets, put them in the football and closed the lid. He tied the loop to the gill of a fish he'd caught the previous summer during a rafting trip and had later mounted. As a final touch, he set the football in the fish's open mouth.

He studied the ceramic ring. It could only be some kind of art piece that he didn't get. But he decided, as it fit perfectly on top of a snow globe one of his elderly customers had brought him from a trip to Colorado, to use it for thumbtacks. He placed the ring on the globe, dug some thumb tacks out of a box in the supply room and was rather pleased with the result. He wouldn't tell Bailey what he'd done; he'd hate her to know that her work was lost on him. He couldn't help thinking, however, that she was right about her visions not coming out exactly as she'd planned. He figured it was probably best that she'd chosen to go into teaching.

Just thinking about having a teacher like Bailey, Gabe grew hard. He was turned on by so many things about her. Her looks, certainly. The woman had a body that could enslave a man forever. But he loved her openness, too. Her ability to talk about anything at any time—a perfect complement to his reticence. He loved her intensity, the life she brought to a room just by being there.

He'd never met anyone like her.

The pot was still sitting in the middle of his desk, staring up at him. Certain that it had significance, that there was a specific point to it, he racked his brain. And came up blank. Until his roving eye stilled on the mini bar across the room. A brandy warmer. That was it. The little pot was just big enough to hold a shot or two.

He had no idea how Bailey had known he liked his brandy warm, or even that he liked brandy, but he was glad she'd guessed so accurately. He wasn't going to leave the pot in the office, however. He'd been enjoying brandy after dinner since he was fourteen years old and his parents had invited him to join them in their evening ritual. He was going to take this thoughtful gift home with him.

And think of Bailey every time he used it.

Chapter Four

"EVE, ARE YOU ABSOLUTELY sure you were right? About Gabe Stone?" Bailey asked two days later. And then, "Ouch! That hurt."

Eve continued to beat Bailey's body into pulp. "Of course I'm sure." Her voice had no business being so calm, considering the agony her hands were creating. "You know I'd never tell you anything unless I was one hundred percent certain," Bailey's masseuse/healer/astrologer/ best friend said. "Now lie still or I'll never get this knot out."

After a couple more deep rubs between the back of Bailey's neck and her right shoulder blade, she reached for some rose oil and started in again. Bailey lay quiet for a few minutes, appreciating Eve's ministrations.

"It's just that I'll never be the kind of woman men like Gabe Stone marry," she said after a while. "I've already—*ouch*—blown it a couple of times."

"What's it hurt to try?"

Bailey's silence said it all.

"You're falling for him," Eve said. Her friend's lack of surprise calmed Bailey a little.

"I'm scared," she admitted, and then shuddered as Eve's hands found another knot. "In some ways, he's like me. But in other ways, he's just like my father, and I've never managed to live up to *him*. Or his expectations."

"Shh-hh," Eve said softly, lightening her touch as she worked down Bailey's back. "Let the rose oil work, Bail. It'll soothe all these worries. Relieve the stress that's got you wound tight as a golf ball."

"Yes, but is it going to help me sleep?" She'd spent the past couple of nights wide awake, wandering around, restless, wondering what Gabe was doing, wishing she could call him. Gladys had kept her company the first night, but last night hadn't even come out of her shell.

"It's good for insomnia, yes." The gentle cadence of Eve's voice was relaxing in itself. "It also enhances love."

Bailey immediately shot up. "Get it off me!" she said, grabbing the sheet from the lower half of her body to begin wiping off her back.

Eve almost left her healing persona behind to

crack a smile. Almost. "Come on, Bail," she said, pulling the sheet away from Bailey as she eased her down to the table again. "When have I ever led you wrong?"

Well, there might have been a time. Maybe. So long ago that she couldn't remember. Eve's calm influence had touched Bailey the day she'd arrived at the institute when she was fourteen, hurt by her father's rejection, frightened. She'd been leaning on her friend ever since.

She let Eve settle the sheet back around her.

"But..." she started again as soon as she felt Eve's oily hands on her shoulder blades.

"Trust me," Eve interrupted. "Did you give him the neroli?"

"Yeah," Bailey grunted. "But I don't know why you were so certain he needed it. His confidence and self-esteem seem in pretty good shape to me."

"Now, don't be shocked, but it's also an aphrodisiac."

"Oh." Bailey pondered that. Between her deadline for marriage and her attraction to Gabe Stone, maybe she'd overreacted earlier to the idea of Eve's potions for "enhancing love." As long as Gabe was getting one, too...she'd take whatever help she could get. "What if he falls for me only because his olfactory gland has been stimulated by oil?''

''It's not a magic potion, Bail.'' Eve laughed—and punched. ''It's a natural enhancer. Now, no more talking until we're done, and then we'll talk until your heart's content.''

Bailey wasn't sure either one of them had voices that would last that long.

''SO TELL ME AGAIN what you felt,'' Bailey said as soon as she was showered, dressed and sitting outside on a blanket in Eve's herb garden. The weather was perfect. Warm, but not warm enough to make her sweat. ''What you felt about me and Gabe Stone.''

''It's time, Bailey,'' Eve said, completely serious. ''Your spirit is crying out for a mate.''

Bailey could have told her that. ''But what about Gabe?''

Stringing flower stems together to make a chain, Eve looked over at her, gaze steady. ''I researched him.''

Sitting straight up, Bailey stared. ''You *what?*''

''Well, you weren't doing anything, Bail. Lonnie's ultimatum came a long time ago, and you were just going to let it all slip through your fingers—everything that's ever meant anything to you—without even trying to salvage it.''

"You *researched* him?" Bailey croaked. "What happened to visions and astrological charts and—?"

"Nothing wrong with helping the spiritual processes along." Eve's nimble fingers continued their weaving. "You've been going to his store every week for more than year, so I figured there must be something that kept you coming back," she said, her long dark hair hanging down on either side of her face. "I asked some friends to find out what they could, talked to people, checked his store's site on the Internet…and every single thing I learned told me I was right. He's the man for you, Bail. Responsible, reliable, intelligent—and he's got a great bod. Tell me you hadn't noticed him."

Bailey couldn't tell her friend that. She *had* noticed Gabe. She'd just never in a million years thought she'd ever have a chance with him. He certainly hadn't noticed her.

"What I can't figure out," Eve said, her flower chain falling onto her crossed, denim-clad legs, "is why you took up with that hobo, Danji or whatever his name was, in the first place."

"You know why." Bailey had the grace to

look down. "And his name was Alongie. I needed a man in my life. I was lonely. And I had no hope in hell of attracting a steady man like Dad."

"But a man you barely knew, Bail? If you wanted an artist, why not grab one a little closer to home? One you had more hope of having an actual relationship with than some reprobate you met at a Colorado art show?"

Okay. Bailey felt bad about that. Eve had no idea how bad she felt. But... "How was I to know he was a con artist? How was I to know he was going to use me as his front man to sell fake turquoise?"

"Fake turquoise?" Eve, of course, didn't let it go at that. "What about the fake diamonds he put in his jewelry?"

Bailey tried not to think about that time in her life. Ever. "I got off," she said now, reiterating, for her own benefit, what mattered most. "I cleared my name," she reminded her friend.

Not that her innocence had made any difference to Lonnie.

"Yeah, after spending almost a week in jail," Eve said relentlessly.

"Don't..." Remembering, Bailey shuddered.

The filth, the language. The woman who'd come on to her.

"You can't blame Lonnie for being skeptical."

"But to close the institute rather than sell it to me?" Bailey still couldn't believe her mentor would do such a thing. For years, she'd been saving every damn penny she'd had to buy that school. She and Lonnie had had an agreement since she'd come back from New York. "The institute's reputation is world-renowned. We accept only a couple of hundred students a year, at most, and the tuition is so prohibitive that fifty would support us. And we still have a waiting list a million miles long. How could Lonnie even think about turning his back on that?" Bailey tried to get angry. Anger took away the hurt.

"Turning his back on *you*, you mean?" Eve asked softly. Her flower chain lay wilting in her lap.

"That, too." Bailey couldn't look at her friend. Eve saw far too much.

"So maybe he's not turning his back on you."

Bailey raised her head. "How can you say that?"

"Maybe he thinks you've left him no choice.

He knows you'll never let the institute go, that the school, your work there, completes you in a way nothing else ever has.''

"Yeah." Lonnie had known the Bailey who'd arrived on his doorstep all those years ago, too. "I'm not following you here, Eve. How is selling the school out from under me not turning his back?"

"Because he knows, too, that there's far more to life than you've explored. That it's time for you to reach out, to discover that there are more colors out there than you can see. Finding love, finding the right man, is not something you're doing on your own, Bail, so maybe he's decided to force you into it. He wants you to be with someone who'll balance you, someone whose steadiness and rationality will balance your impulsiveness. And he's right, Bailey."

Bailey considered this logic. And tried to think again, harder, if Eve had ever been wrong before.

"He knows you'll find a way to get married— to a man he approves—before the deadline. He knows the Winston Institute will be safe."

Only slightly appeased, Bailey heaved a disgruntled sigh. "I still can't believe he's really doing this. I can't believe I have to be married within two months or he's closing the institute when he retires. Get real! Two months to get married!''

"And how long ago did he give you this ultimatum?'' Eve's knowing tone grated on Bailey's nerves.

"Ten months.''

The words stuck in her throat. But they weren't what had made her mouth go dry. No, the thought of Gabe Stone had done that. For the first time since Lonnie's ultimatum all those months ago, it occurred to Bailey that she might actually meet his deadline. She would never have gotten married just for the sake of being married, not even for Lonnie. But to live with Gabe Stone—and get the institute, too? Bailey could hardly contain her excitement.

For a moment. Until the excitement gave way to limb-numbing fear. Gabe had begun to matter far too much in the short time she'd known him. He mattered far too much, period. She'd never been so vulnerable in her life.

She wouldn't have dared to think of him as a potential husband, if not for Eve's counsel. Her friend had a lot to answer for. And Bailey was going to hold Eve accountable if the whole thing blew up in her face.

But only because she knew she'd need Eve's love and support to see her through if that happened.

GABE SPENT THE NEXT couple of days roaming the aisles of his store instead of getting through the pile of work waiting for him up in his office. He had no intention of missing Bailey on the off chance she came by again. He'd sent a thank-you to her for the gifts, care of the Winston Institute, but he hadn't heard from her again.

Not that he'd really expected to, he thought as he leafed through a copy of Twain's *A Connecticut Yankee in King Arthur's Court*. It wouldn't take long for a woman as vital, as vibrant, as Bailey to lose interest in him. Especially since they'd never been to bed together. His performance in the sack was the one thing women came back for.

"Hi, stranger."

He turned, thinking he'd imagined her voice. And suddenly she was there. Standing in front of him in some of the widest-legged pants he'd ever seen, in every color known to man. And a man's ribbed T-shirt that had been dyed a strange shade of orange. As he'd suspected on the other occasions he'd seen her, she wasn't wearing a bra.

He just stared. And let the relief flow all over him. Along with the lust.

"You're not glad to see me?" she asked, making an obvious effort to sound nonchalant.

For the first time Gabe allowed himself to accept the fact that Bailey might actually see something in him. He glimpsed in her eyes what her words weren't saying. Regret, a little bit of fear that she might be right.

"Of course I'm glad," he said. And then, because of that vulnerability in her eyes, he added, "The whole reason I'm prowling around down here, making my employees nervous, is that I was hoping to catch you if you came in."

"You were?" Her grin was worth every word of the difficult confession.

"I was."

"Well, I'm here."

"I see that." But he couldn't come up with a line of sassy banter that would have her end up in his arms.

"Wanna go for a walk? There's a park not too far from here." She was still smiling at him. "It's cloudy outside, but not really any cooler, and I have it on good authority that it's not going to rain until this evening. But we could always take an umbrella in case it does, or hide out someplace until it passes, if you'd rather. Or—" she did a little jiggle thing with her feet "—we could just get wet."

"I'd rather you came to my place for dinner." He had no idea where the words sprang from. Certainly not his brain. He might as well have invited her right up to the bedroom and saved himself the trouble of an extra step.

"I'd love to."

The words were so quiet, so un-Bailey-like, he almost missed them.

"You would?" He had to make certain he'd heard her right.

"Yes."

"Tonight?" He had no idea what he was having for dinner, but Mrs. Ingall always made enough for two. Just in case.

Even though, in the three years she'd been with him, there'd never been a single "just in case." There'd been a couple of one-night stands, but they'd been at the woman's house. He'd never brought a woman home before.

"Tonight would be great," Bailey said as he started to panic. Could he take back the invitation? What in hell was he going to do with a woman in his home for an entire evening? How was he going to keep her entertained?

"May I pick you up on my way home?" he heard himself ask when he'd meant to tell her he'd just remembered a prior engagement.

"Sure." She rattled off an address in a lower rent district in Pilsen.

"That's not far from the Loop," he said, pulling a pen from his pocket to write the address on one of his business cards.

"I wanted to be close to the institute."

Something about the way she said the word made the school sound more like a lover than a place of employment. Gabe knew he was a sick, pathetic goner when he felt a pang of jealousy toward an old brick building.

BAILEY'S FIRST THOUGHT when she saw the near mansion that Gabe called home was that Lonnie would sell her the institute for sure if he could see this house. But only because an irreverent reaction was better than giving in to the intimidation she felt. Even through a haze of rain, the place was beautiful. White with green shutters and awnings, it reminded her of a million storybook settings.

It also reminded her of any number of places

she'd lived with her father. She wasn't dressed for a house as nice as this, wasn't well-mannered enough—as he'd told her more than once.

She didn't care what people thought of her. At least not since she'd taken the story about Androcles and the lion to heart. So why was Gabe's opinion so damned important? Important beyond any plans or goals?

"You live here alone?" she asked as she followed him from the garage straight into the largest kitchen she'd ever seen in a single-family dwelling. This was worse than the houses she'd lived in with her father. Gabe must have an entire staff to keep up the place.

"Yes."

He sent her a questioning glance, as if he was offering her a chance to change her mind about being there if she didn't like his answer. But she was actually relieved that she wouldn't have to meet anyone else tonight.

Being different was an asset to her, gave her an identity and the freedom to be true to herself. But suddenly, standing there, Bailey felt ashamed. Of her weird clothes, her intense emotions, the fact that the one respectable thing about her, the one thing she'd managed to do completely right—her job—was in total jeopardy.

She considered, for a brief moment of insanity while he put dinner in the oven, telling him the truth. But then she'd have to tell him about Alongie. About the time she'd been in jail.

And then she'd lose him for sure. Respectable men like Gabe didn't consort with jailbirds. Her own father hadn't spoken to her for two whole years after that episode. As a matter of fact, he still wasn't speaking to her all that much. Only when she'd called at Christmas.

No, there was no reason to tell Gabe about Alongie. He was in the past. A mistake she'd already atoned for. It made no sense to ruin her future over something like that.

Did it?

GABE WAS A MESS. After he'd put the chicken enchiladas in the oven, pulled the bowl of freshly cut fruit from the refrigerator and tossed a salad, he was sweating. Bailey, who usually talked nonstop, hadn't said a word since she'd stepped into his house. This was exactly the disaster he'd feared. He'd brought the woman who was haunting his dreams to his home, taken the first real chance he had in years, and he was already failing.

All he could think about was taking her to bed.

He had no idea how to entertain her until the enchiladas were done. Kissing her senseless wasn't going to do it. Though he was pretty certain he could manage that successfully. He was certain, too, that if he touched her, the enchiladas would burn. Dinner would be ruined. And the evening would be a repeat of so many others. Into bed. Out of it. And nothing left but goodbye.

He poured them both some iced tea and handed her a glass. Then, out of the blue, it hit him.

"Come, I want to show you something."

Looking around her as they went into the dining room, through the living room to the family room across the hall, Bailey followed slowly.

"Did you do your own decorating?"

Was she asking because she liked it? Or because she didn't?

"No. I hired someone."

"I'm glad."

Because she liked it or because she didn't? He wasn't sure he wanted to know.

She told him anyway. "It doesn't look like you. It's too formal, too cold, too generic."

Which was pretty much how he saw himself.

"So what would you do differently?" At least she was talking.

She stopped just inside the family room. "Add more color, personalize things, make the place your own. Get rid of the fake flowers."

Grabbing the centerpiece on his coffee table, he dumped it in the trash.

Laughing, Bailey said, "I didn't mean right now." She picked up some fishing, computer and financial magazines from the to-be-read pile on his desk and spread them on the coffee table where the flowers had been.

He liked them there. Suddenly he remembered that he hadn't put on any of the cologne she'd bought him. The scent had been so strong, he'd been unable to wear the stuff since that first day, but he'd intended to try again that evening.

"So what did you want to show me?" she asked, taking in his green leather sofas, the entertainment center with his large-screen TV along one wall.

Moving to the case of books behind his desk, Gabe carefully pulled out a well-used volume. "This." He handed it to her.

"Oh, my gosh! It's the original, isn't it?"

Nodding, Gabe smiled as he watched her turn immediately to "Androcles and the Lion." He'd searched out the volume of *Fifty Famous Stories Retold* the night before when he'd been missing her, and now he was glad he had.

"Do you have a favorite?" she asked, still grinning as she finished perusing her story.

"It's the very next one." She wasn't the only one who knew the book by heart.

"'The Sword of Damocles.'" Her eyes flew across the pages. "Why?"

"Because it's true." He met her gaze. Held it. "Being rich and important doesn't bring happiness. People do. This is the first week I can ever remember being happy."

Her eyes filled with tears.

Acting purely on instinct, Gabe reached out to her, drying the drops that fell onto her beautifully soft cheeks before pulling her into his arms.

Lowering his head was the most natural thing he'd ever done. Her lips were soft, warm, beneath his. And they parted with the abandon that was Bailey. She tasted of orange and tea. She felt like hunger. And he couldn't get enough. Enough of her. Enough of the passion. Enough of the joy she'd so unexpectedly brought to his life.

Her hands skimmed his body, touching everywhere, landing nowhere. He was so hard he hurt.

"Whoa." He broke the kiss, backing away from her, his breathing embarrassingly heavy as he tried to get control of himself.

"You didn't like it." Her eyes were shadowed, but not really surprised. "I know I'm way too forward. I try not to be, but then, boom, it just happens without my even being aware."

"You're wrong, lady." He wanted to haul her into his arms and show her just how wrong, but he didn't trust himself to touch her. "I liked it." He motioned to the bulge straining against the fly of his slacks. "Too much."

Bailey glanced down, and then, turning a little red, back up at him. "Oh."

"But we're going to do this right." He took her hand and led her to the kitchen. "We're going to have dinner."

Laughing, Bailey gave him an odd look. "Okay..." The word was drawn out in a question.

"Pretty much every woman I've ever been with has been nothing more than a trip to bed," he found himself explaining. "You're different.

I want this night to be different. I want there to be something between us *before* I make love to you—so there's also something afterward.''

"I want that, too." He saw the sheen of tears in her eyes again, but she didn't let them fall. She smiled up at him and it took everything he had to keep his hands off her.

He was going to get this right if it killed him. And considering the way he was feeling, it very well might.

Chapter Five

DINNER WAS DELICIOUS. Gabe was certain it must have been, because Mrs. Ingall's chicken enchiladas were always delicious. Although he didn't taste a bite.

But he'd managed to go through the motions. He'd chewed. Swallowed. They'd talked. About his manager, Marie. About a couple of her students. He'd lived through the meal. Barely.

"Let's leave the dishes," he said as soon as Bailey had put down her fork. She hadn't eaten all that much, either.

"Okay." She stood as he pulled out her chair for her. Slid her hand into his. "What do you want to do instead? Take a walk? The rain's stopped and I'd love to see your grounds."

He'd intended to share an after-dinner brandy with her. He wanted to show her how happy he was with her gift, the brandy warmer. He'd failed, however, to include one factor when he'd made those plans: how badly he wanted Bailey.

The brandy could wait. He couldn't.

Taking her in his arms, he covered her lips with his own, a silent answer to her original question. Her mouth opened beneath his, coaxing, inviting, and Gabe couldn't turn down that invitation a second time.

The walk up the stairs and down the hall to the master suite seemed to take forever, each step filled with almost painful anticipation. Her hand was like silk against his, sliding along his fingers, holding tight.

She smelled like a candle shop and the heady scent had been affecting him all evening.

"Now this is you," she exclaimed as she followed him into his room. "A huge bed, books everywhere, a picture of a ship on the wall. I love it!"

And I love you. The words came unbidden to his mind as he watched her. He knew better than to utter them or to trust them, given the circumstances. But whatever name he put to the way he was feeling, he knew it was something far beyond lust. Something he'd never felt before in his life.

Gabe covered her lips with his own, needing to validate their togetherness, temporary though it was sure to be.

He made slow, wet love to her with his lips

and tongue. His hands started their own sensual foray, discovering her curves and indentations. Touching softly. Molding. Pulling her against him. He made love to her with the confidence of a man who knew that arousing women was one thing he did well.

And loving Bailey was something he'd been dying to do since he'd first laid eyes on her.

BAILEY'S LIPS WERE HOT. Her entire self was burning up. She'd had lovers. Enough to feel that she was reasonably experienced. Until Gabe's lips consumed hers. Until his charisma swept over her, took possession of her, swept her up into a gale of passion so furious she lost consciousness of everything but him.

She returned kiss for kiss. Lost herself completely to the sensations he was arousing. Not only in her body, but in her heart. Given complete freedom, her sensitized fingertips explored every inch of him. His shoulders, the muscles in his forearms. His neck and back. And for every brush of her skin against his body, she felt another shock of desire course through her.

Taking her lips from his so she could look up at him, she flamed anew, lit by the heat in his eyes. Turning on men like Alongie was something she knew she could do. But never, in her most daring moments of hope, had she imagined that someone like Gabe Stone would be so moved by *her,* Bailey Cooper.

"You are so beautiful," she whispered, unable to tear her gaze away from his. His body shook with his passion—almost as much as hers.

"No, my sweet angel, you are." He kissed her again. And then again. "You are every fairy tale I've ever read come to life."

Their clothes melted away. The covers were pulled back and as they fell together to the soft white sheets of Gabe's bed, as he eventually sheathed himself, entered her, loved her with his hands, his body, his words, Bailey knew that she wanted nothing more out of life than to spend it in this man's arms.

In some strange, elemental way that probably wouldn't surprise Eve at all, Gabe, Bailey's complete antithesis, fit her perfectly.

THE NEXT TWO WEEKS were *better* than any fairy tale she'd ever read. Gabe didn't speak of love. But he showered her with love every single day. With tickets to modern dance concerts. With touches and caresses that set her body on fire. With smiles that melted her heart. He insisted on seeing her every day. And she finally allowed herself to believe that their relationship was real. That their love was real.

She could feel. She didn't need the words.

Gabe wasn't a man of many words; Bailey understood that, accepted that about him. He was much like her father in that regard. Bailey knew the colonel loved her, although he'd never actually said the words. She also knew how uncomfortable her father had become the couple of times Bailey had spoken aloud of her affection for him. Which was why, every single day, she told Gladys how much she loved Gabe Stone. And why she told Eve. She wasn't going to make Gabe uncomfortable by voicing her feelings to him.

Eve was thrilled with the relationship, encouraging Bailey every step of the way to believe in this "happily ever after." The only disagreement the women had concerned Bailey's refusal to tell Gabe about Alongie. About Lonnie's ultimatum.

"It just doesn't matter," Bailey insisted for the third time in one conversation. Her stomach was starting to knot and she was tempted to hang up the phone if Eve wouldn't let this go. "I'm not in love with Gabe because of Lonnie's ultimatum.''

"But you're lying to him just the same."

"I haven't said a word. How can I be lying?"

"By omission."

Bailey shook her head. "You don't get it, do you?" she asked her friend, rubbing her finger lightly along the back of Gladys's shell. "I'm not going to ask Gabe to marry me. I've decided I'm not giving in to Lonnie's ultimatum, so it's a moot point. If we do get married, it'll be for the right reasons. So there's absolutely no reason to go into it. Besides, if I told him what Lonnie wants, I'd have to tell him about Alongie, too."

"Exactly."

"Why should I ruin my life over one stupid mistake? Haven't I already paid enough?"

"Yes, of course, but—"

"Not only that," she said, carried by the momentum of her protest, "I don't want to take a chance that if Gabe hears about the ultimatum, he'll ask me to marry him because of it. It's just the kind of gentlemanly action he'd feel compelled to take. If he ever does ask, I want to know it's because he can't live without me."

"I can understand that," Eve said, her tone

softening. "But, Bailey, promise me something?"

"What?"

"Search your heart carefully. I sense some uncertainty within you. If this does get more serious between you and Gabe, and he does ask you to marry him—or you blurt out a proposal in the heat of the moment—are you absolutely certain Lonnie's ultimatum won't play a part in your answer? Promise you'll search your heart and know for certain that the ultimatum has nothing to do with your decision. Because if it does, if that's the main reason you agree to marry him, the marriage won't last. Even if it's only a small part of the reason, you have to be honest with him. Otherwise you'd be trying to build a relationship on a false foundation."

Eve's words sent cold shivers through Bailey. Or maybe it was the cold water Gladys had just splashed her with as the turtle plopped down off a rock into her water.

"I promise," she said. As she hung up the phone, her hand was shaking. Of course Lonnie's ultimatum was on her mind. A lot. She panicked every time she thought about not having the institute to give her life completeness.

The kids. The talent she spent her days discovering, exploring, nurturing.

But her feelings for Gabe were separate from that, a different part of her life. What she felt for him had nothing to do with the institute. Nothing.

So, could she be blamed for a perfectly natural surge of hope now and then that maybe *all* her dreams would come true?

SHE SPENT SO MANY NIGHTS in Gabe's bed, he cleared a drawer for her in his dresser. And once in a while, they spent a stolen afternoon at his place, too. They'd just come from a particularly moving Sunday dance concert on one such afternoon. Gabe had hardly unlocked his door before he'd grabbed her and carried her upstairs.

Laughing, teasing him about his barbaric attitude, Bailey had his slacks undone before he'd made it to the second floor. And the love they made was a more moving dance than any choreographed piece could ever be.

Gabe was inside her, moving with slow, hard, deliberate thrusts and she was barely conscious of the world around them, so lost was she in the passion he aroused.

One more thrust and she was over the edge. Climaxing around him.

"Marry me."

She barely heard the words he groaned as he joined her in ecstasy. His orgasm stimulated her to a third, tumultuous one of her own and she clutched his back, her body convulsing under his, his weight a comfort, a shield, on top of her.

Unable to think of anything, only to feel, Bailey hung on to Gabe until he finally relaxed and rolled them to their sides. He was still inside her, still connected. Still real and solid.

"Wow," he whispered, gazing at her as though she'd just invented sex—and invented it for him alone.

"Yeah." She smiled. She couldn't imagine what she'd done to bring that look of wonder to his eyes, but whatever it was, she hoped she could keep doing it forever. Forever.

Her faculties returned slowly. Forever.

"What did you say?" she asked him. Her face was only inches from his, but not so close that she couldn't see the satisfied haze in his eyes.

"Wow."

"No." She traced his lips with her finger, lingering when he slowly licked her index finger. "Before that."

"I think I said marry me."

"You aren't sure?" Bailey started to panic. Had he changed his mind already? Or worse, had the words been meaningless, said only in the throes of passion?

"I'm sure I want to marry you," he said, a silly grin on his face. "Just not sure I actually managed to get the question out."

Relief flooded Bailey, making her giddy, drunk with well-being. "I'm sure you did," she told him. "Yep, now that I think back, I know you got the question out. I definitely heard it."

"And?" His brows pulled together in a frown, his penis slipping out of her.

She missed him. As he took his body away from hers, he took her confidence, her security, as well. Their differences intruded. His similarities to her father. He'd never said he loved her. Would he begin to find her a burden, as her father had? When the sex wore off, would he find that he didn't understand her at all? That he didn't like her?

"I can't imagine why you'd want to marry someone like me," she said finally.

Supporting himself on one elbow, Gabe stared down at her, seriousness in every line of his body.

"You are everything I am not."

"And that's a good thing?" She didn't quite see it. She'd spent her entire life trying to be more like him. Like his kind of person.

Gabe lay back against the pillows, staring up at his ceiling. "The old Gabe wouldn't be asking a woman to marry him after knowing her less than a month, but the old Gabe wasn't happy, either." Head turned, he looked at her. "You've brought a whole new dimension to my life, Bailey. You've brought vitality. Anticipation. Since I met you, I get up in the morning because I'm looking forward to what the day might bring, not because the alarm clock went off. I find that rather addictive."

"Oh, Gabe, I think I'm addicted to you, too, but what happens when the novelty of me wears off?"

Hand splayed wide, he covered her breast, squeezing lightly. "I don't think this kind of thing wears off."

Bailey smiled, brought his other hand to her other breast and held it there. She wanted so desperately to believe that what was happening was real, that his feelings would endure.

"Your life is so settled," she whispered. She couldn't bear to talk him out of this, and yet, some part of her knew that if she was going to lose him and survive, it had to be now. "You have a secure job, live in a socially acceptable neighborhood, are highly respected. You instill confidence in people. You don't say the wrong things at the wrong times. And you wear suits."

Flat on his back, Gabe once again studied the textured paint on the ceiling. "But I'm not happy," he admitted for the second time. "At least, I wasn't until you came along."

"You've lived such a blessed life," she said, unable to keep some of the envy from her voice.

Gabe shook his head. "Maybe, but growing up the only child of elderly parents was a lonely thing."

Bailey had a feeling, from the way he chose his words so carefully, the way he kept swallowing as though they were sticking in his throat, the way he wouldn't look at her, that he was telling her something he'd never told anyone else.

She bit her tongue, forcing herself to remain quiet, hoping he'd continue. She needed to hear whatever he'd tell her, needed to understand that somehow this was going to work. She might actually be teetering on the brink of "happily ever after."

"I was raised at the bookstore, learned to walk there, was potty-trained there. We were never home before dark, never home on weekends when I might have played outside, met kids in the neighborhood, made friends."

He stopped, glanced at her as though to see if she were still listening. Bailey smiled at him, encouraging him to continue.

"I think that's why I went into sports when I hit junior high. Just so I could spend time with kids my own age—get outside. Roughhouse a little."

"I guess your parents were a little like my dad. No late-night pillow fights or wrestling over Saturday cartoons, huh?" she asked. Although they were outwardly complete opposites, perhaps she and Gabe had something in common, after all.

"None of that," he said. His gaze returned to the ceiling.

Bailey lay beside him, taking the opportunity to admire his physical beauty. She railed silently against her lack of ability to express an artistic vision in tangible form. She'd give just about anything to be able to create an image of Gabe's perfection. An image that would last for all eternity.

"Luckily I loved books," he said eventually. "I read early, and voraciously. My playmates became the characters in the stories I read. And later, I found my real companionship in the same places."

"Inside books," Bailey said. Reaching down, she slid her fingers between his larger, stronger ones, holding on.

Gabe nodded, then glanced at her as if to gauge her reaction. "Pretty pathetic, huh?" he asked.

"Not at all," Bailey told him in all honesty. "At least you *had* friends."

He watched her silently and when he started to talk again, his gaze never left hers. "You are the embodiment of my fairy-tale lovers come to life," he told her. "You're beauty and magic and friendship."

Not at all sure she could ever live up to his expectations, Bailey knew, suddenly, that she was willing to spend a lifetime trying. "I'm not perfect," she felt compelled to tell him.

"Neither am I," he said, as though letting her in on a secret.

And he might as well have been. Any faults he might have would be news to her.

"You bring life into an existence that's been

barren far too long," he whispered. "I'm tired of experiencing everything in my imagination. Please say you'll marry me, Bailey."

Her promise to Eve flashed through her mind, but there was only one reply she could possibly give.

"I'd be honored to marry you."

They were the last words she said for a long, long time.

GABE WANTED TO BE MARRIED as soon as they could make the necessary arrangements, and Bailey threw herself into the plans with typical Bailey gusto. During the four weeks it took her to prepare for a wedding, she was around all the time, introducing him to her weird, extremely loyal best friend Eve, meeting his attorney and the closest thing *he* had to a best friend, Brad Sommers. She and Gabe attended two modern dance concerts, arguing over her more intense and his more logical interpretations of the pieces they saw. And they made love every chance they got. They were in his office the day before the wedding, having just climbed back into their clothes, when she suddenly frowned.

"You're all out of oil?" she asked.

Still recovering from the incredibly erotic half

hour he'd just spent on top of his desk, Gabe frowned, unable to keep up with her. "Oil?"

She pointed to her artwork, a little skewed, sitting on the water globe. "You've got thumb-tacks in there."

Clammy with embarrassment, Gabe remembered her gift.

At about the same time, her gaze settled on the football hanging from the fish's gill. "And the terra-cotta isn't in your car."

Frowning, he realized that he was missing some vital piece of information about her artwork. Something to do with oil.

He wasn't sure how critical his lapse would prove to be.

"I didn't expect you to use up the oil so fast," she said. "but I'm glad you did. You know you just had to ask, I'd have gotten you more."

"And..." Gabe paused, swallowed. "What exactly would I do with it if you got me more?"

"You didn't..." Bailey's brows furrowed, and then widened, her eyes glowing with mirth as she glanced back at this thumbtack holder.

"You actually thought..." She broke off and grinned.

Standing there, still not understanding, Gabe felt like a complete fool.

Yet, wasn't this what life with Bailey was all about? Learning, expanding, every day a new experience? Wasn't this exactly why he was marrying her?

Of course, that still didn't explain why she was marrying him. Or why she'd still *want* to when things like this made it so unmistakably obvious that he lived on another planet—a very boring planet.

"Since your entertainment is at my expense, you mind explaining it to me?" he asked.

Wrong question. In Bailey's attempt to explain—at least that was what she *seemed* to be doing—she lost complete control. She was laughing so hard she couldn't get a word out. Tears were streaming down her cheeks.

"Y-you t-thought the d-diffuser was a t-thumbtack holder?" she finally choked out.

What the hell was a diffuser? In his opinion, using the strange little object for thumbtacks was pretty creative. After all, there'd been no instructions, directions or diagrams. He remembered the football-shaped pill holder balancing in the fish's mouth behind him. He could only pray she didn't inspect any further. If she cried over thumbtacks, he'd hate to see what she'd do with aspirin.

He was about to find out. Bailey moved in for the kill. And Gabe lunged for the football. He already felt sheepish enough.

"Let me see that," she said, reaching for the football. Gabe held it up high.

He'd forgotten whom he was dealing with, this woman who was changing his life so drastically. Before he could read her intent, she reached down, grabbed his crotch with one strong artist's hand, and squeezed. Gabe dropped the football and watched, cringing, when the aspirin tablets spilled out to roll beneath his desk.

"Aspirin?" she squealed. "Oh, Gabe, I hate to ask what you did with the oil and the diffuser pot."

His brandy warmer was a diffuser pot. Although he still didn't know what a diffuser was. And with all the evidence in front of him, he'd have to conclude that the cologne at home, unused in his bathroom, was the "oil" to which she kept referring. That tiny vial held the key to this whole ridiculous mess.

"I didn't know it was oil," he admitted, but only because she was so beautiful when she smiled. And because he'd never made anyone laugh so hard before. And because he wanted to know what in the hell this crap was for.

"What did you think it was?"

She'd let go of his crotch, but she hadn't moved. He wished he had the cologne—no, oil—there, instead of at home, and could hold that above his head next.

"Cologne."

Bailey sniffed. "I've never smelled it on you."

"I don't wear it." Thank God for small favors.

"Oh." She nodded, looked away, but not before he saw the grin spreading once more across her face.

"I'm to assume that these things all have to do with this oil?"

She nodded, obviously trying very hard to control her mirth. "Uh-huh."

Gabe waited. Either she was going to tell him, or he was going to strangle her. Or maybe he'd strangle her, anyway. Anything to get his hands on her again. All this mental exercise was making him hungry. But not for food.

"The football is terra-cotta." She managed to stay serious long enough to get that out, and then started to laugh. "You apply a drop of oil to the outside and hang it in your car. The sun diffuses the scent."

"That stuff?" Gabe asked, horrified. "You want me to die? The smell is so strong my eyes would water, the road would blur and I'd drive into a tree." He'd barely been able to breathe that one day he'd put it on; he'd had to go home to shower it off.

"It's not so strong one drop at a time." She picked up his thumbtack holder. He was sorry to see it go. He'd grown rather fond of the thing. "This is a diffuser ring. You put a couple of drops of oil here." She ran one finger along the indentation that was no longer holding his thumbtacks. "Then you put it on a light bulb and the heat diffuses the scent."

"Let me guess, I put a couple of drops of oil in the pot, too, plug it in and it diffuses the scent."

"Right. What are you using it for?" The merriment filled her eyes again.

"A brandy warmer." He couldn't deny her anything, it seemed.

Bailey burst into another fit of laughter—until Gabe joined her at her own game. He grabbed a handful of one luscious, unbound breast and squeezed gently. Her laughter died immediately. Her warm, hungry eyes were almost his undoing, but he wasn't ready to let her off the hook so easily.

"You think I need scented oil because my surroundings stink?"

"No!" She stepped back, out of his grasp, laughing.

Disappointed, Gabe let her go. Surely he deserved more than a five-second feel for the humiliation he'd been through.

"Neroli is aromatherapy oil," she told him, still grinning. And then she wasn't. Moving back within reach, she didn't stop until she'd pressed up against him, her hand once again in possession of his most vital organ. "It's an aphrodisiac."

Already hard, Gabe became rock-solid as he considered how early on in their relationship she'd been sending him a sex potion. "I've got your aphrodisiac," he growled, pushing himself roughly into her palm.

Bailey proceeded to soothe his injured ego—and other parts—in a most satisfactory way.

THE NEXT DAY, the thirtieth of April, a whole four weeks after he'd proposed to his crazy angel, Gabe and Bailey finally came together to be joined as husband and wife. They were married in the bookstore—at Bailey's insistence. Gabe had demurred, but when she'd explained so passionately that he'd come into the world in that bookstore and she felt she should enter his life in the same way, he'd relented. He hadn't given in on the preacher, however. Bailey had wanted her best friend to perform the ceremony, ordained for the day. Gabe hadn't even known such a thing was possible and certainly hadn't wanted his life with Bailey to begin on such a temporary footing.

Bailey was beautiful in yards of flowing, off-white lace wrapped around a simple lavender blouse and full-length, flowing lavender skirt. Her hair had fallen, as always, in uncontrolled ringlets around her face and down her back.

And while Gabe felt like a stuffed shirt in the tuxedo she'd begged him to wear, he'd also been unable to imagine wearing anything else for his wedding. Bailey's father had flown in for the occasion and Gabe had liked the man immediately, getting along with him as well as if he'd been his own father.

He met Lonnie, too. And liked Bailey's mentor tremendously. Other than Marie and Brad and Eve, the two men were the only guests at the ceremony, at Bailey's request. She hadn't wanted the importance of their vows to be lost amid the need to entertain.

There was no reception, unless you counted the entire next week, which they spent celebrating by themselves. He'd offered to fly her to Hawaii, but Bailey had wanted only to spend the time alone with him, uninterrupted, in his home. Her new home. She'd even refused to move her stuff in until after that first week, not wanting to waste a second of their week off from work with more work. She'd paid her rent to the end of the month, anyway. He coaxed her out occasionally, for barefoot walks in the park, food, more champagne when they ran out and occasional trips down to her place to feed Gladys. And once, late at night, to go skinny-dipping in Lake Michigan when he'd confessed that he'd never done it before. Mostly she kept him chained to the bed. Metaphorically speaking.

Gabe was glad she did. It saved him from having to chain her there.

The week's only disappointment, if he could call it that, had been the lack of any words of love. Not that he needed them. Bailey told him she loved him in a hundred different ways. With her body, certainly, but also with her looks. With the tender little ways she tried to make life more pleasant for him. The way she insisted on bringing him coffee in bed every morning, the patient way she'd drawn him out of himself, listening tenderly while he struggled to speak of things he'd never spoken of before. The way she made him laugh.

And now, in true Bailey fashion, a full week after their wedding, his wife was on the phone calling everyone she knew, and every name in his address book, as well, inviting them all to an impromptu gathering to celebrate their nuptials.

They were sitting, glued to each other's sides, on one of the sofas in their family room.

"We could've done this last week and gotten it over with," Gabe told her. Although he wasn't thrilled to be hosting a party, never having been much of a partygoer, he was happy to indulge her. He'd rather have her to himself, of course, but he'd known he was going to have to share her eventually. Bailey's light was too bright to shine only for him.

"I'd never have been able to sit through a party last week," she told him, phone at her ear as she waited for the line to be picked up at the other end. "I'd have been impatient and rude and told everyone to go home so I could be alone with you."

"And now you're no longer impatient to be alone with me?" He toyed with a ringlet, pulling her close for a quick kiss before he let her go.

"Now I'm anxious to have everyone see that you're mine," she told him, leaning forward for another, juicier kiss.

"Hello, Brad?" She broke off the kiss to speak into the phone. Gabe groaned, wishing his attorney had been too busy to answer. Another couple of seconds, and he was sure he could have had Bailey right where he wanted her. Beneath him.

Not that she hadn't shown him a few other incredible ways to have her over the past week.

"What are you planning to serve at this party?" he asked his wife when she'd hung up the phone.

"We'll order pizza."

Gabe was pretty sure his neighborhood had never witnessed a pizza delivery.

"And what are we going to do with them after we eat?"

"Play Chatter Matters."

Gabe choked. Chatter as in talking? Could he ditch his own wedding reception, as it were? "How do you do that?" He was afraid to ask, but even more afraid to have it thrown at him unprepared.

"It's an old game Lonnie and his family used to play. Basically you just answer questions from a stack of cards."

"What kinds of questions?"

Bailey shrugged, her slim naked shoulders distracting him. "Like...what's your favorite family memory, or sing a song that expresses your feelings for the person on your right."

Gabe went cold. He was never going to survive this. "And why would we want to do that?"

Her eyes, filled with love and excitement, practically glowed as she looked at him. "I think it's the best way to get to know each other's acquaintances and friends quickly—so that we're all connected from the beginning instead of taking years for yours to become mine and mine to become yours. I want them to belong to both of us right now."

He couldn't think of a single objection to that.

"THAT WASN'T SO BAD, was it?"

Gabe's body hardened as his wife bent to whisper to him from behind. He was outside, lounging in a chair on the sundeck, watching

Brad make a fool of himself over Bailey's astrologer friend Eve.

"No."

They'd just finished a round of Chatter Matters and Gabe had actually found the game to be something of a relief. He'd only had to speak when it was his turn, and the question had guided him in the direction of what he was to say.

"I think everyone's having fun, don't you?"

Looking out over the yard, at the clusters of his bookstore employees, a few close customers and Bailey's arty people, he had to agree with her. His wife knew how to throw one hell of a party. He tried to pretend her chin wasn't resting on his shoulder, that he couldn't feel her warm breath tickling the lobe of his ear.

"How soon you think we can get rid of them?"

"Gabe!" she laughed. And slid onto his lap. "I'll hide the evidence, does that help?"

The brat. She knew exactly what she was doing to him. "No, it does not help," he growled as she wriggled around, settling herself more comfortably.

"We could always slip away." Her voice grew husky and Gabe felt a thrill of power. He was having the same effect on her that she was having on him.

"Do you think they'll notice?" he asked.

"Do you think they'll care?" she countered.

"Let's go."

BY THE TIME Gabe finally let Bailey up for air, all but a few of their closest friends had left. Lonnie was still there. And Brad and Eve were sitting out at a table by the pool, drinking champagne.

Pouring herself a glass, Bailey went over to join them. Gabe could hear her riling her friend over the way she'd been keeping Gabe's attorney to herself all evening.

"She's something else, isn't she?"

Busy admiring his wife, Gabe hadn't even noticed Lonnie approach. "Yeah."

He stood at the outdoor bar, debating between a glass of champagne and the brandy he really wanted. Lonnie leaned one arm on the bar and glanced over at Bailey and the others.

"I can't tell you how relieved I am she made that deadline," Lonnie said.

Deadline? Gabe hadn't even known Bailey was working on anything, let alone that she'd finished a project. Or that she'd had one to finish.

"I hated doing it," Lonnie continued. "It would have killed me to let the institute go, to see it die." He paused, looked back at Gabe.

Gabe nodded. Bailey hadn't breathed a word about the institute being in trouble. Of course, they'd had other things on their minds. Even so, he didn't like not knowing what was going on in Bailey's life and made a mental note to leave a bit more time for talking.

"But worse," Lonnie went on, sipping from the flute of champagne he'd brought with him, "it would have killed me to refuse to sell it to Bailey. She and the institute are like two parts of the same whole. One wouldn't be complete without the other."

Funny, Gabe had thought that was *his* role in Bailey's life.

"You figured Bailey was going to buy the institute?" he asked. Not only had she never given an indication that she had any such plans, Gabe knew for a fact that she couldn't afford a decent roof over her head, let alone purchase an entire school. He'd seen her apartment.

"I didn't think it, I know it," Lonnie said. "We signed the papers the week before the wedding. All it took to finalize the deal was her marriage to you.''

Suddenly everything happened at once. As if from outside himself, Gabe saw surprise and then horror cross the older man's face.

"You didn't know...." His voice trailed off and his eyes swung toward Bailey.

So did Gabe's. He saw his wife spill her glass of champagne all over herself. She'd just glanced his way, seen Lonnie speaking to him. She and Lonnie shared the nonverbal communication experienced only by truly intimate acquaintances. A kind of communication she'd never had with Gabe. Her face mirrored the horror on Lonnie's as her gaze flew to Gabe.

Excusing himself, Gabe left the bar, left the few remaining guests, and locked himself in his study. He was being ridiculous, of course. Acting like a child, running away to hide. He recognized that even as he chose to do nothing about it.

Bailey could say goodbye to their guests for both of them. Gabe couldn't stomach the celebration another second.

"Gabe?" He'd never heard that note of fear in Bailey's voice. Heart quickening, he rose automatically to go to her, take care of whatever was bothering her. He was halfway to the study door before he caught himself.

"Go back to your party, Bailey," he commanded. She'd never heard that tone of voice from him, either.

"I asked them all to leave. Gabe, we need to talk."

He didn't think so.

"Please, Gabe?" The doorknob rattled. "Please talk to me."

Gabe remained standing in the middle of the room, his hands in the pockets of the slacks he'd pulled on—without underwear—after loving Bailey so thoroughly less than an hour before.

Something thumped against the door, brushed all the way down it. Bailey's back as she slid to the floor. He could hear her weeping softly, just outside.

And couldn't stand to be trapped in there. Listening.

He pulled open the door so quickly, she fell against his ankles. In spite of himself, he bent to her, almost as though to pull her into his arms. To hold her and tell himself he was never going to let her go.

He hadn't heard from her yet. He could be

drawing all the wrong conclusions. He owed it to her, to their love, to listen to her.

Of course, he reminded himself as he helped her up, he and Bailey had never spoken of love. Not even in the wedding vows she'd written for them.

Clinging to him like a child lost in the dark, Bailey finally spoke. Her words were muffled against his chest. "Lonnie told you."

"It depends," he said, keeping his voice calm with great effort, "on what there is to tell."

"He told you about the ultimatum—that if I wasn't married by next month, he was going to close the institute rather than sell it to me like we'd always planned."

Nope. Lonnie hadn't laid it out anywhere near that clearly.

"You can afford to buy it?" What in hell did it matter? But he couldn't focus on anything else at the moment. Except this. She had enough money to buy an elite art school. And he hadn't known. She had *plans* to buy the school. And he hadn't known. And the real kicker—she'd had to get married to sustain the plan. Basically, he didn't know her at all.

Bailey nodded, her head moving up and down against his chest. Moments ago he would've found that movement incredibly erotic. Now he couldn't bear her touch. Pushing her away, he waited until he was certain she was standing on her own, then dropped his hands from her shoulders. They still burned where he'd touched her.

Her eyes were searching his imploringly. Swallowing, Gabe refused to look at her.

"I've been saving for years," she said. He wasn't sure why she was bothering to explain, or why he was bothering to listen. He just couldn't figure out what else to do. "The insurance settlement from my car accident was what got me started."

He nodded. Her words were logical. Unthreatening. Made perfect sense.

"But then, a couple of years ago, I got into a bit of a scrap...."

Gabe listened as the story spilled out—Bailey's relationship with her past lover, her arrest, her time in jail, the eventual trial that cleared her name but sent her lover to prison for ten years. He didn't know why he was surprised. He'd known Bailey was as unconventional as they came.

Still, he could hardly believe the story she was spinning. Nothing at all like the fairy tales he'd spun for her. And about her.

He couldn't help thinking, as she talked, that he'd done a much better job with his storytelling than she had.

"I thought everything was going to be fine when it was all over. I'd proven my innocence...."

"Your ignorance," Gabe said, telling himself to shut up. He was in no frame of mind to speak to anybody.

Bailey lowered her head, acknowledging the accuracy of his hit. "But more importantly, I'd learned my lesson."

"What lesson was that?"

"That my father was right all along. My judgment wasn't to be trusted...."

He had to agree with her father there.

"That I needed to find someone solid and respectable and pray that he'd have me. Or..."

"Or?"

"Or make up my mind to live alone."

Gabe said nothing.

"I was wrong about everything being okay," she continued, still standing where he'd left her in the middle of the room. She had her arms wrapped tightly around her middle, bunching her colorful caftan—Bailey's version of a swimsuit cover—at her waist.

"Lonnie said I'd gone too far in my episode with Alongie. He said he just couldn't make excuses for that one. He said...he was no longer sure enough of my stability to turn the institute over to me when he retired. I needed a keeper, he told me, or at least a husband who'd give me some...perspective. That is what he called it."

Turning in a circle, Bailey faced the open door, and then Gabe again. "He wouldn't budge," she said, her eyes begging for his understanding.

Gabe would have liked to oblige. But he couldn't. He didn't understand anything about this nightmare except that he wanted it never to have happened. He wanted to move the clock back an hour, do things differently. He wished he'd kept his wife in their bed instead of letting her talk him into rejoining their wedding party.

"He gave me an ultimatum. Either I get married—to a stable, respectable man—by his retirement or the school was retiring with him."

That about wrapped things up.

What a damn fool he'd been. Hands in his pockets, Gabe walked over to the window and stood staring out into the night, counting the lights along his driveway. He had the most idiotic sensation that he might have tears in his eyes and he couldn't bear anyone to know that.

Especially not the woman who'd just ripped every good feeling he'd ever felt to shreds.

It was his own fault, really. How could he have been fool enough to believe that someone as vivacious as Bailey Cooper would ever have a real interest in him? Of course she'd had ulterior motives for approaching him. It was no longer astonishing that she'd hung around longer than the rest. Now he knew why she'd tried so hard, why she'd pretended to find his minimal conversation stimulating. Her miraculous interest in him wasn't miraculous at all. He'd been living in his world of stories—medieval legends and fairy tales and the great sagas, in which wondrous and magical things occurred with regularity. Where a farmer's son could win a princess... Life wasn't like that.

"I was the stooge who happened along?" He didn't spare himself as he sought the truth. There was nothing left in him to hurt.

"No." He could hear the tears in Bailey's voice and didn't turn around. He didn't want to see her this way. "I'd noticed you more than a year ago, one afternoon around five. I'd just come into Stone's and you were leaving. I couldn't stop thinking about you and went back purposely at the same time hoping that we might run in to each other.''

"We never did."

"No."

"And you needed to meet me so badly you finally got up the nerve to approach me, anyway?" He summed it up, still outwardly unemotional. Inside he was grasping for anything to hold on to.

Seemed incredible to him that he'd inspire such need in her, but what did he know?

Maybe they could salvage something here.

Bailey hesitated and that was all the answer he needed. She'd caught him out again. But this was the last time, he vowed. The very last time.

"Eve told me you were the man I had to marry."

He heard the words, but he'd already closed his heart to the forthcoming pain. He'd known when she hesitated that whatever she had to say was going to hurt.

"She'd done some research."

The blood drained from his skin. He'd had no idea the truth was going to be that bad.

"I was a research project?" He'd been wrong.

There was more in him to hurt. He could feel the pain, twisting ever tighter.

"I didn't know," Bailey whispered. "But, Gabe, listen to me..." She grabbed his hands, clasping them to her breasts, her voice filled with desperation. "After our second date I knew I wanted to marry you, but not for the institute. I wanted to marry you because I couldn't imagine living the rest of my life without you."

He'd have to be an idiot to believe that.

Pulling his hands back, he faced her. "Tell me something." He tried to soften his tone, but he couldn't.

"Anything."

"Did you or did you not purposely keep the truth from me?"

She didn't say anything for so long, words no longer mattered. Her silence convicted her.

Gabe headed for the door. He was through.

"I did, but not for the reasons you think." Her words reached him in the hallway. Stopped him.

He turned back to her, a disgusting, needy fool. "Then you didn't use our marriage to get the institute? You would have married me, just as quickly, if buying the school hadn't been an issue? If Lonnie hadn't given you an ultimatum?''

She didn't have anything more to say. He could see the futility in her eyes.

"I'll pack my things and go," she said, brushing past him.

Gabe didn't try to stop her. He went back into his study and remained there, standing at the window, until she was gone.

Chapter Six

BAILEY TRIED TO STAY AWAY from Gabe, to leave his life before she did more damage, but then she'd go to sleep at night, back home in her dingy little apartment—so dingy and little that it was still available despite the notice she'd given. She'd go to sleep and dream about the joy she'd shared with him. The joy he'd shared with her. He'd been happy. Briefly, it was true, but she'd made him happy. And he'd made her happy, too.

When she thought she might lose her mind from the backlash of pain, she sought out Eve.

"The thing is," she sniffed, sitting on the floor in Eve's tiny bungalow living room. "I couldn't honestly tell him I'd have married him anyway, without doubts."

"You were head over heels in love with him on your wedding day, Bailey. I was there. I felt it."

"I know."

"So?"

"You made me promise to search my heart."

"And if you had, you'd have found out you were head over heels in love with him."

Shaking her head, Bailey reached for another tissue. "I did search."

"And?"

"I was afraid, Eve. I knew I loved him, but I'm still not certain he ever loved me. Men like Gabe do things slowly, deliberately. I moved so fast he couldn't possibly know what hit him. So what was going to happen when things moved to a normal, everyday pace and he had time for regrets?"

"Why do you assume there would have been regrets, Bail? You're a great person, a beautiful woman, the best."

Bailey smiled through the tears slipping down her cheeks. "He's too much like my father to be content with someone like me. You should have seen him after you guys left that day, Eve. So cold, so logical. It was a replay of the time Daddy shipped me off to Winston's. There was no caring left."

"Your father *was* caring for you, Bail. He did the absolute best thing he could ever have done when he sent you to Lonnie."

"He had no way of knowing that."

"I don't believe that, Bail. I know your father. He doesn't do anything without checking all the angles. He couldn't, not with all his responsibilities."

"So? You're saying I was a job to him? A responsibility? I want to be more than that."

"I'm saying that he'd have done his research before sending you to Lonnie. He'd have been certain Lonnie could help you. And he cared enough to get you help. If he was just looking to get rid of you, he could have shipped you off to any old boarding school."

Bailey pondered that. The thought comforted her. For a moment. "But that doesn't have anything to do with Gabe."

"Sure it does. Your father cared. Maybe Gabe does, too."

"Maybe."

"Are you saying you wouldn't have married him if not for the institute?"

Bailey stared at the carpet, picking at a thread. "I don't know." She looked up at her friend through a fresh wave of tears. "I wanted to, so badly, but if it hadn't been for Lonnie's ultimatum I probably would've chickened out. I knew losing him afterward was going to kill me."

"Not if you don't let it," Eve said firmly, just before she pulled Bailey into her arms and rocked her, her own eyes wet with tears.

THE NEXT DAY, two weeks after her fairy-tale wedding, Bailey lingered outside Stone's, knowing she shouldn't be there and unable to stay away. She'd been in the middle of an oil class at the institute, had burst into tears and walked out. She was hot and bedraggled, as well as paint-spattered; she'd walked from the Loop halfway up the Magnificent Mile, but she'd needed to do something before she lost whatever grip she had on reality.

And being close to Gabe helped. She kept thinking about the things Eve had said the night before. The things she'd finally admitted, to her friend and to herself. She was so confused now, she didn't know where to turn.

With survival in mind, she opened the heavy door of the beautiful old building and went inside. She couldn't hesitate, couldn't worry about the stares she was getting. Instead, she marched up to the counter and asked Marie if Gabe was in his office.

"He's busy, this morning, Miss Cooper," Marie said. She was looking everywhere but at

Bailey. Bailey didn't think the woman's barely concealed aversion had much to do with the grungy pants and oversize shirt she was wearing.

"It's Mrs. Stone," Bailey said. "He's in his office?"

"He doesn't want to be disturbed this morning."

Half aware of the customers gathering around, Bailey tried to keep her voice down.

"He's my husband, Marie. I have a right to see him."

An older woman gasped and whispered to her friend so loudly Bailey and Marie could both hear her. "Gabe Stone married that?"

Bailey ignored the old biddy. "Don't you think you ought to let me go up before I shock anyone else, Marie?" she asked, but didn't wait for a reply. She didn't need the woman's permission to see her husband. She knew where Gabe's office was. She'd made love with him on his desk the day before their wedding.

A fact he'd obviously forgotten, Bailey thought when she opened his office door a couple of minutes later. Judging by the expression on his face, his memories of her in that room weren't good ones.

In true Gabe fashion, he didn't say a word.

Just sat with that horrible frown on his face and stared at her.

"I can't sleep. I can't eat. I couldn't leave things like this," she blurted, wishing now that she'd taken time to at least change her clothes. She was going to need a miracle to get him to like her again.

"Guilt will do that to a person," he said. But he had rings under his eyes, too.

Bailey took a strange sort of comfort from that. She moved closer to the desk, then stopped when his expression grew even colder.

"I wish you'd let me explain," she tried again. "I wish you could believe me when I—"

"Believe *you?*"

"Give me a chance, Gabe," she begged. "Let me show you how much you mean to me."

He lowered his chin to his chest. Swallowed. And when his gaze returned to hers, she felt physically sick. He'd said his goodbyes. She could see that in the thinning of his lips, the hardness of his eyes.

"What's the point, Bailey? We're from two different worlds. It's best to end things now, before there are any further complications."

Complications. Fair or not, that was all she'd ever felt she was in her father's life. A complication. Was it the same for Gabe? Had her fears before the wedding been more real than unfounded?

More than anything, she had to know. "Do you love me, Gabe?" She faced him as she asked the question.

"Exacting your pound of flesh, Bailey?" He used one of her father's famous tricks, answering a question with a question.

"No." She shook her head. "Just looking for the truth."

He sighed, looking so unhappy for a moment that her foolish heart took hope. "The truth is, we probably rushed into this and should never have gotten married in the first place." His calm logic was a familiar brick wall.

"Is that what you think?" She'd been right all along. Give him a little time to consider things, a little bump in the road, and he was ready to sign off.

She'd never fit into her father's life; why in hell had she thought she'd fit into Gabe's? After all, in many ways, those two were so alike.

"Don't you?" His gaze, as it finally met hers, was strangely vulnerable.

He read her answer in her eyes. Bowed his head.

"It would be best if you don't come by here again, Bailey," he said, looking back up at her. "Further contact between us can only bring further...discomfort."

Without another word, without a backward glance, Bailey turned and walked out of Gabe's life.

THE FOLLOWING MONTHS were the toughest of Gabe's life. He lost count of the number of times he drove by Bailey's old low-rise, hoping for even a glimpse of her. He'd seen lights on occasionally, but that was as close as he got to any indication of life.

He didn't know what was the matter with him, why he couldn't bounce back, but six months after she'd gone, he still felt as though he were only half alive. He worked. He dated. He took more time off than he ever had before. He no longer cared if he had anything to say when he went out, only cared that he not be stuck at home with his memories of Bailey. And found that not caring went a long way toward loosening his tongue.

He still wasn't a sparkling conversationalist. He was still serious-minded and more interested in Shakespeare than in current trends, but he could hold his own if he had to.

The one thing he didn't do was divorce Bailey. He had no need of his freedom, no plans to remarry. He never intended to try that experience again. And insane though it was, as the months passed and he received no decree from her, he breathed a sigh of relief. He told himself that this was due to the protection his non-marriage gave him on the social scene; maybe, if he had another ten years, he might even start believing it.

Christmas came and went, and he thought, for a day or two there, that he wasn't going to make it. If it was possible for a man to die simply from lack of wanting to go on, he knew his number was coming up.

But to his surprise, he didn't die. After the holidays had finally passed, he made up his mind to start living again. Disgusted with his tortured hero act, he made a conscious effort to find something in life to interest him. Something he could take pleasure in.

He discovered a passion for Tae Kwon Do, an ancient martial art. Gabe began to rely on the mental discipline it required to keep him sane. In the month of January, he went just a couple of nights a week, but by the first of February, he was attending class at least five times every week.

With his Grand Master, he finally worked out the pain of Bailey's initial betrayal and then started on the agony of living without the joy she'd brought to his life. He released the tension that had been building to an exploding point these past months. He kicked and moved, sparred with his classmates, learned to control the demons inside him, and felt alive again for the first time since Bailey had left. He'd even begun to forgive himself for not being able to hold on to someone such as Bailey. He knew they'd done the right thing in separating. He and Bailey were too different to have made their marriage last.

Or so he told himself. Many times a day.

He even started reading again. Spy thrillers, mostly, because he needed something that was going to keep him on the edge of his seat long enough to keep him *in* his seat. But slowly and surely, he was coming around.

Until the fourteenth of February arrived and Gabe found himself home. All by himself. On the day meant for lovers. What came to mind, mocking him, was a thought he'd had on his wedding day—that he'd never be spending another Valentine's Day alone. He'd woken up so grumpy, he'd decided to stay home for the day.

Feeling morose and resigned, he hauled the aromatherapy diffuser/brandy warmer that Bailey had given him from the back of the cupboard. His first shot of brandy, his usual after-dinner drink, was warmed and ready before lunch. He was just about to take his first sip when the doorbell rang.

Who in hell would be coming to visit him on Valentine's Day? he wondered irritably. It was Monday; he was supposed to be at work.

Gabe strode to the front door, a firm goodbye on his lips for whoever had dared interrupt him. Couldn't a guy feel sorry for himself in peace?

But when he opened the door, there was no one there. At least, no one he could see. He felt a presence, though, and looked around, wondering if some new little kid in the neighborhood was playing a prank. He'd take the kid straight home to his mother the second he caught him. The kid ought to learn to respect other people's rights.

A movement on the ground caught his eye. Gabe glanced down automatically, thinking there must be a cat on his porch.

"What the..."

There was no cat.

He couldn't believe what he was staring at instead. His breath caught and his heart stopped. Completely. Just stayed frozen, right in midbeat. He started to breathe again. His heart started to pound. Nothing else moved.

Except the bundle in the basket at his feet. It moved once. Then it blinked.

Gabe blinked back. He couldn't tear his gaze away, and couldn't figure out what else he should do.

The blanket surrounding his guest was pink. That finally registered. He knew it should mean something. But he didn't remember what.

He continued to stare. To take deep calming breaths. To try to control the rapid pounding of his heart.

And all the while his brain just kept drumming out the same message. *There's a baby on my doorstep. There's a baby on my doorstep.*

Gabe would probably have stood there for the rest of the afternoon, but the baby apparently got tired of waiting for him to figure out what to do. Its little face screwed up and it emitted the most godawful sound Gabe had ever heard. At least in his own home.

That spurred him into action. Reaching down, he grabbed the handle of the basket and swung the cumbersome thing inside. Slamming the door with his foot, he plopped the carrier down on the tile floor of his entryway and stared some more.

That was when he noticed the note attached to the fuzzy pink blanket. And recognized his name scrawled on the front.

Gabe reached for the note. Not because he felt it would have any significance, but because it was there. He was mildly curious. Mostly numb.

He had someone else's baby on his floor.

Correction. Gabe's blood ran cold as he read the note. And then read it again. Her name was Mignon—and she was his. Chest constricted almost to the point of suffocation, he looked down at the squalling pink bundle and read the note a third time, certain it would say something different.

It didn't. He dropped the note. Then he tore outside, turning wildly to the right, to the left; he ran down into the yard. *Where was she?* Aware of the baby inside his house, he didn't go far, but he scanned the entire neighborhood. She was gone.

But not for long. The note had said she'd be back.

Confused, befuddled, Gabe went back. He leaned against the door, too weak to stand, too afraid to move. In the time it took for one doorbell to ring, his entire life had changed forever. Compelled by things he couldn't hope to understand, he looked down. The wet, big blue eyes of his four-week-old daughter stared up at him.

She was so bundled up that was all he could see—her eyes, pert little pudgy nose and a rosebud mouth currently tensed into a diamond-shaped pout. Sliding down the door, Gabe knelt beside her, afraid to touch her. Knowing he'd have to. She'd suffocate if he didn't get some of that stuff off her.

With trembling hands, he finally reached out to his daughter.

"It's okay, little girl," he whispered, afraid his voice would scare her. "Daddy's just going to pick you up now, okay? It won't hurt, I promise. Daddy's just going to pick you up."

He waited another couple of seconds, giving her time to register a complaint about this plan. After that, he ran his hands along the inside edges of the carrier until they met at the bottom, and then he gently lifted. The bundle popped out like a cork.

"See? That was easy as pie, little princess," he said, still whispering. "Daddy's going to carry you into the family room now, okay? It's just over there..." Bundle held out in front of him, he continued to whisper all the way to the other room, hoping his voice would be enough of a distraction in case there was any part of the journey that met with her disapproval.

Mission accomplished. Not wanting to test his luck, Gabe set her down on the leather sofa closest to the door—and jumped when she started to squall even more loudly than before.

"What?" he asked, leaning over to stare down at her. Could there be something on the couch? He thought of "The Princess and the Pea." Or under the cushion?

He lifted her carefully to check, and the horrible sounds stopped immediately. Deciding the problem was, indeed, the couch, Gabe set her on the other sofa. But the second he let her go, she howled again. She didn't like the chair, either. Or the floor. Not the kitchen table, any of the counters or even his bed. By the time he'd pretty well decided he'd just hold her until her mother came—no matter how long that took—he was as sweaty as she had to be, still bundled in her fuzzy blankets and funny little cap.

Exhausted, back in the family room with her carrier now close by, he fell to the sofa, laying her in his lap. She blinked, gazing up at him, her little brow furrowed in a frown.

"I know, little girl, I don't get it, either." He was still whispering in spite of the fact that his throat was getting sore from the strain. "Your mother has a lot to answer for."

Bailey. Even thinking her name sent a jolt through him. She'd been on his doorstep and he hadn't even known it.

She'd given him a baby and he hadn't even known it.

Well aware by now of his daughter's sensitive nature, Gabe started—with extreme caution—to remove the things covering her. A blanket. A second one. The tiny cap. Covering the finest little ears he'd ever laid eyes on. She was zipped into a body jacket, which he removed ever so carefully, crooning reassurances the entire time. When he'd finally made his way through all of the layers, he was shaking again. Shaking with love. And with fear. She was the tiniest creature he'd ever seen.

And he was a daddy. A father. Part of a family. He wasn't alone anymore.

AN HOUR LATER, still sitting outside on the cold ground, ears numb, Bailey wiped away a fresh spate of tears. Waiting. Her heart was breaking with every second she sat there, knowing she'd just lost half of her daughter's life. Knowing she'd had no choice but to bring the baby to the father who would love her. After Gabe's last painful words to her all those months ago, she'd been unable to share her pregnancy with him, unable to go to him while she was so vulnerable, but she was well now. Recovered. Strong. She was ready to be accountable, to accept whatever fate had in store for her. To be fair and rational as she discussed sharing Mignon's life with the man who didn't want her mother.

She just wished it didn't hurt so damn much.

Chapter Seven

GABE'S LEGS WERE NUMB. His little girl had fallen asleep on his lap almost two hours ago, and he hadn't moved a muscle since. She needed her sleep. He only wished he'd been able to join her. That he could find some escape from the torment he'd been suffering as he sat there loving her so damn much it hurt.

And, even though he willed it to be not so, loving her mother, too. His lower extremities might be numb. His heart most definitely was not.

For the better part of an hour he'd been torturing himself with memories of Bailey. Interspersed with imaginings of what the past several months must have been like for her. Had she taught all the way through, or was she running the institute now? He'd bet she'd looked glorious pregnant.

He added another regret onto the rapidly growing pile. If he didn't stop soon, they were going to crush him.

He'd missed Mignon's birth. Hell, he'd missed naming her—although he approved of Bailey's choice. She's taken the name straight from *Fifty Famous Stories Retold.* From the final story in the book.

He'd missed Bailey like hell.

He was going to be seeing her sometime. Soon, he hoped, since she'd left no food for the baby and he had no idea what Mignon could eat.

She'd said in her note that she intended to be completely cooperative about sharing Mignon's custody. She intended to discuss the future. Until a few hours ago Gabe hadn't even known he had a future.

He tried, as he sat there, to speculate about what the future might bring, to form some kind of realistic expectations so he could slide through the next hours with the least possible damage. But he couldn't picture an end that satisfied him. Not a realistic one, anyway.

The only certainty was that, one way or another, he was going to raise his daughter. He couldn't think beyond that.

The doorbell rang fifteen minutes later. His little girl was still asleep and Gabe considered not answering until she woke up.

But he couldn't leave Bailey standing out

there in the cold. She didn't even have a car. For all he knew, she'd walked from the public transit stop. He sure hoped she'd had insurance through the institute for Mignon's birth. He should have taken care of them both.

When the doorbell pealed again, he knew he was going to have to do something. Continual ringing might wake his daughter. Of course, moving her might do the same, but Gabe had no choice. Placing his precious bundle on the couch, carefully secured by a strategically placed cushion, he stood. He had to brace himself against the chair across from the couch—or fall. His legs were screaming in protest. He wasn't sure, for a second there, if he'd ever walk again.

But he did. And he made it all the way to the front door before the bell rang a third time. Taking a deep breath, pretending he was ready to see his wife again, he pulled open the door.

Bailey's eyes soaked him up. And then flooded with tears. None of his expectations had prepared him for that.

SHE DIDN'T KNOW what to do when he just stood there in the doorway, watching her sob like an idiot. Needing him to hold her more than anything in the world, she waited, hoped, but to no avail. He stood there a total stranger, not even inviting her in.

Her mind went blank. What should she say? How did she stop crying? She finally took the only option left to her. She moved forward. She stepped up to him, slid her arms around his solid, secure middle and buried her face in the crook of his shoulder.

Even when he stood frozen, arms at his sides, she didn't move away. Truth be known, she couldn't. She'd borne his baby for him. She'd survived her aloneness and pain.

So slowly she hardly dared believe it was happening, his arms stole around her, pulling her inside his house, inside his life. He held on even after he'd kicked the door shut, silently waiting while she cried out the anguish of the past months.

"I'm sorry," she mumbled, and felt him nod. She wondered which of her many apologies he'd just accepted. And then figured it didn't matter. Beggars couldn't be choosers.

"What the…"

Gabe pushed her gently away to glance down at his sweater. There were two telling wet patches on his chest that matched the ones marking her thigh-length men's shirt. She'd been sweating so much she'd unbuttoned her army jacket on her way up the walk.

"Mignon's dinner," she said when Gabe continued to stare at the front of her shirt.

"You're huge!" he blurted.

And Bailey smiled for the first time since she'd left her baby on his doorstep. A watery smile, perhaps, but… "Yeah."

Right on cue, her baby let out an earth-shattering howl and Bailey's breasts began to leak in earnest. It was a little embarrassing how abundantly she provided for Mignon's needs.

She and Gabe hadn't really even said hello, but first things first. Bailey headed toward the sound of her daughter's pathetic cries and scooped her up into a hug as soon as she reached her.

"I missed you, little funny face," she said, rubbing her nose against the baby's tear-streaked face. Recognizing her mother—at least that was Bailey's take on the situation—Mignon stopped crying and immediately turned her open birdlike mouth to Bailey's chest.

Reaching to unhook her maternity bra, Bailey had the baby settled even before she'd sunk down on the couch. Only when Mignon had begun nursing, relieving some of Bailey's immediate physical distress, did she look back to Gabe.

He was standing a couple of feet away. Watching intently.

"She was hungry," Bailey explained inanely. What did one say to the man who'd just found out he'd fathered her child?

Gabe nodded. And the move was so familiar, so Gabe-like, Bailey had to fight more tears. She kept hoping that eventually she'd be all cried out.

"Think she could get any noisier there?" Gabe asked suddenly, still staring at Mignon. When she looked up at him, Bailey's heart stopped in her chest. Gabe was smiling.

"She throws herself one hundred percent into everything she does."

Gabe nodded again. "I guess she's like her mother in that regard."

Raising her brow in question, Bailey continued to gaze at the man she'd been fantasizing about every day for all these months. He wasn't right for her, so why did it still feel as if he was the other half of herself?

Bailey fed the baby in silence for a while, feeling just the tiniest thrill of pleasure at the enthralled way Gabe continued to watch. When the baby had finished on one side, she quickly moved her to the other, having learned from experience that she didn't have time to cover up before her daughter started protesting.

Her stomach churned with desire when, in one unguarded second, she saw the heated way Gabe was staring at her moist, uncovered breast. At least something between them still worked.

A little reluctantly, she covered it.

She wanted to talk with him about the future, get everything out and done, but she had to wait until Mignon was done eating. The baby nursed lustily, burped, and then, as usual, fell promptly asleep.

"What else does she do?" Gabe asked, his hands in his pockets.

She buttoned her shirt and settled Mignon back on the couch.

"You've seen her whole repertoire." Bailey smiled down at their daughter. "Eats, sleeps and cries." She knew she should look up at him, but concentrating on Mignon was safer. It also gave her strength.

"And goes to the bathroom," she added when she realized she hadn't changed Mignon before she'd fed her. She'd been thrown off their normal routine.

Gabe seemed content to stand in front of the couch until the world ended. Bailey wasn't that patient.

"Are you angry?" she finally asked, meeting his eyes. She should probably get up, but she felt safer on the couch, next to Mignon.

"I don't know what I am."

That was fair. She didn't know, either, much of the time.

"Was it a hard pregnancy?" He rocked back and forth on his feet, his gaze locked on the baby as he asked the question.

Not if you didn't count how agonizing those months had been without him. She shook her head.

"No problems?"

"Not even morning sickness."

"And the delivery?"

"Eve was there," she said, remembering those difficult hours. There'd been a time or two when she'd been certain she couldn't go on, but once Eve had arrived at the hospital, she hadn't let Bailey quit. And the prospect of seeing her baby, the baby she'd been loving for so many months, did the rest. "It was relatively short."

"Did you have her naturally?"

Bailey grinned. "Would you expect me to do anything else?"

Gabe conceded her point with a nod, and then frowned. "Did you have her in the hospital?"

She hadn't wanted to. Probably wouldn't have if Gabe had been around, but, alone, she hadn't wanted to take any chances. "Yeah."

"You had insurance?"

"Yes."

The questions were suffocating her. Not because she didn't want him to know the details, but because there were other, more important matters at hand.

"Has your father seen her?"

Bailey didn't think it was a coincidence that they'd both been thinking of him at the same time. She shook her head. He'd barely spoken to her since she'd left Gabe. Not that she intended to tell Gabe that. "He's been out of the country for the past six months."

He was quiet for a few minutes, a brooding expression on his face while he watched the baby sleep.

"Thank you for bringing her."

"I couldn't not." And she couldn't continue like this much longer, either. They'd made a baby together, for God's sake. They weren't strangers.

"Have you taken over at the institute yet?" The question was asked as unemotionally as the rest, and Bailey started to feel afraid. Did he really care so little? Had she only imagined those weeks of a loving so warm she'd thought she'd never be cold again?

"No," she said. "I didn't buy it."

His gaze shot to her face. "Lonnie didn't sell it to you?"

"I didn't buy it." There was a big difference.

"It's closing?"

Was he worried she wouldn't have a job? Wouldn't be able to support herself? That she was going to ask him for help?

"No," she assured him. "A group of teachers from the university bought it and will be running it through a board of directors. I still have my job for as long as I want it."

"Why?"

Bailey was starting to feel uncomfortable beneath that probing stare. "Because I love what I do, the kids need me, and I need to do something with my life. Mignon won't be a baby forever, you know."

"I mean, why didn't you buy it?"

He hadn't raised his voice. There were no visible signs of any change, yet she sensed a tension in the room that hadn't been there moments before.

Whatever it was, it gave Bailey the courage to tell him the complete truth. "Because I didn't need it anymore."

He digested that silently, rocking back and forth slightly, as he had before. "Mind explaining that?" he said eventually.

"From the first day I arrived at the institute it'd been my family, the place I went to for security, acceptance, maybe even love. After you, it didn't work anymore."

"Why not?" He'd stopped rocking. Stopped moving completely.

"Because I'd had the real thing."

"But you wouldn't have married me if not for the institute."

"In one sense, that's right, Gabe." Bailey rose slowly, careful not to disturb their daughter. She approached him, stopping just before her body touched his, and gazed up at him. "Because I was afraid to marry you and needed a push, something to get me past the fear. I can honestly tell you that the reason I married you wasn't to buy the institute. It was that I couldn't imagine my life without you."

Something flickered in his eyes—and then was gone. "You're not remembering correctly, Bailey," he said. "You told me yourself why you approached me. Lonnie gave you an ultimatum. Eve gave you a solution."

"That's why I approached you that first day, yes. Or at least, that's what I told myself. I'd been looking for an excuse to talk to you for a long time," she admitted.

"Then what were you so afraid of when it came to marrying me?" The question was little more than a hoarse whisper. And loaded with feeling.

"You waking up and finding yourself tied to me. And regretting it."

He hadn't backed up an inch. Bailey took heart from that. And from the warmth she could feel traveling from his skin to hers.

"Did you love me, Bailey?"

"Exacting your pound of flesh, Gabe?"

"No."

"Yes, I love you. With all my heart." Relief, tangible and weakening, engulfed her as she finally let him know how she felt. It didn't even matter that he couldn't return the feelings. Not anymore. She just needed him to know, to release all the intensity inside her.

"You never said so."

"Neither did you." He still hadn't.

"We're very different," he said instead. She knew what he was really saying. Nothing had changed. They were still two very opposite people who'd happened to end up in the same place.

She swallowed. Nodded. "I understand."

"Do you?" he asked, holding her gaze with an intent, searching look. "I wish you'd explain it to me, then."

Frowning, Bailey asked, "Explain what?"

"Why half of my soul's been missing since the moment you walked out of my life."

"It...has?"

Gabe nodded. "If we weren't meant to be together, why haven't I been able to get you out of my mind, my heart?"

"Your heart?" She felt the tears coming.

He nodded again.

"But I don't have what it takes to hold you in the long run, Gabe. I'm too intense and too emotional. I think with my heart and not my head. I'm not comfortable in your kinds of clothes, your kind of neighborhood...."

"You're strong spirits and I'm stale tap water."

"No!" She shook her head, her curls shaking vigorously. "How can you even *say* that?" she cried. "You're everything I've always wanted! Solid and dependable and loyal and smart and logical and reliable and so sexy it hurts…" She watched him for a minute, as though deciding how much more to say, and then continued. "These past months without you have been agony, Gabe. If I ever doubted for a second how I felt about you—which I didn't—these months would have shown me that my love for you is eternal."

"You never doubted your feelings for me?"

"No," she answered instantly. "It was always your feelings for me I wasn't sure of."

And in that second, Gabe finally got it. He and Bailey weren't different at all. They were from the same mold, suffering from the same insecurities. He'd never doubted his own feelings, either. Only hers.

He'd never been able to understand what she saw in him, what there was about him that could possibly hold her attention—other than sex. He'd also never understood why she didn't appear to recognize what an amazing, incredible woman she was. Why she didn't seem to have a clue about her own value. Could the truth be that he was exactly the same way? That he had worth of which *he* wasn't aware?

That what she saw in him was as real as the things he saw in her?

"You really love me," he said, hardly able to accept it, yet filled with a certainty that he'd just hit on the truth.

"I really do."

Hands in pockets, he stood there, staring at her. "I really love you, too."

"No, you don't." She backed away from him.

"Yeah," he said, moving in on her. "I do."

"You can't." She was crying.

"If you can love me, I can certainly love you," he countered.

"How can you say something like that and still sound so logical, so calm?"

"Because it's important."

Her whole body swayed forward and then, after gazing at him for a couple of long, interminable minutes, she was in his arms. Laughing, crying, holding on for dear life. It wouldn't have mattered if she'd let go, he had a firm grip on her.

"I can't believe you love me," she said moments later, shaking her head.

"Without you," he told her, "there's no point in me."

Taking his face between her hands, Bailey looked up at him. "You mean that?"

"Believe it, Bailey," he whispered.

"I love you, Gabe." Her voice was soft, tremulous.

"I love you, too."

The doubts were gone, almost as if her friend Eve had set a spell on them. But Gabe knew with everything in him that this was more than a spell. This love was going to last their whole lives and beyond.

Epilogue

One month later

WITH MIGNON SLEEPING in the sling strapped across her chest, Bailey moved among their guests, greeting everyone, laughing, so obviously happy, Gabe couldn't help grinning as he watched her.

"She always could work a room."

Turning, Gabe saw his father-in-law lean an arm against the same bar that had been holding Gabe up since they'd returned home from Mignon's christening almost an hour before.

"Do I detect a note of disapproval?" he asked, more because of the view Bailey believed her father held of her than because he heard any negative tones in the older man's voice.

"Not at all," Colonel Evan Cooper answered, pouring himself a shot of brandy. "Perplexity, probably, but I'm proud as hell of my daughter."

"She doesn't think so."

The colonel shook his head. "I'm not surprised," he admitted. "I've never known what to do with her, how to talk to her. It's like she's from a different planet. When she was growing up, whatever I tried to convey would invariably end up meaning something entirely different."

Knowing Bailey, Gabe could sympathize with the older man. But where his father-in-law had been stumped, Gabe was only enlivened. He loved every second that he spent trying to keep up with his unpredictable wife. "Maybe you should tell her that."

"Maybe." Evan finished the brandy. "She's mellowed."

Gabe thought of the way she'd awakened him that morning, stark naked, kissing him from his toes up. "She's just on her best behavior because of the occasion," he assured the older man.

The colonel nodded, clearly heeding Gabe's warning. "I can't tell you how relieved I am that you took her back," he said.

"Actually..." Gabe looked at his wife, wondering how soon they could be alone again. "It's more like her taking me back," he said. And he thanked God every day that she had.

Laughter and loud greetings came from the front door.

"It's that weird friend of hers," Evan said, eyes turned toward the living-room entrance. "Who's she with?"

"My attorney."

"Oh."

"Yeah." Gabe couldn't have said it better. Except that, unlike the colonel, Gabe was thrilled about the unusual union that had sprung up between Eve and Brad. "They're good for each other," he said, hoping to explain what he was still trying to understand himself. "She tempers his logic and knowledge with intuition."

Bailey would have been proud of him if she could've heard him. At just that moment, she looked over at Gabe...and everything stopped.

I love you, her eyes told him.

I love you, he replied with his.

The party raged around them. Laughter abounded. Food was plentiful. Mignon slept. And her parents, with one look, escaped into a world made for them alone.

A world where a wacky artist and a stodgy bookseller lived happily ever after.

MY MAN VALENTINE

Jule McBride

Chapter One

TURN INTO THE SKID.

Gripping the steering wheel, Dr. Tom Cornell pursed his lips in dissatisfaction as he always did at any discovery that the forces of nature weren't completely under his control. Then he calmly wrestled the car into submission while everything on the dashboard—stethoscope, Beanie Babies, thermometer, valentine card and a page he'd ripped from a phone book—slid toward him.

"Hang on, Belle," he tossed over a shoulder. "Daddy swears the gall bladder surgery he did this morning was more dangerous than this, and besides we're doing less than ten miles an hour. In fact, sweetheart, maybe we'll just pull over and let you drive. What say?"

From the back seat, his two-year-old daughter giggled.

As the car slid to a slow, graceful halt on the ice, Tom glanced into the rearview mirror, and in the split second before his eyes caught

Belle's, he saw his own sandy hair, mustache and warm brown eyes. He looked like a decent guy, not the sort who'd leave a baby on a doorstep after a snowstorm. But then, looks could be deceiving. Tom shot Belle a grin. "You enjoyed our little spin, huh, Belle?"

Shaking an empty juice cup, she bobbed in the car seat, wisps of strawberry-colored hair curling beneath what she called her "ha-ha"— a red hat printed with white hearts. Staring through the rear window at the snow, Tom wondered if he shouldn't give up this crazy mission and take Belle home. It was nuts to drive all the way up to Braxton County with eight inches covering the ground.

Besides, leaving Belle with a stranger could be dicey. Lately she'd given separation anxiety a new name—to the point that even Annie was teasing Tom, saying she was going to use Belle in a case study about arrested childhood development. Tantrums aside, Belle had taken to hiding Tom's car keys, wallet and watch. By controlling objects associated with her father, she seemed to think she was controlling *him*. Wincing, Tom tried not to think of the watch he'd fished from the toilet bowl yesterday; it was just a good thing he wore a Timex, not a Rolex, since the toilet bowl was where more than one of his belongings had gone when Belle got mad.

Of course, Tom knew Belle got her controlling nature from him. He'd never learned to take no for an answer, which was why—on a snowy afternoon—he was pressing the gas pedal, inching down the unplowed road with fresh determination. White powder blanketed the faraway, pine-thick mountains, and closer, it looked like magic dust sprinkled on the sloping suburban lawns. Taking in the nearly identical brick houses along the tree-lined cul-de-sac, Tom decided Belle would be fine here. Yeah, he was definitely heading for Braxton County today...and Annie.

"With the help of Eloise Hunter."

Groping a hand across the dashboard, he lifted the page he'd torn from the phone book, as well as the valentine card, on which a gold cupid aimed an arrow toward black calligraphy that said:

Happy Valentine's Day from Eloise!
     This heart entitles the bearer to one free day of baby-sitting.

According to Annie, her best friend, Eloise, handed out these homemade gift certificates every holiday. Recipients could redeem them throughout the year, and Annie, always playing the matchmaker with Tom, had passed Eloise's valentine onto him, hoping he and Eloise would hit it off if she baby-sat Belle.

Not that Eloise didn't sound nice. Amusing and thoughtful, too. As a home ec teacher, her pet project was introducing adolescent males to homemaking, and it was her efforts that had put Annie's three rambunctious teenage boys back on track this year, during Annie's painful divorce.

"Tom, Eloise is amazing," Annie had assured. "Somehow, she keeps her hand in five pies at once, and even though she's only twenty-five, she's incredibly mature. There's nothing she can't do." With wistful sighs, Annie had spoken of Eloise's beautiful hand-sewn quilts and to-die-for pineapple upside-down cakes. Eloise was not only a neighborhood block representative, but she also painted theatrical sets and taught weekly crafts classes to seniors. Not a beauty, Annie would admit, but Eloise possessed big brown eyes, and lush brown, shoulder-length hair.

"All she needs is a warm, caring, gentle man

like you, Tom,'' Annie had urged, pressing the valentine into his hand.

Annie, he thought with a frustrated sigh. She was a staff psychologist at the Charleston Area Medical Center where Tom was a surgeon, and although she was a certified grief expert, that never stopped her from analyzing the general populace, including him, Belle, Eloise and, most recently, even the chief of staff's prize Pekinese, whom she claimed was suffering from depression.

According to Annie, Eloise Hunter's father had immersed himself in his job as CEO of National Aerodynamics after his wife's death when Eloise was three, which was why, at age twenty-five, Eloise was intent on attracting the attentions of unavailable men. Eloise's unresolved fixation on her father, Annie claimed, was the reason she'd been pining for her uninterested next door neighbor, C.D. Valentine, for the past two years. And it was why Dr. Tom Cornell needed to intervene ASAP and take Eloise out for a night on the town.

"Please, Tom,'' Annie had begged, "just meet her. You know I have a sixth sense about people, and I think you're tailor-made for each other. She's wonderful, and she loves kids....''

Reminded of how much his little girl needed a mother, Tom felt tangled strains of emotion—protection, fear, love and pride. Already, Belle was beginning to look exactly like his wife whom Tom had lost last March...the loving mother Belle would never remember, except in photographs.

So what if Annie says I'm spoiling Belle? he suddenly thought defensively. Why didn't Annie understand that he'd rather err on the side of smothering than inattention? Tom wasn't about to risk being like Eloise Hunter's father, who'd withdrawn from his daughter after his wife's death.

"I just hope Eloise is home," he muttered.

In order to surprise Annie at the cabin in Braxton County, he had to leave Belle in town. More road closings had been announced, and he couldn't risk getting stuck in subzero temperatures with Belle. He couldn't tell Eloise Hunter who he was, either, or why he was leaving a baby. Eloise would only pick up the phone and warn Annie of Tom's plans—and that he couldn't have. His jaw set with purpose. Before the sun set this Valentine's Day, he was going to tell Annie how he felt. She'd gone to the cabin with her sons, Tom wasn't on call for the next forty-eight hours, and because school had been canceled, Eloise should be home. The timing was perfect. His eleven months of grieving was long enough....

"Usually Annie helps patients' families," the chief of surgery had said all those months ago. "But you should talk to her, Tom. I'm not saying professionally. Just invite her to share a cup of coffee. Annie's a good woman. And you're a great doctor. We all want you to work this through and come to terms with your loss...."

The whole staff at CAMC had hung in with Tom during the crisis, but it was Annie who'd made all the difference. When she'd first waved from a secluded corner of the hospital's cafeteria, he'd barely noticed her, but by the time they'd finished their third cup of coffee, he'd wound up covering her hand with his, drawing strength from her natural warmth and vitality. Unexpectedly she'd begun talking about her husband leaving her, and as Tom listened, he'd been reminded that he'd become a surgeon because he loved helping people. That evening, he'd gone home to Belle, no less torn by grief, but feeling changed, as if things might turn out all right.

Now, after a near-year's worth of shared

lunches, Tom was noticing a whole lot more about Annie than her personality. At night, when he shut his eyes, he kept seeing every inch of her: her endlessly long legs, the charming over-lap of two lower teeth, the fine texture of her touchable blond hair. She'd appeared so magi-cally—the right woman, at the right time, in the right place, and she'd said the exact healing words Tom needed to hear. He owed her, just the way Annie owed Eloise Hunter for helping put her sons back on track, but somewhere along the way, Tom's gratitude had turned into more. Lust, love, he wasn't sure which yet. And be-cause Annie was still stinging from her lousy divorce, she wasn't even giving him the chance to find out.

"At least, not yet," he muttered. Then he took a closer look out the car window. "This looks like the place where you and I part com-pany, Belle."

A scarecrow was in Eloise's side yard, just as Annie had said. In the summer, it kept a watch-ful eye on Eloise's vegetable garden, but today its straw hands held a big red heart, and red pan-taloons encased its legs. The woman definitely had a sense of humor, Tom thought with a chuckle, and if Annie hadn't so thoroughly captured his imagination, maybe he would try to tease Eloise loose from her unrequited passion for her neighbor.

Instead Tom turned in the seat, and seeing his wife's face in his daughter's, felt his heart suddenly ache. Even now, he sometimes berated himself for the small failures of his near-perfect marriage, wishing he'd concentrated less on the future, more on the here and now. Foolishly he'd believed they had a lifetime of tomorrows. Now, because he knew differently, he resolved not to wait another day with Annie. And he certainly wasn't telling Eloise who he was. No, Annie wasn't getting the chance to gather her defenses.

"Belle," he said matter-of-factly, shoving the valentine into his inner coat pocket and glancing between Eloise's trim brick house and his daughter. "Daddy really needs your help."

Sensing imminent separation, Belle's eyes began to narrow.

"Annie's evading me," Tom explained, his voice soothing, "and she's trying to fix me up with Eloise Hunter. But now I'm going to..." Pausing, he laughed. "Never mind, sweetheart. Your tender ears shouldn't hear what Daddy's got in store for Annie," he amended as he unstrapped Belle from her seat. Grinning encouragement, he continued, "Now, you're going to do Daddy a favor and charm Eloise, right?" he asked.

And that's when Belle started to scream.

"SHE *WOULD* PUT ME ON HOLD," Eloise muttered. Wedging the phone receiver between her jaw and shoulder, she continued rolling dough, then cut hearts with a cookie cutter and laid them on a baking sheet while she waited, hoping her father would come on the line soon. "Oh, c'mon," she whispered. Then she glanced at the cookies in front of her. "C.D. had better like these." He'd loved the angel-shaped sugar cookies Eloise had made for him at Christmas, so she'd used the same recipe, and as soon as these cooled, she'd decorate them, take them next door and...

Ask C.D. if he wants to make love.

"No," Eloise corrected in a nervous whisper. "Fool around. That's how I'll put it. I'll be very casual."

As if there could actually be something casual about propositioning C.D. Valentine! Nevertheless, she'd already prepared herself, dabbing patchouli oil behind her ears, tugging on cowboy boots and tucking a transparent white blouse into her snuggest jeans, so that hints of a lace camisole showed from beneath. Now her heart pounded in anxious anticipation as she glanced through the window in the top portion of her side door, past the scarecrow and across the flat, snowy expanse separating her and C.D.'s houses. Her gaze lingered on his car—a four-wheel drive equipped with two sports racks. Twenty minutes ago a florist had pulled up behind it, delivering a basket of roses. Who were they from? Connie the bartender? Bonnie the redheaded accountant? Maybe they were from Cory, the new chef...

Unlike most of the women who swarmed over C.D. like locusts, as a single mother working to support her two children, Cory seemed to have some substance, a fact that made Eloise nervous, since no matter whom C.D. dated, he always claimed he'd continue to rely on Eloise for "more mature companionship." God knew, the man usually needed it.

Last Valentine's Day was a case in point. When she'd seen movements in C.D.'s darkened kitchen, Eloise had become convinced he was being robbed. Armed with mace and a lamp, she'd rushed next door—only to find Nancy Nottingham, then head hostess at C.D.'s Mountain Lounge, eating mint ice cream in the dark, clad only in a zebra print bra, no panties. Not that C.D. had exactly looked offended by Nancy's outfit when he'd appeared, naked except for briefs.

Now Eloise fought a wave of renewed mortification, followed by something akin to depression. Dammit, this past New Year's, she'd resolved to approach C.D. by Valentine's Day, but she still hadn't made any progress toward her goal. Why was she such a wuss?

"And why make such a big deal of it?" she murmured, boosting her own confidence. She and C.D. were good friends, weren't they? Whenever she went to Minneapolis to visit her father, C.D. drove her to the airport, waited in the terminal and waved as her plane took off. And last Thanksgiving, when his mother was recovering from hip surgery, Eloise had helped C.D. prepare a turkey dinner for the entire Valentine clan. "Besides," she whispered now, "C.D. sleeps with so many women...why not me?"

Thoroughly irritated at her lack of initiative, she deflected it by muttering into the phone receiver, "I haven't got all day, Dad." Opening the oven door, she slid in the baking sheet, spun the timer and imagined herself saying, "Happy Valentine's Day, C.D. Brought you some cookies. Mind if I come in?"

The phone clicked on. "Eloise?"

Hearing her father's assistant's voice, she realized she'd already braced herself for disappointment. "Mrs. Mesinger?" Static crackled on the line, breaking up the reply, then Mrs. Mesinger's voice boomed loud and clear again.

"Eloise?"

"Yes. Sorry, Mrs. Mesinger, but we've had a snowstorm. Even though it's not snowing now, the phones keep going out."

"Oh...I see. Well, I did catch your father," Mrs. Mesinger continued, "but he was late for a meeting in the fifth-floor boardroom, and you know how the people from the Flights Coordination Association can be!"

Actually, Eloise didn't. She took a deep breath, vaguely aware of the clutch of her heart. *Couldn't Dad take a minute to come to the phone?* "Should I call back?"

"Well...let's see." Eloise heard Mrs. Mesinger leaf through an appointment book. "I'm afraid he has a lunch engagement. But not to worry, Eloise. He wishes you a Happy Valentine's Day, too..."

Oh, really? Eloise tried to deny the deep undercurrent of panic and anger that never quite made it to the surface at moments such as this. While Mrs. Mesinger continued talking about the exciting week Eloise's father had planned, Eloise found herself picturing the offices of National Aerodynamics. A home away from home during her childhood, she'd spent hours entertaining herself in vacant offices, curled on the floor with books and crayons spread over the muted gray carpeting.

Once, she'd gotten lost while exploring—she couldn't have been more than five or six at the time—and she'd never forgotten how her panic mounted as she roamed the scary, mazelike stairwells and endless hallways of identical doors. Only when she found the fifth-floor boardroom had she been comforted. The walls were hung with photographs of her father: leaning over unscrolled maps, waving from cockpits, or fulfilling his duties as CEO, cutting ribbons at National Aerodynamics facilities all over the world. *But you never found your daddy that day, did you, Eloise?*

"Well...happy Valentine's Day, Eloise," Mrs. Mesinger said.

"You, too." Hanging up with a sigh, Eloise

glared at the browning cookies, thinking maybe Annie was right. Maybe Eloise *was* a fool to bake for C.D. He didn't care about her any more than her father did.

Not that Annie's analyses ever helped. "Nothing can," Eloise muttered, her voice suddenly vehement. Not when C.D. was so gorgeous! This summer, he'd started mowing Eloise's grass—just to be neighborly—and she'd served him tall, cold glasses of homemade lemonade as he'd worked. Carrying them outside, her eyes had riveted on the sweat glossing his tanned chest, and she'd fought shudders as droplets slid past rippling muscles into lush, curling blond chest hairs. She had soaked in the wild, barely restrained strength that emanated from his body just as surely as her skin had soaked in summer sun.

But could she really proposition him? On New Year's Eve, turning her fantasies into reality had seemed so right in theory.

Before she could reach a final decision, the doorbell rang. Glad to put the question on hold, she headed down the hallway, dusting flour-sprinkled hands on an apron, wondering who might be calling in weather like this. She swung open the door, shivering as winter wind rushed inside.

"Hey there," said the man on her porch.

He was tall and lanky, with sandy hair, a mustache and warm brown eyes. In addition to holding a baby girl, he was laden down with diaper bags and a car seat. Not Cyrus Dale Valentine, Eloise thought, sizing him up. But not bad looking, either. Self-consciously, she untied her apron, looped it over the doorknob and flashed the stranger a quick smile. "Can I help you?"

He scrutinized her a moment too long, and at the suspicious gaze, she felt a sudden prickle of indignation—until she looked at the toddler again. Guilt flooded her. No doubt, she was taking out her pique at her father on the stranger. "Are you looking for the Willises' house?" The Willises had a child about the same age as his. "Theirs is the white brick house by the stop sign. You can't miss it. Number four-twelve." As block representative, Eloise knew everyone's address by heart. When the man didn't respond, she continued, "Uh...are you lost?"

His previously narrowed warm brown eyes suddenly sparkled with mild flirtation. "No," he said, resituating the girl on his hip. "You're definitely the woman I'm looking for."

"Really?" Eloise returned dryly. She spent half her life fielding C.D. Valentine's flirtatious remarks, so she knew how to handle them. Every time C.D. looked at her this way, he wanted something—usually for her to bake a pineapple upside-down cake, or to water his plants for the weekend while he went skiing with one of his flighty girlfriends.

"Here..." Before she could protest, the man leaned, expertly pressing the child into the crook of Eloise's arm. "Her name's Belle. She's two years old, and if you wouldn't mind holding her for a second..."

"No problem," Eloise managed to say, refraining from pointing out that the toddler was already in her arms. She stepped over the threshold and onto the porch as the man patted various pockets, probably looking for an address or directions. "Looks like she's been crying," Eloise added. It was an understatement. Her dark eyes, squinted in anger, were filling with fresh globular tears as the girl glared at Eloise.

"Where did I put that..." The man's voice trailed off and he sighed as he began searching inner coat pockets.

Eloise eyed the girl. She wasn't one to think badly of two-year-olds, but Belle's lips were drawn completely inward like an old woman's, and her eyes, which were framed by strawberry-blond hair, were mere slits of cold, furious, infantile rage. One look, and she'd obviously decided Eloise was the enemy. "Uh...I think she's about to get fussy..." Another understatement. The child looked fit to kill.

"She'll get over it," the man assured jovially, suddenly reaching past Eloise and swinging Belle's diaper bags inside.

"Wait," Eloise protested, her heart missing a beat when she got the sudden, strong impression the man meant to leave his daughter here.

"What do you think you're doing?"

"Ah," he murmured, sounding relieved. "Finally."

Eloise watched in confusion as he pulled one of her heart-shaped valentine certificates from a pocket and slipped it into her free hand. He said, "According to this, you're good for one free day of baby-sitting."

"I don't even know you." Just as she said the words, she whirled anxiously toward the kitchen, since she thought she'd heard the oven timer. "Wait," she continued, turning back to the man as he edged guiltily down the porch steps. "Who are you? You can't just leave! You need to tell me who you are!''

"Sorry—'' Now he was backing down the walkway C.D. had so kindly shoveled for Eloise this morning. "I can't tell you who I am, Eloise. But if there's any kind of emergency, just call the number I put in the bag. I'll be checking my messages regularly. All I can say is…this is a special Valentine's Day surprise.''

"For *whom?*'' Eloise gasped. Her heart suddenly stuttered. Oh, she may have been ambivalent before, but this was supposed to be her and C.D.'s special night! How could she seduce C.D. if she was baby-sitting? "I have plans!''

The tall, lanky man turned and all but ran for his Volvo sedan. As Eloise raced after him, his little girl drew a quavering breath and released a long, piercing scream that might have torn Eloise's heart if she wasn't so damn mad. Suddenly, Eloise was positive she'd have seduced C.D. tonight. If it weren't for the stranger, she'd have lost her virginity in a wonderful night of lovemaking. "You don't know what you're doing to me!'' she shouted furiously.

She watched in horror as the stranger hopped into his car, waving as he pulled out. Her heart pounded in protest, her lungs burned from the sharp air, but she could only gape at the receding car. Just as it reached the end of the street, she registered that a sticker from the hospital where Annie worked had been stuck to the bumper.

She groaned. "The cookies!" Whirling, she ran toward the house, clutching Belle to her chest and trying to ignore her jagged sobs. Belle released another scream. Outside of low-budget horror films, Eloise had never heard anything like it.

"Please stop," she begged, hopping over the threshold, slamming the door and racing down the hallway. "I don't care what you think. I'm not an awful person. I baby-sit all the time, and other children like me." Reaching the kitchen, Eloise deftly whisked open the oven door and pulled out the cookies, but it was too late. Steam rose in dark wisps from the charred, blackened hearts, and tears suddenly stung her eyes.

Her Valentine's Day couldn't be worse. The hearts that were meant to be a precursor to sex with C.D., were now ruined. Rattlesnakes had kinder eyes than the baby in her arms. Not even her own father had bothered to come to the phone!

Just as Eloise angrily swiped the tears from her cheeks, she heard two loud pounding knocks at the side door, and then C.D. Valentine waltzed into her kitchen, gorgeous as ever, his huge, broad-shouldered body filling the doorway while his luscious gray-blue eyes homed in on the baby like radar.

Chapter Two

"WILL YOU EVER LEARN to knock?" Eloise sounded unusually flustered, and her tone made C.D. narrow his eyes since, if he didn't know better, he'd suspect she was masking tears. "C.D., I could have been in a bathrobe or something!"

"Or something. That I'd like to see," he returned easily, his usually flirtatious patter covering the fact that everything inside him froze as he stepped into her peach-and-mint-green kitchen and saw her holding a child.

"And you didn't wear a coat, either, C.D.," she admonished, gesturing toward his open chambray work shirt and threadbare jeans.

"You really can be bossy sometimes, you know."

"It's cold out there."

C.D. thought he heard a catch in her voice, but surely he was wrong; she hadn't been crying. Eloise never cried. He glanced next door, at his own nearly identical brick house, then his gaze returned to hers. "At least I got dressed," he offered with an engaging grin.

"My," she returned dryly. "A red letter day."

"It is," he agreed. "Besides, you know I never catch colds." His gaze swept quickly over the kitchen table, which was piled high with projects, then he took in Eloise. Even though he'd shoveled her sidewalk this morning, he now had the distinct, if false, impression that he hadn't seen her for many years and that during his absence, she'd somehow given birth to a baby. Shaking off the oddly jarring thought, he decided the cute girl in her arms couldn't be more than two years old—about the age of his latest niece, Kitty. The child had quit crying when C.D. came in, and now an exaggerated frown made her look almost comical.

Not that C.D. smiled. "Jack Stuart's daughter?" he guessed, trying to sound casual as he brushed white-blond strands of wind-whipped hair from his cheekbones and headed for the coffeemaker to help himself to a cup. When he turned around, Eloise was staring at him, her eyes turning dark again, just like those of the squinty-eyed baby at her hip.

"*Who?*" she asked.

"You know." Reaching past Eloise and the girl, C.D. lifted a cookie from a baking sheet. "That guy Annie's friend keeps wanting to fix you up with, the professor from over at West Virginia State." Suddenly C.D. realized Eloise was staring intently at the heart-shaped cookie he'd begun happily munching. "For somebody else?" he guessed guiltily, about to take another bite.

"They were for...oh, never mind. They're burned, C.D."

"Crispy," he corrected, crunching again. "Hmm. I like them this way, too. Same recipe you used on those Christmas angels. Now, do you mind telling me why you're so upset? When I walked in, you looked as if you were six years old and someone just stole your lunch money. Did I do something wrong, precious?" He knew the endearment riled her, but that she secretly liked it, and there was nothing Cyrus Dale Valentine loved more than seeing Eloise riled. He watched with satisfaction as color rose in her cheeks, and her warm eyes turned as glossy as her shoulder-length chestnut hair.

She drew an annoyed breath. "The real question," she challenged, wagging a finger at him like a Sunday schoolteacher, "is why you've come barreling into my house."

C.D. hesitated before answering. He'd felt... unsettled, worried, and although he'd hated to admit it, uncharacteristically jealous. Fact was, he'd been so upset that he'd completely forgotten to bring over the basket of Valentine roses he'd ordered for Eloise.

"Whoever the guy is, he looks nice," he admitted. "But he has to be thirty-five, Eloise. Maybe even forty. Not that I was..." Pausing, C.D. decided *spying* seemed too strong a word. "Anyway, the point is, I happened to look out my window and see him. And while I know it's none of my business, you haven't mentioned anyone since you broke up with Glenn." Glenn was a man she'd dated for four months the previous year, a gangly guy with glasses who, in C.D.'s humble opinion, looked far more suitable than the good-looking, well-dressed older man who'd appeared on her doorstep moments ago.

"I mention a lot of people." A quick toss of her head sent dark chestnut strands swirling against her pale opal cheeks. "And if you came over to talk about Glenn," she warned, "you might as well go home right now."

"I didn't. But I'm your friend and I worry

about you. I'm just saying that a ten-year age difference is something you should think about. You should look before you leap, Eloise."

"What makes you think he was ten years older than me?"

"I took a good look."

"Hmm." Her eyes and the little girl's seemed to narrow in tandem. "I don't spy on the people who come to your house, C.D.," she reminded. "And my love life's none of your business."

"Maybe not." But it was Valentine's Day, and a man should be taking Eloise to dinner instead of asking her to baby-sit. Couldn't she see that? Sighing in frustration, C.D. pulled out a chair and frowned down at folded stacks of camouflage-print material, wire mesh, leather strips and chains. "Starting a new career as a dominatrix, Eloise?"

She rolled her eyes. "Yes," she returned darkly. "I'm getting tired of teaching. I felt in need of a new career, and I assure you, C.D., you're going to be my first victim."

"A dominatrix," he murmured, still staring at the camouflage-print fabric. "That, or you're starting a war."

"More like you came over to finish one."

Glancing up, he found himself wondering at

the sudden hint of a smile that tugged at her plump pink-lipsticked lips. Nothing in the world, he decided, could be more mysterious to him than the ever-shifting moods of Ms. Eloise Hunter. He didn't mind sparring with her, no more than he minded her bossiness. The way he saw it, it was refreshing to be around a woman who knew her own mind. Unlike a lot of women, Eloise didn't pretend to share his tastes. In fact, she hated many things closest to his heart, such as ice hockey, tacky underwear and fast food.

"The boys at school are making skateboard covers and throw pillows," she explained, nodding at the items in the chair. "Leather and chains encourage them."

C.D.'s thick blond eyebrows knitted together. "Is this really the only way to get boys interested in sharing household responsibilities?"

"Unfortunately, yes. If you want to sit while you drink your coffee, why don't you move all that stuff to the table?"

"All I'm saying," C.D. continued as he seated himself, "is that you might want to think twice before you date an older man who already has a child, Eloise. I mean, it's easy to see what's in it for him, since you'd make a great mother, but—''

Eloise's huge brown eyes widened as they always did when he opened his mouth and inserted foot. ''Hate to cut you off, C.D.,'' she said, a touch of censure in her voice, ''but do you mind if I say something?''

He never had anything but Eloise's best interests at heart, so he felt strangely taken aback by her present attitude. Shrugging, he took a long draft of coffee, noting the faint, honey-nut aftertaste and wondering why his never tasted this good. ''Uh...sure, Eloise. Shoot.''

''You're in no position to lecture about suitable partners.''

He winced. Lately his love life had been a mess. ''You've got a point there.''

''And if you weren't so nosy, you would have figured out by now that the man who left Belle here was a complete stranger.'' Eloise paused. ''Belle,'' she repeated. ''That's her name.''

C.D.'s mind was still processing other information. ''A stranger?''

As Eloise edged closer, the scent of patchouli perfume, which just happened to be C.D.'s favorite, washed over him. Drawing in the scent, he watched as she stood Belle on the floor and began wiggling tiny, chubby arms from a red coat, exposing a navy sleeper beneath. He listened as Eloise told him the whole story.

"You're saying the guy left a valentine certificate?" C.D. reiterated when she finished. "And then he just drove away?"

Now she sounded stunned. "Yes, in a green Volvo sedan."

He bit back a soft, angry curse. "We'd better call the police."

"But, C.D.," she protested, "I can't do that. I obviously know the person who gave that man my valentine."

"But why didn't he tell you his name?"

"I don't know."

"Can you guess whose valentine it was?"

Glancing down at the heart-shaped card on the table beside the baby, Eloise shook her head. "No, all the baby-sitting certificates were the same."

"Well," C.D. scoffed. "Just because the guy had a certificate doesn't mean he can drive up and leave his child."

"No," Eloise agreed thoughtfully. "At least not without giving me more information." Her gaze flew to his. "I just remembered. He said he left a phone number." She raced to the diaper

bag and routed out a slip of paper, then hurried
to the phone, Belle at her hip again.

She returned a moment later, her face grim.
"It was just a machine and the outgoing message gave no information, not a name or anything."

As C.D. mulled things over, he tried not to
notice that Eloise was dressed up and wearing
lipstick. Not that her choice of a white top and
jeans was particularly provocative, but this
blouse was sheer with full sleeves and a fancy
collar that draped her shoulders. Beneath was a
camisole printed with tiny pink flowers, and her
jeans were faded to perfection, cupping what
C.D. generally thought was Eloise's best feature,
her backside. "Wait a minute," he suddenly
couldn't help but say, pushing aside the fleeting
illogical thought that she'd lied to him. "If you
didn't have a date, why are you so dressed up?"

Eloise shot him a long, sideways glance.
"C.D.," she said levelly, "if you didn't notice,
I have on blue jeans and a shirt."

Oh, he'd noticed. Lifting his eyes from her
plainly visible underwear, C.D. decided her
words didn't require a response, especially not
when he saw her blushing. Eloise knew exactly
what kind of male reaction her outfit was capa-

ble of provoking, especially since she usually only wore sweatpants and oversize T-shirts around the house. But whom was she dressed up for?

She blew out a perturbed sigh. "Anyway, a stranger left Belle here—" As she shifted her hold on the baby, Eloise's blouse pulled taut across her chest, accentuating her full breasts in a way C.D. couldn't help but notice. "So, I guess any plans I might have had need to be back burnered."

C.D. fought not to ask once more what she'd planned today...or tonight. Why wasn't she being straight with him? Usually she was more forthcoming. Noting that dark storm clouds were gathering in her eyes again, he racked his brain. Maybe he'd forgotten to take care of some chore for her...but he'd had her car inspected Saturday, then rigged up the new clothesline in the basement. No, he'd broken no promises. So, why was this exchange carrying so much low-level tension? Baffled, he offered a casual shrug. "I just asked if you had a date. I mean, you do have on lipstick, Eloise."

Something, maybe sadness, touched her eyes, and a quick flash of insight made C.D. sure she'd called her father to wish him a happy Valentine's Day. She always called him on holidays. C.D. figured Terrance Hunter had been busy as usual, but before C.D. could coax the story from Eloise, she murmured, "Uh…no. No date, C.D. Really."

Sensing a hint of pain, C.D. decided that someone had canceled on her and he gentled his voice. "Well, baby-sitting a stranger's baby is a helluva way to spend Valentine's Day. But I'm here for you if you need me." Unlike that damn father of hers who paid her about as much attention as a piece of furniture. Casting a glance at the child, he added, "And if it's any consolation, the little one looks as confused as you about the situation."

Eloise suddenly chuckled, the sound as soft and warm as the room. "With her face all squinched up, she looks like a little prune. Don't you think so, C.D.?"

"That or a shar-pei dog." His lips stretched into a wide grin that made his eyes light up, and the tension that lay between them vanished like smoke. "Now, you say the man knew your name?"

She nodded. "He called me Eloise."

"And he had a sticker on the back bumper from the hospital?"

"Yes, but that doesn't help, C.D. I gave out seven baby-sitting certificates to the nurses there...Annie's introduced me to so many people."

He snorted in frustration. "Seven!"

Her lips parted in surprise. "What's wrong with that?"

"You're running yourself ragged, that's what. Why not stay home one night and take a nice long hot bath? Or watch some videos with me? Friday you had a block association meeting, Saturday you were decorating classrooms, and Sunday was the quilting group..." Realizing she looked sorely offended, his voice trailed off.

Shifting the baby on her hip, she shot him a look that was pure Eloise: head tilted, chocolate eyes wide in her pale skin, the lower lip of her plump pink mouth thrust out. "I didn't exactly hear you complaining about *your* valentines."

"True." She'd promised to iron his shirts when he was "pressed for time," and to bake him a pineapple upside-down cake, whenever he wanted. He suspected he was the only person who'd rated two certificates, and she was right. C.D. didn't feel the least bit guilty. "Well, I'm not moving until you call all seven of those women and find out who gave away her valentine. Maybe it was Annie. You must have given her one.''

Eloise was taken aback. ''Annie would never give a certificate to a stranger.''

''If you say so. Now, c'mon. Let me hold that cute little girl while you make those calls.''

As Eloise snuggled the baby into his lap, he felt an unexpected rush of tenderness. ''Don't worry,'' he found himself assuring, taking in Belle's fine, hat-flattened strawberry hair, chubby, tearstained cheeks and quivering lower lip. ''We'll find your dad, kid.'' C.D. considered the emotion that had flooded him when he'd seen her dad. *Soon enough, some man's going to figure out what a sweet deal Eloise Hunter is.* That was C.D.'s first thought. Eloise was nothing like the women who'd seemed so fun when C.D. was younger…women who, over the past couple of years, had started seeming too clingy. Or possessive. Or hell-bent on besting him.

It was always something. Sighing, he glanced around the kitchen he'd helped Eloise paint last summer. Bright inviting light illuminated the peach walls and mint trim, taking the somber winter-gray out of the day. Colorful projects littered the chairs—weaving yarns and quilting scraps. Lately the electric buzz of productivity that hummed through Eloise's house had made spending time at his club feel dull by comparison. Years ago, when he'd bought C.D.'s Mountain Lodge with a family loan, he'd loved it, but the late nights had started wearing thin. He was thirty now, and he'd begun considering opening something more sedate, maybe a supper club.

"Karen didn't give away her valentine," Eloise announced as she hung up the phone. "Neither did Mary, Sue or Ellen. Annie and Gertie aren't home, and that only leaves Jane."

"Guess you'd better call her then."

As Eloise ran a finger down her phone directory, C.D. realized she'd painted her nails pink. He frowned. "Are you sure you didn't have a date tonight?"

"What?"

His heart went out to her. "Did somebody cancel, Eloise?"

She shook her head. "No, C.D."

"But you painted your nails."

She glanced up, her dark eyes settling on his for a charged, penetrating second, and when they darted away, he was left breathless, his heart pounding. No doubt, he'd imagined it, but he could swear he'd seen...raw sexual desire? In the eyes of... *Eloise Hunter?* He was still gaping at her when she glanced at him again.

She frowned. "What, C.D.?"

His chest felt strangely tight. He told himself he must have imagined the way she'd looked at him. "Uh...nothing, Eloise." But he'd definitely felt a jolt of something. And everything male in him had responded.

As he bounced the toddler on his knee, Eloise's pink-tipped fingers flew efficiently over the keys, punching in Jane's number. She eyed C.D. as the phone rang. "Maybe you can stay and help me with her until her father comes back," she invited casually.

He wished he could. "I've got to go to the club. Later I've got a..." *Date* was too strong a word, he suddenly decided, despite the fact that he'd made late-night dinner reservations at one of the best restaurants in town. "I said I might hang out with Cory awhile. You know, the new chef at the club."

Eloise nodded, as if to say that was expected. "Oh...hello? Jane?" she said as the other woman picked up the phone.

C.D. winced, cursing himself for making plans with Cory. But how was he supposed to know Eloise might need help? He suddenly smiled, thinking of how Eloise had shown up on his doorstep two years ago with a pineapple upside-down cake. She'd caught him at a bad moment—shirtless with his tattered jeans unsnapped—and she'd blushed to beat the band. Quickly thrusting out her cake-free hand, she'd rushed into a monologue, saying, "Hello, I'm Eloise Hunter from Minneapolis, Minnesota, and I've always been best known for my pineapple upside-down cake. It's damn near famous."

Before C.D. could get a word in edgewise, she'd told him she was twenty-three years old, just out of college, and that she'd moved here because West Virginia schools were offering great salaries to attract teachers, since so many locals were moving out of state.

"Precious," he'd finally said, "I don't know about you, but that breathless introduction sure left *me* winded. Want to come inside?"

She had. And something about the perfunctory, almost manly way she'd shaken his hand had absolutely killed him. Up to that point in his life, C.D. couldn't recall ever having shaken the hand of a woman. He'd kissed women, yes. Felt up, yes. Danced with, yes. Significant eye contact, always. But handshaking? Never. Not even once.

Since then, he and Eloise had helped each other whenever the need arose, which meant conflicts such as this one with Cory were bound to arise. It wasn't the first time. Chewing his lower lip, C.D. suddenly wondered if he should call, tell them not to expect him at the club, then cancel with Cory and stick around Eloise's for the evening.

"So, Jane didn't give away her valentine?" he asked as Eloise recradled the receiver. Rising, he nestled his coffee cup in the dishwasher, then handed her the sniffling child.

"Shh..." Eloise lightly bounced Belle, soothing her. "No," she said to C.D. "But I'll keep trying Annie and Gertie. I guess you have to go?"

"I'd better." He frowned, brushing away a stray wisp of the girl's hair. "Sure you'll be all right alone?"

Eloise shot him a droll look. "I'm a grown woman, C.D."

Before he thought it through, he flicked a finger against the shoulder of her blouse, his gaze drifting to the low collar, which exposed a hint of her ample cleavage. "I realize that, Eloise," he murmured, then catching himself, quickly said, "If the guy comes back, do me a favor and call the club, would you? Just so I'll know."

She nodded. "Okay."

"Mind if I take another cookie?"

"You like them, huh?"

"They're great."

Obvious disappointment he couldn't begin to fathom crossed her features. She swallowed hard, then skirted around him, opened the refrigerator and handed him a plastic container. "Here. Have some gazpacho. And you can take the whole tray of cookies."

"Not until you ice them." As he leaned to grab another burned heart, he could smell the sweet patchouli mixing with the sugary scents of baking. The perfume smelled different on every woman who wore it, and at that second, C.D. discovered he liked it best on Eloise. Her natural scent turned it into something complex and hard to define, making him more aware of her as a woman than he wanted to be. "You smell good," he couldn't help but say. "And no matter what you say, I think you had a date."

She glanced at the sniffling toddler who was eyeing the cookie. "I sure do."

C.D.'s eyebrows shot up.

"With Belle," she explained.

Barely registering his relief, C.D. leaned, and suddenly, without thinking, he dipped his head, lightly brushing his lips across Eloise's cheek. He had no idea what possessed him—and the kiss left her staring at him in awkward disbelief since they'd never parted this way—but as he turned and headed outside, into the bitter-cold day, C.D. wasn't at all sorry.

In fact, he wanted to kiss her again.

WHEN C.D. RETURNED a few hours later, the digital bedside clock read 9:00 p.m., and since the toddler was napping in the middle of Eloise's bed, he wound up sitting on the mattress to call Cory. Wedging the phone between his jaw and shoulder, he tried not to dwell on the electric jolt he'd felt earlier as his lips swept the warm, soft velvet of Eloise's cheek.

He watched her place the basket of roses on her bedside table. "Thank you so much," she murmured.

He smiled. He'd known the flowers would be a hit. As she casually seated herself next to him, her thigh brushed his, and he tried to tell himself that Eloise wasn't making moves on him, despite the slow-building heat that coiled in his belly. No, arousing him was the furthest thing from

Eloise Hunter's mind. She simply wasn't that kind of woman.

"You have a date," she whispered insistently.

He covered the mouthpiece while Cory talked. "But you need help," he whispered back. Poor Eloise looked like hell. He'd found her lying in bed with a cold compress pressed to her forehead, staring warily at the baby. Not only had Belle wept for hours, but C.D. had found—and recovered—Eloise's car keys, which the girl had tossed into the commode.

Now C.D. sighed. It had been hours since the mystery man had abandoned his child here...and hours since C.D.'s realization that another man would someday claim Eloise Hunter. Not that C.D. had a right to his jealousy. It was pure selfishness. Still, *he* was the one who gave Eloise pep talks after her lousy visits with her dad, and she was the only woman C.D. had ever met who enjoyed spending lonely weeknights alone watching his favorite Kung-Fu movies. Suddenly, his mouth watered at the thought of her vegetarian eggplant lasagna and—selfish though it was—he decided he really didn't want her to get married.

"Really," she said again. "You don't have to stay, C.D."

"You need help." As he continued listening to Cory, he glanced through the airy white curtains that framed the snowbound winter night. A full white moon brightened the black, star-dotted sky and rolling West Virginia hills. Inside, soft light from converted oil lamps bathed a pastel quilt Eloise had made last winter. Lace nightclothes slung over an armchair looked startlingly luminous, and C.D. found himself shifting uncomfortably on the mattress, fighting a pang of arousal. He'd had no idea Eloise wore such scanty underthings to bed. Nor could he recall the bedroom—where he'd hung curtains and changed lightbulbs—seeming so rife with romance. The scent of patchouli was definitely taking its toll. Tightening his hand defensively around the phone, C.D. tried to concentrate on Cory's harangue, but he was still thinking about how he'd kissed Eloise earlier. Like her room, the kiss had been romantic, nothing more than a near-touch and quick mingled breath.

"Sorry, Cory," he finally said, glancing helplessly at Eloise when he managed to get a word in edgewise. "But Eloise is alone here, and we haven't decided if we should call the police, or go over to the hospital to hunt for Belle's father." Eloise still hadn't reached Gertie, and Annie was at her cabin in Braxton County, but the phones there weren't working due to the weather.

"We were supposed to have dinner after my shift," Cory reminded him. "And I already got a sitter for the kids." There was a long, seething pause, then she added, "Everybody said this would happen."

He told himself to stay calm. He and Cory had only begun casually dating, and she was over-reacting, probably because she was still prickly from the breakup of her marriage. "*What* would happen, Cory?"

"Everybody at the club said you're seeing Eloise."

"Cory," he said, chuckling, "I really don't know where you got that information." Glancing at Eloise, he rolled his eyes. "There's a baby here, and we don't know who she belongs to. Have a little compassion." The remark, offered with good humor, only riled Cory, and it was long moments before he managed to extract himself and hang up the phone. He shook his head. "We've only been out a few times."

"Your affairs get hot and heavy awfully quick," Eloise said knowingly.

He laughed. The supposed intensity of his affairs had long been a focus of Eloise's curiosity. "I don't have nearly as much fun as you seem to think."

Eloise's jaw dropped. "Nancy Nottingham," she said simply.

That had damn near been the last time C.D. had sex, but he was hardly going to admit it. "That was a year ago," he defended.

Eloise shrugged. "Well, on the one hand, Cory sounds too possessive."

"You're being gracious."

"On the other hand," Eloise continued, "you did break a Valentine's date. I know women at the club chase you, C.D., but maybe you should quit dating them."

He only did so casually, Nancy being the one exception, but C.D. didn't offer the information because he'd suddenly become aware of the room again—of the silence, the low lighting and the wind whistling seductively through the pines outside. He was aware of Eloise's enticing scent, too, and of the warmth where her thigh pressed his. Even though he tried to break their gaze, he was riveted by her soulful dark eyes and translucent skin.

Desire came with the force of a revelation. His heart missed a beat, his groin throbbed almost

painfully, and a wild, dark, crushing need to pos-
sess Eloise Hunter overwhelmed him. He was
stunned by the force of it, and, feeling strangely
shaken, he glanced away. What was he thinking?
Eloise was just a fraction shy of downright
bossy, so if she had any interest, she would have
come right out and told C.D. long ago.

Her voice was low, and, he could swear,
husky, though no doubt he wanted to hear it that
way at the moment. "C.D.?"

Licking his lips against their sudden dryness,
he said, "Look, precious, I think you'd better
bundle up that little girl."

Eloise frowned. "Why?"

*Because if you don't, I might forget we're
friends and take advantage of the fact that we're
in bed.* "Because by the time I pull my car
around front, it'll be warmed up for you and the
kid. I figure we'd better run to the hospital. You
said the guy had a sticker from the hospital on
his bumper." C.D. nodded at Belle. "So, maybe
we can find out who her father is."

Chapter Three

"COULD YOU GUYS TURN OFF the music? Or the TV?" As one of her sons lowered the music, Annie recradled the phone and leaned against the island separating the kitchen from the main room of the cabin where her sons were entertaining themselves. Rooting under a bulky sweater, and using the cabin window as a mirror, she dug into a jeans pocket, found a plastic-coated band and swept her blond hair into a practical ponytail.

The weather had worsened in the mountains, and outside, snow was falling in blinding sheets while high winds shored deepening drifts against the front porch. Not that it mattered. Although phone service was spotty, the roads would be plowed by morning, and Annie had brought plenty of supplies in case she and the boys got stuck.

She just wished she could reach Tom Cornell. Placing her hand on the phone, she prepared to try again. She felt like an idiot, calling him every five minutes, but she'd realized she never should have given Eloise's valentine to Tom. What would Eloise think! Not only was the gift certificate meant for Annie, but Eloise might misunderstand Annie's motivations, and that would be awful, since Annie was deeply appreciative of the offer to baby-sit. Her boys adored Eloise. Unfortunately, Annie had gotten so irrationally fixated on getting Tom back into the dating scene that she'd been become exactly like her own mother: intrusive and controlling.

Annie thoughtfully chewed on her thumbnail. Well, maybe she was justified in her matchmaking. Over the lunches they shared, Tom always reminded her to leave her analytical skills in her office—and God knew she tried—but if she didn't intervene, poor Eloise would never give up her crush on C.D. Valentine, now would she?

The more Annie ruminated about C.D. Valentine, the angrier she got. Every time C.D. did anything the least bit neighborly, such as trim Eloise's hedges, mow her grass, or shovel her sidewalks, it was as if he'd performed a minor miracle. Oh, Annie didn't want to burst Eloise's bubble, but the flower boxes C.D. built her last spring weren't exactly the eighth wonder of the world. To hear Eloise tell it, the pink flamingos he'd left on the lawn on her twenty-fourth birthday were right up there with Stonehenge and the Hoover Dam.

Didn't Eloise understand how she was debasing herself by effusively meeting C.D.'s needs? Countless times, looking hopelessly breathless and flushed, Eloise had given Annie lengthy blow-by-blow accounts of how C.D. executed the most mundane household chores.

Why couldn't Eloise take up her own space? Stand up for herself? Annie felt a sudden rush of righteous white-hot anger. How many times had Eloise saved C.D. Valentine's houseplants from extinction? Or fed the man something more nutritious than the fast food he apparently thrived on? Eloise even helped him clothes shop, since, just like Annie's ex-husband, C.D. was clueless when it came to new styles. Left to their own devices, men would still be wearing loincloths, Annie thought with disgust.

Suddenly she frowned, recalling Thursday's lunch with Tom. He'd had the nerve to imply that Annie's anger at C.D. was really aggression Annie secretly wanted to aim and fire directly at her ex-husband. Well, Annie had set Dr. Tom Cornell straight, hadn't she? *She,* not *he,* was the psychotherapist, she'd reminded. Now a smile curled her lips as she recalled how handsome he'd looked, dressed in green scrubs and a lab coat, reaching over the table to steal celery sticks from her plate.

"I'm not claiming to be Sigmund Freud," Tom had said. "And I wouldn't know gestalt from an inkblot, but I'm beginning to understand what makes you tick, Annie."

And she'd said, "Well, now that I'm lying on your proverbial couch, Tom Cornell, what's that?"

He'd said, "The same thing that makes most women tick: a need for love and understanding."

And then she'd—

"Mom, you're talking to yourself again."

Startled, Annie glanced up, guilty warmth heating her cheeks. Years of her own analysis had made her realize she had plenty of flaws— among them, the uncanny ability to carry on long, argumentative conversations with herself. "I know," she murmured, distractedly. "But I'm thinking."

"About Tom Cornell?" one of the boys teased, sending the other two into gales of laughter.

Standing stock-still, her hand still on the phone, her eyes widened. Was it possible she'd been rationalizing? What was her real motive in wanting to take back the valentine she'd given Tom? Maybe she secretly didn't want him to meet Eloise.

Shutting her eyes, Annie employed a visualization exercise she frequently offered to clients as a tool for exploring their true feelings. She pretended that her matchmaking had been completely successful. Tom and Eloise were standing at the altar....

Sucking in a deep, calming breath, Annie let her attention linger on Tom's tall, lanky, tux-clad body as he turned toward Eloise, who was barely recognizable, dressed in a long-sleeved, beaded gown. Slowly Tom lifted the veil—and Annie grimaced. She should have known! The bride wasn't Eloise; it was Annie. And the flower girl was Belle!

Apparently, in her anger over her divorce, she'd managed to obscure her own developing feelings for Tom. As a standard, defensive reaction—so common in therapeutic situations—she'd protected herself by attempting to marry Tom off to someone else. It all made perfect sense. Human psychology always did.

"There you have it," Annie whispered. "People are right. Therapists, not clients, are the real head cases." It was definitely a good thing she'd left couples counseling. Besides, everybody agreed grief was her real forte.

"Mom!"

She'd been so lost in thought that her son's calls had barely penetrated. "What?"

"Someone's at the door."

Probably a stranded motorist. Frowning, she headed toward the front of the cabin, hoping the person hadn't been walking. It was beautiful here, but the snowdrifts were deep, and without city lights, the surrounding woods were pitch-dark. Feeling a rush of concern, she opened the door, and then stepped back in surprise. "Tom?" She flushed guiltily as her eyes flicked over him. This seemed so strange, since she'd just been thinking about him, although Annie had to admit she often thought about him. "Where's Belle?"

"With Eloise Hunter."

She tried to ignore the sudden stab of jealousy. "Oh? So, you met Eloise? Did you like her?"

He raised a staying hand. "Annie," Tom said levelly, "before you start psychoanalyzing me or Eloise again, I'd like to have a word with you."

Her lips parting in surprise, she peered into the bitterly cold, snowy night, then into his eyes again. Usually a warm brown, they'd darkened with seeming pique. Snow glistened in his hair and mustache. "What possessed you to come here on a night like this?" she asked. "Where did you get the directions? And where's your car?"

"Please," Tom said again. "Don't start the analysis."

She was still in shock. "What were you going to say?"

"I *was* going to give you the watered-down version," he began, sounding none too happy. "But that was earlier. Annie, it's now taken me eight hours to drive here when it should only have taken me two. The car was skidding, so I had to leave it in some backwoods town I'll probably never find again. I had to coerce the owner of a car dealership to open his business and rent me a four-wheel drive. That vehicle got stuck in a ditch and a tow truck had to pull me out. Otherwise, it's a long story. Suffice it to say my child's with a woman I don't even know, and who doesn't know who I am—although,

God knows, she came with a good reference. I'm tired, I'm hungry and my shoulders ache. So, like I said, you can just forget the watered-down version."

"Okay," she said. "Give it to me straight."

"I'm in love with you, Annie."

THE PEDIATRIC FLOOR of the hospital was quiet, and the mauve and royal-blue furnishings and carpet were bathed in the soft, soothing glow of low fluorescent lights. "Gertie," said Eloise. "Finally. I've been calling both here and your house for hours, looking for you."

"I'm filling in for somebody," Gertie explained apologetically as she tossed a long dark braid over the shoulder of her nursing uniform. "They've been rotating the schedule so much that no one can ever track me down." Her eyes followed another nurse who'd kindly taken Belle from Eloise's arms, and who was now amusing her in a glassed-in day care nursery. "Anyway," continued Gertie, "that's definitely Dr. Cornell's little girl. Tom Cornell," she clarified.

"He's a doctor?" C.D. asked, unzipping his parka. "You're sure?"

Gertie's eyes trailed over C.D., lingering longer than Eloise cared for. Not that Eloise could blame Gertie for looking. Worn jeans hugged C.D.'s muscular legs, fitting his rock-hard thighs like leather gloves to hands. And between the steel-gray parka that matched his eyes and the heavy climbing boots, he looked as if he was a fearless outdoorsman about to perform some daring mountain rescue.

"Oh, it's Belle Cornell. I'd know that munchkin anywhere," Gertie continued with a smile. "Her screams are legendary. While her dad's working, Belle always stays in the nursery. We've actually thought of auditioning her for horror films. She would have sounded great in the remake of *Psycho.*"

"My thoughts exactly." Eloise glanced anxiously toward the patients' rooms, hoping the nursery was soundproof. "She's been crying for hours, Gertie," Eloise continued with concern, glancing at C.D. "She cried the whole time you were at the club. I tried everything. I walked her, rocked her, fed her...I was sure I was doing something wrong." The guilt had been the worst of it.

"Nothing can be done," Gertie assured. "Annie says it's just a phase, and that she'll outgrow it over the next few months."

"Well, right now my head's pounding."

Belle's ear-shattering shrieks had started a tension headache that had spread throughout her body. "I think I took a whole bottle of Ibuprofen."

"Separation anxiety." Gertie nodded sympathetically. "That's what it is. Belle lost her mother last year, when she wasn't more than a year old, and she has a hard time."

"Poor thing," Eloise murmured, suddenly feeling blessed that she'd at least had a mother for her first three years of life. She exchanged a quick glance with C.D., suspecting he'd read her mind. He'd asked her once, and she'd shared her scant memories of her mother. They were vague, of course. Nothing concrete, just free-floating feelings of warmth and nurturing. And then there was nothing but a big black hole where her mother should have been.

Now Eloise braced herself against emotion, and she felt C.D.'s big hand settle on her shoulder, offering a reassuring squeeze. "She'll be fine," he murmured, making Eloise wonder if he was talking about her or Belle.

"Annie's doing all she can to help," Gertie continued. "We all are. Belle's a strange kid, though. She'd taken to hiding Tom's belongings as if they're magical talismans. Annie says keeping objects associated with Tom assures Belle that he'll never abandon her.''

"Maybe that's related to why she threw your car keys in the toilet," C.D. said. "Maybe she was mad."

"Could be. Annie's so wonderful with analysis," Eloise added, then she suddenly gasped. "Oh! *That* Dr. Cornell. Now, I remember him."

C.D. didn't look pleased. "You've heard of him?"

She could swear the words, though innocent enough, held an undercurrent of jealous emotion. Looking into C.D.'s gray eyes, she suddenly felt ungrounded, almost as if the floor had disappeared and she'd started floating. He was a full head taller than she, and as her eyes searched his chiseled face, taking in the wind-tanned cheeks and white-blond hair brushing his collar, she felt a slow, undeniable shiver of longing. Powerless to fight it, she remembered her earlier plans to seduce him, and only wished she had the nerve. For two years, she'd spun countless wild fantasies, but the second she was face-to-face with C.D., she always thought the better of making a move.

"Well," she said, fighting breathlessness. "I

don't really know Tom. But Annie's always wanted me to meet him.''

Gertie laughed. "Annie wants you to *marry* him, Eloise. She says you two would make the perfect pair. And Annie ought to know. Before she started working here, she was mostly doing couples counseling.''

"Marry him?" C.D. said. "That's a little extreme. They haven't even really met.''

Was it her imagination or did C.D. sound perturbed? Jealous even? At the thought, Eloise felt faintly woozy, and her head started swimming in earnest. No matter how hard she tried to convince herself she was suffering from an overdose of Ibuprofen, she knew better. She'd been dizzy since four o'clock this afternoon.

She still couldn't completely believe that kiss had happened. It was as surprising as the fact that C.D. had brought her roses for Valentine's Day. Over and over, she kept telling herself that the kiss had been merely perfunctory, and that the gift was merely a neighborly gesture. Against her cheek, C.D.'s lips had felt like the faintest trace of a finger, nothing more. Maybe he'd been leaning toward the cookie tray, and the brush of his lips was an accident....

But no.

Eloise was just as sure the kiss had been intentional. Realizing her heart was hammering, she glanced away from C.D., wishing she knew what he was up to. Had he decided he could have feelings for her? Was he coming on to her? Testing her response? Did he intend to slowly build intimacy, taking their friendship to a new level? As impossible as that seemed, the tension of not knowing for certain was unbearable.

Gertie was still talking. "You know Annie's been desperate to fix you and Tom up for months. Maybe you should go, Eloise."

"Maybe I should," she murmured politely.

C.D. gaped at her. "You want to go out with a doctor?"

Gertie's eyes widened. "You have a problem with doctors, C.D.? Tom Cornell's a good-looking, highly paid professional man with strong family values and a social conscience."

Trying to be as coldly critical as possible, Eloise kept her eyes riveted on C.D. and casually said, "You've got a point there, Gertie. Maybe I should at least go on a date. He was good-looking, even C.D. said so."

"Definitely handsome, in an every day, average kind of way," Gertie agreed.

Eloise could swear C.D. sounded relieved. "Average?"

Gertie nodded approval. "Average is good. I've never gone for those cocky types. You know, like the guys who played football in high school? They always turn out to be jerks."

Eloise winced. C.D. had been a high school quarterback, and now he looked offended. He said, "Not all football players are jerks."

He sounded so testy that Eloise had to conclude he was jealous, not that she understood why. They certainly weren't involved. "Well... anyway, C.D.," she managed to say lightly, wondering if the remark would further goad him, "men with medical degrees aren't average. Tom Cornell's got to be brilliant."

"Oh—" Gertie blew out a quick sigh. "Excuse me a sec." Grabbing a file, she headed toward a doctor who was beckoning from a patient's doorway.

C.D. barely seemed to notice her leaving. Leaning casually against the countertop of the now-deserted nurses' station, he said, "Brilliant? Is that what you're looking for in a man?"

"I'm not looking for anything," Eloise assured him.

"Glenn was a teacher," C.D. countered,

"which means he was smart. And now it sounds as if you're interested in this doctor."

It seemed impossible, but there was no mistaking the watchful wariness in C.D.'s wolfish eyes, nor the determined set of his lips. He was definitely digging for information. She bit back a smile, pleased for once to have the upper hand with C.D. Valentine. Not that the jealousy was anything more than an issue of ego. Nevertheless, she couldn't help but goad lightly, "Now I remember. Annie said Tom owns a house in South Hills with a big yard and in-ground swimming pool, and she said we've got similar interests...gardening, kids, volunteer work."

"Last year I was part of the Business For Kids program," C.D. reminded her.

Eloise had spearheaded the community program and involved C.D. who'd done a bang-up job, treating kids to lunch at his club while he spoke to them about starting his own business. "You were great, C.D."

"Really?"

She nodded.

Edging closer, he glanced around quickly as if to make sure they were unobserved, then he lowered his voice argumentatively, the soft huskiness sending a thrill through her. "Anyway, you can't go out with this guy."

If his proprietary attitude wasn't so irksome, she might actually start enjoying this. "Is that so?"

C.D. looked appalled. "He left his child at your house."

She hadn't noticed before, but now she realized that C.D. smelled of citrus aftershave. He'd come so close that her shoulder was wedged solidly against his chest, too. Awareness flooded her, and then, just as quickly, a rush of thoroughly unexpected hostility broke through the irksomeness. Why couldn't she get it through her head? He hadn't meant anything by the kiss earlier, and now he wasn't intentionally making her nerve endings dance. C.D. was a flirt by nature, and she'd be a fool to take anything other than his friendship seriously, no matter how much she wanted him physically.

C.D. was still eyeing her. "You're not going out with him, are you, Eloise?"

"I might," she returned, her voice becoming cool. "No one's perfect."

"Perfect?" C.D. echoed with stupefaction. "Eloise," he repeated, "I can't believe you'd really go out with a man who abandoned his own child."

"I'm sure he had good reasons for leaving Belle. He's a doctor," she countered. "Maybe he was delivering a baby in the snowstorm. Or visiting a sick child." C.D., she realized, was looming over her now, and his voice, which had grown both angrier and huskier, was sending shivers through her bloodstream. "Maybe doctors were needed elsewhere because of the storm," she continued. "At a shelter or something."

"I very much doubt it," C.D. said darkly.

"Tom Cornell's a very nice man," she defended.

C.D. took the comment as a direct affront to his own character. "You don't even know him, Eloise."

The genuine glint in his eyes should have given her pause, but it only served to further tweak her temper. Truly, C.D. had no right whatsoever to keep her from other men. "You don't know him, either," she returned.

C.D. scowled. "Why are you defending him, Eloise?"

"Oh, I don't know!" she suddenly burst out.

"Dammit," C.D. suddenly cursed, blowing out a murderous, frustrated sigh. "I do."

She swallowed hard, her heart skipping a beat. "Do what?"

"Know what we're fighting about."

She eyed him cautiously. "You do?"

"Yeah, I do, Eloise. We're fighting because I want to do this. I've wanted to do this all day," he said. And then C.D. simply leaned down and covered her mouth with his.

Chapter Four

C.D.'s KISS GAVE ELOISE the privilege of tasting something she never had before on a man—jealousy. He'd controlled it masterfully, heat and raw possession flavoring the touch of his mouth with just enough danger to titillate without causing alarm. Now that they were back at her house, she sucked in a quick sizzling breath and shuddered, wondering if he'd try to kiss her again. He was pacing in front of the bed, cooing soothingly while Belle cuddled, asleep on his shoulder, her fingers relaxed on his chambray shirt.

"I got into the jewelry box and slipped one of your necklaces around her neck," he whispered, rubbing a hand down Belle's back. "The beads are big, so she can't swallow them, and wearing it calmed her. Guess your stuff has become acceptable now. You know…how Gertie said Belle likes to hide her dad's stuff."

"I definitely wish I'd thought of letting her wear a necklace," Eloise returned, savoring a warm maternal rush. She'd held Belle for hours during the crying jag, and apparently they'd bonded. She liked thinking that her belongings now made Belle feel safe. "Where can we put her, C.D.? If we leave her alone on the bed, I'm really afraid she'll fall out."

"What about on the floor near the armchair? The carpet's soft. We'll watch TV in here until her dad turns up."

"Sounds good. I'll get some bedding." Turning to go, Eloise's gaze dropped over C.D., and she felt tension explode inside her once more. Her heart fluttered, butterflies invaded her stomach and the anxious excitement that made her turn on her heel and head down the hallway suddenly seemed dangerously unstoppable. She might have been confused about the chaste kiss that afternoon, but there was no mistaking what C.D. Valentine had done at the hospital. Wonderfully thorough and invasive, the deep plunge of his tongue had been as warm as the winter night was cold and as restless as the wild winds blowing between their houses.

Opening the linen closet door, she stared unseeingly at stacks of freshly laundered sheets, her mind still occupied with C.D.'s welcoming, practiced mouth. In the car, after they'd strapped Belle into the back seat, C.D. had threaded his fingers through Eloise's, resting their joined hands on his thigh. She'd sat stock-still as he

drove, enjoying the feel of his flexing leg muscles and fearing that any movement might end
the moment, making him withdraw his hand.
Funny, she thought now. She'd gabbed freely
with C.D. for years, but in the car, she hadn't
been able to think of anything to say. She'd
racked her brain, wanting to make casual conversation, but she'd wound up only staring
through the windshield, the slow, romantic songs
on the radio reminding her it was Valentine's
Day, just as the magical moon haunting the sky
reminded her that C.D. had really kissed her.

All the way home, she'd watched that full,
yellow moon drift through the marbled snow
clouds, and she'd wondered what action to take
next. Had he enjoyed the kiss as much as she?
she wondered now, lifting bedding from the
shelf and heading back to the room. Should she
initiate another kiss? Or was it better to let sleeping dogs lie?

Stopping on the threshold at the sight of him,
emotion lodged in her throat and she tried to
swallow it, but it remained—just a pure longing,
a slow-burning ache. After the feeling vanished,
Eloise wished she hadn't felt it. She was a fool
to keep dreaming about this man.

He was seated in the armchair, his eyes shut,
diffused light from the rewired oil lamps making

his hair look more yellow than blond. Belle was stretched dreamily over his chest, still bundled in her blue sleeper, her chubby legs dangling, her arms spread. Most women wouldn't guess, but C.D. loved kids. He was the youngest in his family, and between his four married siblings, he now had seven nieces and nephews. Last Thanksgiving, when Eloise helped him cook dinner for his family, she'd been amazed to see how he doted on the children.

"I wish he'd settle down and have some of his own," his sister Tammy had said, laughing and slowly dropping a hand over her pregnant belly. "I don't know what that man's waiting for."

Eloise didn't, either, since she imagined C.D. could start a family with any woman he wanted. Sighing, she tiptoed into the room and, as she reached the armchair, C.D. opened his eyes, surveying her a long moment. He had the best eyes. Early mornings, when he stopped for coffee before Eloise left for school, the two of them would stare out her back window, into fog that exact color, not the dark gray of steel or storms, but the same misty gray that rose between the mountains, warming with daybreak and catching hints of sky-blue and green from the pines.

Slowly, C.D. smiled.

Eloise smiled back, feeling emotion as subtle as the lamplight suffusing her. He'd flicked on the TV, and, the low murmur of sound helped dispel her internal tension. Lifting a hand, he grasped an edge of the baby blanket hanging over her arm and rubbed the fabric, tracing the weave of lavender and pink chenille. His voice was as sensual as the touch, as seductive as a lullaby. Talking low, so as not to wake the child sprawled on his chest, he murmured, "Nice, Eloise. You must have made it."

She glanced down and said, "Yeah," and when she looked at him again, she was powerless to curb the hunger of her own gaze. His cheeks were smooth, shaved planes, dark and wind-tanned from the outdoor sports he loved, and they were made darker still by shadows dancing in the low light.

His voice lowered yet another notch, turning huskier and strangely promising. "It's a baby blanket. Why'd you keep it?" The corners of his mouth curled further upward. "Planning on having a baby sometime soon, Eloise?"

Looking at him, she realized how much she wanted one. "Wouldn't you like to know?" Her smile deepened. "I was going to give the blanket to your sister."

C.D.'s brow wrinkled. "Who? Tammy?"

She nodded. "Uh-huh. Last year, when Kitty was born."

He still looked puzzled. "You made a wool piece for the baby. It was green and yellow. Remember?"

Turning back a corner of the blanket, Eloise said, "I made this for her first, but I messed up the underside. It was supposed to be reversible." She shrugged. "It didn't turn out right, though. Sometimes things don't." Even as she said the words, she became aware of the slow gulping of her pulse. *If we slept together, would things work out? Could we live with it later? Would it destroy our friendship?* Earlier, she hadn't really considered all the implications...the possibility of losing C.D. as a friend.

His lips parted slightly, and he tilted up his head to get a better look at her. "You mean to say you made my sister another baby blanket because of one little misstitch on the back?"

"You know I'm a perfectionist." *And you're perfection.*

He shook his head. "You," he said simply.

"You," she whispered back, aware that their gazes had meshed and held and that the slow thudding pulse at her throat was making her breathless. Nervously she tossed her head, so her hair fell behind her shoulder. How could he be so calm when they were in her bedroom? When another kiss seemed as close as the next breath? When the light was low, the bed so near?

"That's what I like about you, Eloise."

"What?"

He shrugged, searching for the words. "You pay attention to detail. You always get things right."

Did I get that kiss right at the hospital?

"Like?"

"Like when you helped me pick out the new decor for the club last year."

"Thanks." Feeling flustered by the way he was watching her, she stepped behind the chair and busied herself, arranging things for Belle. "Maybe we can pull the other chair over here to block off the corner."

"Wouldn't want our little tigress escaping," C.D. agreed, rising. When Eloise finished with the makeshift bed, he leaned, gently disengaged Belle's fingers from his shoulders. As he placed her on the floor, he slipped the necklace off her and then covered her with the blanket. "Beautiful workmanship," he repeated, then added, "I don't think she'll wake up."

"I figure that last crying jag did her in."

C.D. released a low, rumbling chuckle. "Definitely did *me* in."

"You? I'm the one with a headache."

He frowned. "You still have it?"

"Not really."

Stepping behind her, he settled his hands on her shoulders anyway. Feeling their broad strength, she couldn't help but groan throatily with satisfaction. Through half-shut eyes, she could see the toddler sleeping, a tiny fisted hand nestling the blanket against her cheek, and along with the television's hum, she could hear C.D.'s steady breath. His chest rose and fell against her back as his fingers kneaded her aching shoulders, and his proximity warmed her, making the surface of her skin feel alive, awash with prickles. When his groin brushed her buttocks—casually at first...once, twice, then with unmistakably steady pressure—heat flooded her whole body and she suddenly wished she didn't want him so much. Maybe it was wrong to want *anyone* so much. He wanted her, too, judging from his obvious arousal.

But didn't he understand they were playing with fire? That his kiss had made her mind spin with possibilities? Dammit, hadn't he guessed that her heart leaped whenever items in her house broke, just because she'd have an excuse to call him? Or that she found herself grinning every time he showed up unexpectedly, as he had this morning to shovel her sidewalk?

Don't be an idiot. End things right here. Don't ruin it.

Wasn't sharing C.D.'s life enough? If they slept together, things would become so difficult, wouldn't they? Besides, casual affairs weren't exactly her middle name, and C.D. might find out that the intimacy she'd implied she shared with Glenn was one hundred percent fabricated. Lies, lies, lies. She'd lied to appease Annie, who thought Eloise needed to get her mind off C.D., and Eloise had wanted C.D. to think she was serious about another man, just to keep her pride intact.

Suddenly his hands stilled on her shoulders, and she blew out a quavering breath as he increased their pressure, turning her to face him. Keeping her voice low, she managed to reestablish a conversational tone, even if the tremor in her voice gave her away. "I hope Belle's dad shows up soon."

Obviously C.D.'s mind was on other things. His eyes drifted slowly over her face, lingering on her lips. "I'm sure he will."

She tried to ignore her racing pulse, but their thighs were still touching, and the hard ridge of his jeans' fly was pressuring her. Somehow, she found her voice. "Gertie thinks Tom got caught in the storm. Wherever he is, maybe the phones are down. Wonder if it was an emergency?"

"I'm having an emergency," C.D. whispered. His eyes, still riveted to her mouth, glowed with awareness.

Contrary to her earlier plans, common sense now said that taking things further with C.D. would be the worst kind of mistake. Or maybe the warning came from a sudden mental image of her father. One minute, Eloise was looking into C.D.'s eyes, and the next she was in the past, wandering through empty hallways and boardrooms. She felt her gaze darting around while she tried to deny the panic growing inside her, tried to stifle the small, insistent little girl's cry, *Daddy? Daddy? Where's Daddy?*

Annie was right. Maybe Eloise would never stop asking that childish question. Even now, a pair of Terrance Hunter's monogrammed cuff links were in the jewelry box C.D. had left open on the dresser, which was why Eloise fully understood Belle's impulse to hide her dad's things. One day, years ago, Eloise's father had asked her to put the links away for him, but she'd kept them instead. Now, glancing at the jewelry box, she felt a stab of pain, just a quick jolt that brought her back to reality.

"Eloise?" C.D. probed.

He was watching her carefully, clearly sensing her thoughts had taken a turn, moved elsewhere. "Nothing," she said. But was she kidding herself? Had she really thought, even for an instant, that she could make love to C.D. without consequences? A darker question she'd long denied lay buried beneath that one: *If your daddy didn't love you, Eloise, what makes you think someone else will?* And even deeper still, was that strange, illogical question of childhood, *If Mommy loved you, why did she die? Mommies aren't supposed to leave their little girls.*

Shooting a quick glance at Belle and feeling her heart pull, Eloise abruptly turned from C.D. Without offering a backward glance, she headed toward the hallway. She'd reached the linen closet when he leaned and caught her hand, forcing her to turn around. "Where are you going so fast?"

Away from you, C.D., she thought. But now she wasn't so sure. Looking into his gray, blue-tinged eyes confused her every time. For two years, she'd suffered the worst sort of juvenile crush, and yet she wanted—even needed—to deny the intensity of the emotion. This was *C.D.*, she told herself, reliable C.D., who shoveled her walk, had her car inspected and drove her to the airport whenever she visited her father. She cared about him, and she didn't want to lose what they already shared.

"C.D.," she suddenly whispered. "I really think you'd better go home now."

His eyes narrowed. He was so close she could feel his breath and, when he lifted his hand, she could hear the slow, gentle brush of his knuckles as he trailed them across her cheek. Briefly she shut her eyes, enjoying the contact. Down deep in her bones, she felt rather than heard the soft rumble of his voice. "You think you can get rid of me this easy, Eloise?"

She opened her eyes. "It's late."

"I said I'd watch TV with you until Belle's dad comes."

"You'd better not."

He inched nearer, and her senses went wild when his lower body grazed hers again; he felt so impossibly good. It shouldn't have affected her the way it did—men brushed up against women all the time, didn't they?—and yet his hard, muscular male body sent blood racing through her veins. She'd never imagined so much tension could be held inside a human being, least of all inside *her*. It was getting damn difficult to take, but somehow she mustered her voice. "You really should leave, C.D."

The only thing that budged were his lips, which turned ever so slightly upward as if to say he secretly knew how much she wanted him. "Answer me one thing," he said. "Why?"

"I'm a practical woman," she whispered illogically, barely able to hear herself over the sudden ringing of her ears. "A schoolteacher. A block representative."

Totally ignoring her incredibly valid points, C.D. tilted his head downward, so their lips nearly touched. "A block representative," he repeated, his lips stretching, broadening as he planted his smile solidly on her mouth. His tongue followed, and even as Eloise cursed her own lack of resolve and good old American backbone, she found herself yielding. Even as she denied his power over her, she swooned. Their mouths fit like every good cliché: like a lock and key, puzzle pieces, or half hearts. His lips clung to hers, tasting as fresh as dew on morning grass. And then, suddenly, they were gone. Eloise gasped at the loss of contact, stunned to find how weak he'd left her, how her thighs trembled, how the tips of her breasts had constricted and were aching.

"You're just scared," C.D. challenged softly, his eyes looking glazed with arousal, so very male.

Eloise could barely breathe, but when she did, his strong masculine scent completely filled her lungs, making her knees weaken all over again. "*Just* scared?" she whispered, the words a raspy croak. "Isn't that enough, C.D.?"

"Not hardly, Eloise."

She licked her lips, still tasting him. "Let's show some common sense here."

"There's nothing common or sensible about what we're going to show each other."

He said it as if lovemaking was a foregone conclusion. Internal shivers were moving through her now, their invasive presence another byproduct of his kiss. "This is crazy. We can't."

He didn't look convinced. "What if I disagree? Doesn't my opinion count?"

Temper started mingling with the passion he was provoking. Why couldn't he understand? "Earlier tonight, I was thinking about making love to you, C.D.," she said. "I admit it. But we're friends, and I want to keep it that way."

"Friends," he repeated. "That's all the more reason…"

"Get real, C.D."

"This is as real as it gets," he said huskily, his hand sliding all the way down her back, slipping over her behind.

In her mind's eye, she saw an image of C.D.,

gorgeously naked, aroused and tangled in the rumpled covers. *But I love you. I can't lose you.* He was standing so close, *too* close, and the frightening truth that she loved him was like something palpable. It crowded around her, squeezing out her breath.

He was watching her carefully, sizing her up, obviously not in the mood to take no for an answer. She almost wished he'd be difficult or threatening, since a woman could easily contend with that kind of behavior. Yes, brute force was something a woman could stand up to. But this...

His breath was mixing with hers, his long, strong fingers seductively stroking her cheek again. Gently he tilted up her chin, a heavy-lidded gaze dropping over her face just before his lips met hers again, their coaxing more convincing than words.

She was starting to panic. "Please, C.D.," she murmured.

Those devastating gray eyes pierced hers. "Is the problem the other women I've dated?"

Somehow, she'd survived them. That's what she wanted to say, and yet on another level, she didn't care about them. Some were prettier or perkier, but they never lasted long, often only a few dates, and then C.D. would return. He'd pop in for morning coffee, swearing hers was the best, and then they'd share conversations about the weather, meaningless early-morning conversations, that smacked of domesticity, and that had somehow come to mean the entire world to her. "Yes..." she managed to lie. "Yes, that's it. It's all those women, C.D." Better that than admitting the ridiculous depth of her own feelings.

"Eloise," he returned, his voice barely audible. "Not nearly as much goes on with those women as you like to think."

"But...well, right now, I'm watching the little girl..."

"She's asleep."

Before she could respond, he turned, stepping away and opening the closet door, and Eloise's knees weakened in sudden anticipation. C.D. knew her house inside-out, and even though he was obscured by the door, she knew he was pocketing a condom from the box she'd bought when she was dating Glenn. She'd hoped something would happen, but none of the packets had been used.

"If Belle wakes, we'll hear her," C.D. assured, shutting the door, grasping her hand and pulling her further down the hallway. "Come on. Give me another kiss in the guest room."

He wanted more than a kiss, and Eloise knew it, but seconds later, she found herself next to him, beside the guest room bed, standing in a shaft of light from the hallway. White curtains opened onto a snow-blanketed hillside, and moonlight reflected onto a white quilt and knitted afghan. "C.D.," she whispered as he drew her into his arms.

"I want you, Eloise."

Her sudden nervous laughter sounded too bright, forced. "You're not going to show any mercy, huh?"

"Not in the least." His lips grazed her cheek. "If it's mercy you're looking for, precious, you're in the wrong place."

"Do you remember July Fourth?" she suddenly said, a recollection of the hot, summer night flashing into her mind.

He brushed back her hair, smoothing it over her shoulder. "When we were down at the levee?"

"Some girl named Missy stood you up."

"And we stayed down by the river until midnight."

She nodded, remembering how they'd lay down, their backs resting on the hard, hot concrete, their toes dipping into the cool water. They'd stayed long after the fireworks were over, staring up into the stars scattered across the velvet night sky.

"I thought about kissing you then," he said.

Her breath hitched nervously. "Not really. You're making that up."

"Really." He smiled. "But I forgot until right now."

Despite her anxiousness, she managed to smile back, and she was still thinking about the fireworks—about the multicolored starbursts, shooting ribbons of light and squiggles of red fire—when C.D.'s next kiss exploded against her lips. There were going to be no more chaste kisses, and by comparison, C.D.'s effort at the hospital had only been polite. As hot as July, his searing tongue now dived between her lips, moving with sure, coaxing strokes, and she fell with him onto the bed in a soft tumble of tangling hair and touching lips. Their jeans-clad legs scissored together and his strong arms tightened around her back.

She felt his mouth tremble. It was greedy on hers, thirsty, but he held back, almost as if he feared his need would overwhelm them both.

"Here," she whispered, thinking it was amazingly easy to undress a man. As the soft chambray of his shirt fell away, her palms glided over coarse, wonderfully masculine chest hair, and vaguely she wondered why she'd bothered arguing. Maybe she could have done this long before tonight. Any morning, when he'd been drinking his coffee, maybe she could have simply reached over and unbuttoned his shirt. If she'd only had the nerve to take what she wanted....

When he unbuttoned her blouse, thoughts flew from her mind. When he palmed her breasts, she whimpered. Her jeans, then his, hit the floor. Nothing but skin and desire was left. Heat and long-harbored need. He was all hard velvet. She, ready dampness. This was C.D., she kept thinking as his mouth smothered her breasts. *C.D.* Not the man of her fantasies, but her flesh and blood neighbor, her friend. From under heavy lids, her gaze dropped slowly over his golden chest hairs, down to where he was gorgeous and burnished, touched with fire and need. Her heart stuttered. Aroused and wanting, C.D. Valentine was definitely a man to contend with, everything a man should be.

His tongue flickered out once more, the soft velvet edge sliding along the taut tip of an aching breast, making her cry out as she threaded her hands deep into his hair. Pulling him closer, she arched, straining as he scooted between her legs, the flexing hot solidity of him eliciting fiery starbursts inside her that drew her mind downward, somewhere darker, and left her close to shattering.

"C.D.," she murmured desperately, her breasts feeling unspeakably full with his kisses, her whispered words urging him to draw the stiffened peaks further between his lips, suckling. Arching once more, she sought to join with him, and he gasped, leaned away, rolled on a condom.

"Eloise," he whispered, his strong hands gliding down her bare back. "We're doing the right thing. I know you're worried, but you won't regret it."

"Yes, I will," she said, her gaze seeking his, her soft breathing labored. "But it doesn't matter right now." Every part of her was burning.

His eyes were tender, his mouth gentle as it closed over hers once more. Then a sharp cry escaped her in a second of shock as he guided himself into her and thrust once very hard...oh, damn...so hard. It would have been too hard, except for the tunneling rush of pleasure.

"Oh, no, Eloise," he uttered hoarsely when it was too late, when he was deep inside her. "You're a virgin."

Her voice was strangled. "I was until just now."

"Oh, precious."

"You weren't supposed to guess, C.D."

His breath was a soft pant, his eyes flooded with tender light. "Why didn't you say something?"

Her pulse was racing and every inch of her body ached for more of him. "I wanted you to be the first," she gasped in a moment of weakness, knowing it was too heartfelt a revelation and that the power he held over her could break her heart. "But don't worry. Like I said, it's all right, C.D."

"Sure is," he returned, carefully entering her again and flooding her with ecstasy. "So very right, precious."

ELOISE.

C.D. should have known she was perfect for him. Like a typical male idiot, he'd been concentrating on other aspects of their relationship for the past two years, when he obviously should have had sex on his mind. He wasn't proud of it, but he was prone to the typical male attitude that said some girls were so nice as to be off-limits. Now he shuddered to think of what he'd almost missed.

Even more interesting was the fact that he and Eloise already shared lives. Thoughtfully he watched her set a glass of milk and a plate of iced, heart-shaped cookies on the kitchen table.

"Why didn't you tell me?" he said again, slipping an arm around her waist, feeling her long white silk gown tease his fingertips. She wasn't wearing a stitch beneath, and he groaned with satisfaction, pulling her into his lap and feeling the exciting curve of her bottom on his thigh. He nuzzled her neck.

"Tell you?" She snuggled, her skin hot and damp through the sheer fabric, her eyes drifting downward, curiously lingering on his chest, belly, then briefs.

He was still marveling at her responsiveness, at the many men who'd let her get away, at how easily he could have missed his chance to make love to her. "How did you manage not to..."

Color stained her cheeks. "Sleep with anybody before now?"

Tenderness claimed his heart. "I'm not trying to embarrass you, Eloise."

She shrugged. "I didn't have a lot of friends when I was growing up, C.D. And I was worried about all the usual things, pregnancy and disease. And then...well, I thought something would happen with Glenn, but to tell you the truth, I wasn't all that interested in him. He's a nice person," she added quickly, snagging a cookie from the plate and biting into it. "Anyway, why do you want to talk about this?"

"Because you've been under my nose for two years, and I just now noticed."

"Well, you were right before. It's embarrassing, C.D."

"Not for me." He was on top of the world.

Pink suffused her cheeks and she smiled, dimples bracketing her mouth. She eyed him a long moment. "As many women as you've been with," she said levelly, "nothing would embarrass you, C.D."

He drew her closer, thinking he'd never felt more comfortable than now, sitting here with her shoulder comfortably wedged against his chest. Pressing a kiss to her hair, then brushing his lips to the dark strands, he whispered, "There really haven't been as many women as you think."

"Oh, C.D.," she said as if to say he was impossible.

"Really," he defended. "Whenever you're ready to hear the truth, I'll tell you. Meantime, your accusations just expose your overactive imagination. You've been having fantasies."

"What if I have?"

"When did they start?"

"When I first saw you, C.D."

The information made his soul sing. So did

how she curled against him, ducking her head. His gaze followed hers to a window. Beyond the reflected interior of the kitchen, he could see the scarecrow, and past his house, a hill thick with pines. Snow coated the sloping branches. It was after midnight, and somehow this time with Eloise felt stolen. He rubbed a hand up and down her back. "Let's go back to bed, precious."

"We should check on the little one."

Shutting his eyes, he took a deep breath of her warm, feminine scent that was spiced from lovemaking, and for a second, he fantasized they were talking about their child. He sighed. "Guess Belle's dad's hunkered down somewhere for the night."

"Guess so."

"So, we've got the place to ourselves, no interruptions."

That got a smile. "You didn't seem to be expecting interruptions before, C.D."

"Sure I was. Couldn't you tell I was holding back?"

She elbowed him. "I don't think so."

She was right. He'd never felt such explosive release. No doubt, she could now feel the evidence of his wanting her again. There were so many things he wanted to do with her, to show her. Lifting a cookie, he crunched on it. "Thanks, Eloise."

Her lips tilted further upward at the corners. "Sure."

"For that, too. But I meant for icing the cookies."

Her chuckle filled him with warmth. "I was going to bring those cookies over earlier, and use them to seduce you."

The idea had immense appeal. "Are you serious?"

She nodded. "Ever since last summer, when you started mowing the grass without a shirt..."

He squinted at her. "That's why you were dressed up and wearing patchouli?" When she nodded, he thought again of how she'd made a second baby blanket for his sister. "When you get something in your head, you always do it right."

Her voice was the softest, sexiest purr he'd ever heard. "Did I get it right tonight?"

Just before he kissed her, he whispered, "Nothing's ever been so right." He'd never imagined he could feel so satisfied, or so sure about his future.

Chapter Five

THANKFULLY MORNING BROUGHT Eloise to her senses. Annie was absolutely right. Eloise already loved one unreciprocating man, her father, and she didn't need to love another—her true feelings be damned. Better to end things with C.D. before they ever began. That's what Eloise thought as she crossed her arms over the longest, most concealing flannel nightgown she owned and worriedly tapped her fingernails on the countertop while waiting for the coffee to brew. Surely, she told herself, glancing at C.D., he understood that fairy tales that lasted past dawn meant trouble, so he'd leave after he had some coffee.

"Here you go, cutie," he said, amusing Belle by dunking a spoon into a bowl of applesauce, flying it through the air, then slipping it neatly between her lips. She was seated at the kitchen table, her head just poking over the top of it since there was no booster seat. She was again wearing the beaded necklace, which she'd insisted having the moment she awoke. "Just like a woman," he murmured as she wiggled her arms and legs. "Preening and giggling. Throwing me those wanton glances." Glancing at Eloise, he said. "Wonder why her father never called. It seems kind of strange. Don't you think? Even though we didn't call about any kind of emergency, you'd think he'd at least check in."

"Maybe the phones are still down," Eloise countered, feeling prickly since C.D. hadn't yet mentioned what happened last night. Did it mean so little to him that it wasn't worth talking about? Did he really feel they could simply pick up where they left off? Or did he simply assume it was a one-night stand? She felt too uncomfortable to ask, and as soon as she'd awakened, she'd scooted from bed, quickly dressed and come downstairs to start coffee. "I never got hold of Annie, C.D. And anyway, it's still early. Wherever he is, maybe Tom's not even awake yet."

"Well, Annie's told him all about you, so he probably just figures Belle's in good hands, which she is. Right, Belle?" C.D. glanced up, flashing Eloise a grin. "I hope Annie doesn't take it too hard."

"Take what too hard?"

"Her failed attempt at fixing up you and Tom Cornell."

Even though Eloise knew she'd be a fool to think C.D. cared about becoming steady lovers, her heart lurched. *No, don't be crazy, Eloise. He didn't mean anything by the remark.* Somehow, she managed a return smile as she set a coffee mug in front of him, suddenly wishing he'd save them both some grief and go home. Last night was magical, and she wanted to keep it that way—a fantasy, liberally splashed with stardust and glitter.

He was watching her. "Penny for your thoughts."

"Fifty cents," she countered. "Inflation."

"Really, what's on your mind, Eloise?"

How could she tell C.D. she'd expected him to be gone before she woke up, or that sharing the morning with him only put her in touch with the vision of a domestic life she secretly wished they shared? Last night, she'd half assumed they had a tacit agreement to pretend their lovemaking had never happened, which was why she'd expected to find C.D. gone. She figured it would be as if fantastical things had appeared in the night, then vanished just as mysteriously—just like a pumpkin coach and mice footmen.

But C.D. was still here, clad in tight-fitting,

mouthwatering briefs, and he was so attentive to Belle that he could have been her proud parent. Fighting her deeper feelings, Eloise dryly acknowledged that—sans child—this scene could have been a replay of last Valentine's Day when C.D. had been in his kitchen with Nancy Nottingham, except now *Eloise* was the lucky girl and the setting was *her* kitchen. And, of course, Eloise was not wearing animal print undergarments.

Who knows who next year's Valentine would be? Eloise thought glumly. Her eyes trailed wistfully over C.D.'s hair that had felt as soft as chenille on her naked shoulders, down the thick coarse thatch matting his bare chest, then down to where his underwear hugged firm male contours. By the time her gaze traveled down long legs to his bare feet, she was able to admit the truth. She'd fall to pieces if another female showed up at C.D. Valentine's house anytime soon. Missy, Bonnie, Connie, Cory…Eloise suddenly felt a rush of jealousy about them all.

So, what was she supposed to do?

Unfortunately this wasn't like choosing accountants or phone carriers and, for once, asking for C.D.'s advice was out of the question. Glancing through the window, she searched the foggy, cloud-filled sky, but it didn't portend well, promising colder temperatures and more snow. Watching the flurries whirl against the barely distinguishable white backdrop, she suddenly remembered a similarly chilly day last year, when she'd agreed to be C.D's social date at a business owner's association meeting. She shook her head at the memory.

"Now, you're definitely thinking about something, Eloise."

"I just remembered that awful chicken dinner we had," she admitted, making him chuckle. "Remember? At the business owners meeting? You said it was the worst meal you ever ate, and then, the next morning, you brought me a rubber chicken."

"Something had to commemorate the event."

Despite her smile, she felt another rush of panic. C.D. wasn't just any friend, he was her *best* friend. Last night, she'd wanted him so much she'd lost her ability to reason—she'd waited years for the right moment and the right man—but now she needed to preserve the friendship. "Are you hungry?" she managed. "Uh…I was thinking I might make some biscuits, okay?"

A slow grin spread over his face. "What about you for breakfast? You look great."

"C.D., I'm wearing a flannel nightgown, my

hair's a mess…'' Her breath suddenly caught as her mind filled with images of his long fingers mussing it, threading through the strands and massaging her scalp. ''I've got dark smears under my eyes,'' she continued, thinking she'd better put things in perspective before they did wind up back in bed. ''And no lipstick.''

C.D. considered. ''Gee, maybe you should ask Annie about the superego.''

''Superego?''

''Yeah. Isn't that the name for the part of the personality that can get way too punishing if a woman doesn't get enough sex?''

Sex? She'd had plenty; both her body and heart were still warm with it and aching for more. But why was C.D. ignoring the delicacy of their situation? She forced a scowl. ''I'm not punishing myself, C.D.''

He laughed. ''You do look great, Eloise.''

''Looks aren't everything.'' She'd never *felt* more conflicted. If they'd served no other purpose, the years of perfectly touched photographs that graced the Hunters' Christmas cards had proven that external appearances often masked hurting insides. Year after year, Eloise had basked in her father's convincingly loving gaze as they'd posed, and for a second, she'd been sure her whole world was about to change. A buzz would sound from the camera, a light would flash, but then her father would check his watch, turn Eloise over to a housekeeper, and head back to his office.

Sighing, she took in the picture C.D. was creating, looking so comfortably at home in his underwear and happily feeding the toddler. Unwanted emotion threatened to break through her carefully erected facade, and suddenly she feared she'd go for broke, risk their friendship and, like a fool, confess that she was in love with him. Clearing her throat, she said, "Did you want biscuits or not?"

C.D. lifted an eyebrow critically. "With icing?"

"Cinnamon."

"Swell."

"You know," she said, half to herself, "you're the only man I know who can use words like 'swell' without a trace of irony and without sounding like an idiot."

"One of my many talents."

Last night C.D. had acquainted her with a good many more, which made his easy acceptance of their changed relationship even more difficult to bear. Given C.D.'s seemingly active sex life, maybe he was used to shifting boundaries and alliances. Worriedly chewing her lower lip, she was leaning to preheat the oven when a knock sounded at the side door.

"Oh," she said, agitated at the realization she'd soon be alone with C.D. "That must be Belle's dad. I wonder why he came around back, instead of to the front door?"

"Maybe he knocked and we didn't hear him."

"Probably. Shouldn't you put on a robe?"

"He's a guy. He's seen underwear." C.D.'s laughter filled the kitchen again. "Besides, borrowing one of your bathrobes wouldn't help. I'm not the pink and ruffles type."

"True," she murmured, smoothing her hair. As she opened the door, brutally bitter air swept inside, but it wasn't anywhere near as cold as the scowl on Cory's face. Eyes as black and glossy as her shoulder-length hair flowed from beneath a black knit beret, and her long black coat made her appear imposing to the point of severe. A gloved hand held a red paper plate, and through the plastic wrap, Eloise could see cupcakes decorated with heart sprinkles.

"Eloise," said Cory stiffly.

"Cory," Eloise replied. Stepping back, she watched curiously as Cory breezed past, then she quickly shut the door, turning just in time to see

Cory drop the plate onto the table and put her hands on her hips.

Frowning, C.D. set down the bowl of applesauce, and glanced up at her. "Uh...hey, Cory."

As if she'd barely heard, Cory continued, "I just wanted to see this for myself."

"See what?" Eloise ventured, guilt rushing in on her. She knew Cory and C.D. had never slept together, but they'd had a date last night, and now Cory assumed she'd been stood up because of Eloise. If Eloise hadn't known what to do ten minutes ago, she was even more confused now. Not only had she slept with her best friend, but in less than twenty-four hours, she'd also become the proverbial "other woman." This was definitely a first. She peered at Cory, unsure of the proper protocol. "Would you care for some coffee?"

Cory ignored her, and if she noticed C.D. was clad only in briefs, she gave no indication. "I really can't believe this," she continued, looking insulted. "Do you know how guilty I felt last night, C.D. Valentine?"

"Cory, I'm sorry about dinner—"

"I felt lousy," she fumed. "You said you had to stay here...that poor little defenseless Eloise needed help caring for a baby whose father was missing. I should have known that was only an excuse. What do you know about kids?''

"Actually," Eloise couldn't help but say, hardly liking that she'd been referred to as defenseless. "He knows a lot. C.D. has seven nieces and nephews, Cory."

"Thank you, Eloise," Cory returned, not sounding the least bit appreciative of her commentary. "You should know." Her eyes riveted on C.D. again. "All night long, I berated myself for being angry about your breaking our date. How could I be so selfish when you two were desperately trying to find a child's father?"

C.D. looked vaguely uncomfortable. "No need to beat yourself up about it, Cory."

"Really, there's not," Eloise added.

Cory's eyes pierced around the kitchen. "I guess not."

Even though no explanations were required, Eloise found herself saying, "It wasn't really planned this way, Cory. One thing just led to another..."

"I'll say! And don't play the innocent with me, Eloise."

Eloise's heart hammered, her temper flared, and suddenly she wasn't sure who she was more angry with—C.D. or Cory, whom she didn't even really know. Eloise wasn't used to scenes, and she should have guessed that wherever C.D. went, he'd bring one with him. Nevertheless, his girlfriends didn't usually attack.

"I should have listened," Cory continued with a sigh. "But I took you at your word, C.D. Last night, I felt guilty and made cupcakes with the kids. This morning, I bring them over...and lo and behold, here you are, still at Eloise's, in your underwear."

The gray irises of C.D.'s eyes were turning flinty, and when he spoke, his voice carried a soft warning. "Cory, we've only gone out a couple of times. I really don't think you've got the right—"

"I'm not saying I have the right to intervene in your love life, C.D. What makes me mad is how you keep lying about being available. Every girl at the club told me you're seeing Eloise."

"Oh, no," Eloise assured. "It's nothing like that."

Cory turned, her eyes slowly drifting over Eloise, making a point of taking in her mussed hair and generally disheveled appearance. Suddenly Eloise became uncomfortably aware that she was wearing no underwear under the flannel gown and eyed the matching robe she'd draped over one of the chairs.

"Eloise," Cory said flatly, as she turned,

opened the door, and ushered in another rush of
frigid air. "Has it really escaped your notice that
you slept with this man last night? And haven't
you ever wondered about the fact that C.D.
leaves work ten times a day to run errands for
you?" Cory paused, blowing out a sigh.
"Sorry," she continued, "but my mood has
nothing to do with you. It's just that, some days,
trying to date is enough to make me want my
ex-husband back." Suddenly chuckling, she
added, "And that's saying something." She
stepped onto the porch, turning toward the
kitchen just long enough to scrutinize C.D. and
Eloise. "I really can't believe this. Haven't you
two figured out you're in love?"

Love? Eloise was barely aware of the door
closing, and she didn't realize C.D. had risen
until he moved in front of her. She edged back,
resting against the counter. Of course, Cory was
right. Eloise was in love, which was why she
was now as dizzy as a rock climber with vertigo.
Her hands skated down the counter, seeking purchase, and even though C.D. was taller than she,
she suddenly felt as if she were viewing him
from some precarious height.

In love. She and C.D. were just friends! At
least from C.D.'s point of view. As his palms
slid around her waist, Eloise tried to ignore how

the skin beneath her gown tingled. "I can't believe Cory said that," she murmured apologetically.

"I can."

A dull ache of temper began worming its way to the surface. It was almost as if C.D. wanted to tease her with the idea that last night meant something more. "Can what?"

"Believe Cory thinks I'm in love with you," he returned. "Because I am, Eloise." While she was still gasping, C.D. said something even more shocking. "Marry me."

HER ANGER WAS UNEXPECTED—it darkened her eyes and deepened the color of her cheeks—and it left C.D. wondering what he'd said wrong. "Eloise? Didn't you hear me?"

"I can't believe you said that!"

"Said what? That I want to marry you?" He squinted at her, knowing he was definitely missing something here. "Last night I knew it, but when Cory said it, it hit me again like a ton of bricks. It hit me square in the face, Eloise. However you want to put it. I probably fell in love with you the day you first came over with that pineapple upside-down cake."

It may have been short, but it was the most heartfelt speech C.D. had ever offered a woman, and he was stunned to see that it had absolutely no effect on Eloise Hunter. Her eyes remained strangely impassioned, luminously dark, and since he was now feeling something suspiciously akin to panic, he quickly covered it with a temper he hoped could match hers. He had his pride, and to say he wasn't exactly used to rejection was a definite understatement. "Mind telling me what's going through your mind, Eloise?"

"We slept together, C.D. Or don't you remember?"

"Remember?" Gaping at her, he quickly reached out and closed a hand tightly around her upper arm as if he expected the gesture to make her see reason. "I've waited all my life for something like last night to happen to me. Seems like you're the one who forgot."

"I think we should *both* forget."

He never could. His whole life, he'd recall the first instant their bodies joined. Everything—the scent of shampoo and patchouli, sound of her needy whimpers—were embedded in his cells. Now her eyes, which had drifted so hungrily over his body in the moonlight, looked hot and dangerous. "Never," he vowed.

"C'mon, C.D. You've got to leave."

Leave? Was she crazy? Before he thought it through, he pulled her closer, more forcefully than he should have, but damn if he cared. Trapping her against the counter, he tried to deny how the contact aroused him in spite of his anger, and he gritted his teeth against the excruciating feel of soft flannel brushing his bare belly. "You're running scared, Eloise," he said with deceptive calm, leaning so close he could have kissed her.

"Don't bully me, C.D."

"Is that what you call this?" Pressing harder, letting her feel his arousal, he could see her eyes widen, and could tell she, too, was now thinking of other choice words besides bullying. Her lips slackened, her eyes became temporarily glazed with response, and the soft pant of her quickening breath only served to make him more aware of how perfect they'd been together. "You liked being with me last night, Eloise. Say it."

She tried to scoot past him, but he wasn't about to let her go. "That was last night, C.D.—" Her voice sounded strangled. "This is today."

Something he didn't even know he had inside him suddenly ached. "Quit it. Don't ruin this, Eloise. You're going to make me wish I don't feel the way I do."

"Whatever way you feel will pass," she assured hotly.

"What makes you say that?"

"Because with you and other women it always has."

His hand loosened, the palm sliding to her elbow. As he felt her body heat seeping through the warm flannel gown and into the very fiber of his being, he cursed himself for not being better able to control the wild lust that was still flooding him. Didn't she know what she did to him? "You're different and you know it, Eloise."

"Maybe they thought they were different, too." Her voice quickly turned into the sort of plea that always made him do her bidding. "C.D., you don't mean what you're saying. I know you. You feel this way right now, but—"

"Don't tell me what I feel. Last night, I was holding Belle and pretending she was ours. I was imagining we were living together, Eloise, starting a family."

"You don't know what you're saying!"

"Of course I do."

"You're still under the influence of sex."

"Yeah," he agreed. "And it was the best sex I ever had."

Eyes widening, she tried to slip once more from where he'd pinned her to the counter, but he grasped her wrist and hauled her back. The soft crush of her unhindered breasts against his chest made him draw in a sudden, deep steadying breath that carried her heady scent. "Dammit," he bit out. "You might bring out the best in me, but now I see you can bring out the worst, too."

She looked like a cornered rat. "Just go home, C.D. I'm begging you."

For the life of him, he couldn't understand. "I know you have feelings for me. No woman could have given me what you did last night if it wasn't so. Cory's right. We've been a couple for years. And last night..." His big hands circled her waist, anger and lust mingling as he drew in the thick, deep scent of her hair. "Eloise," he continued, his voice barely audible, "I can still smell our lovemaking. And I think you're running away. You're just scared because of how it was growing up with your father."

"This has nothing to do with my father!"

Looking into eyes that had turned defensive and wary, he realized he'd hit the brick wall of truth, and the closest thing C.D. had ever felt to hatred welled up inside him for the man who'd raised her. No doubt, Terrance Hunter had his own troubles, but Eloise had never stopped offering him her heart. The ravages were obvious every time C.D. picked her up at the airport after a visit. Her father never called, visited or acknowledged her gifts.

"Get out, C.D."

She meant it. Sometimes Eloise could talk about her childhood, but now C.D. realized she actually felt threatened by the idea of someone caring about her. And her need for love was so deep that she couldn't even speak it; her fear of abandonment so great, she wouldn't even try.

"Right now you're acting every bit as cold as he is, Eloise," C.D. couldn't help but growl in frustration. "And you'd better think about it. It's you who's destroying what could be between us. Maybe that's what your dad did after your mother died. Maybe he got scared and walked out before something between you two ever began. But growing up to be your father's daughter won't help matters."

Her posture had gone rigid, her shoulders ramrod straight, her chin tilted up, her gaze haughty. "I don't know what you're talking about, C.D. Valentine."

His gray eyes held hers like a vise. "I'm damning the fact this is happening," he admitted. "Damning it because I've known you such a long time, Eloise. I've watched you, and I know you waste too much time seeking approval from strangers. Now, I can see you don't want a man, and you don't want me. You're after something a lot safer—school activities, baby-sitting other peoples' kids, being a block representative. You spend your time impressing people you barely know, like those nurses at the hospital. But what's in it for you?

"Your relationship with your father never allowed you to ask that question, did it? No," C.D. continued, answering himself. "Because things were set up so Terrance Hunter always got it all. And now that you could ask that question, you still don't. You know why? Because you don't have the guts to claim some love for yourself." Just before he turned and headed toward the hallway, he said, "You know what else I think?"

She'd gone stark white, the color draining from her face. "No. And I don't care to hear."

"I think letting a man into your life would mean facing the one truth you never could."

If he had any doubt, the look she offered him now said he'd gone too far. She hated him. "Which is?"

"That your father never loved you."

Tears of fury sprang to her eyes as he moved toward the hallway. "Where do you're think you're going?" she demanded.

"Exactly where you told me to," he said over his shoulder. "Home."

Chapter Six

ELOISE NEVER WANTED to speak to C.D., not that he'd care. Despite what he'd said, two years of knowing him had taught her to read him like a book. He'd spend the evening at the club, and by tomorrow—or at least within the week—he'd have a new infatuation with a woman he could add to the long list of Bonnies, Connies, Missys, Nancys and Corys.

"And Eloises," Eloise whispered, still shaking with anger. Even if she wasn't so sure her assessment was correct and that C.D.'s feelings for her didn't run as deep as he said, she'd never speak to him again. The things he'd said about her were simply too cruel. She just wished he was even more honest. He'd long thought of her as a sister, not a love object, and now he was only professing his feelings as a way of assuaging his guilt over what happened.

Dread filled her as his heavy footsteps trudged from the bedroom back down the hallway, and as he approached, she braced herself for another exchange. Instead of coming into the kitchen, though, he headed for the front door. So, *that's* how much he wanted to avoid her. She winced as the door opened and shut with a resounding thud, her bright, fiery anger fading to a dull ache. Last night was everything she'd dreamed of sharing with a man—and with C.D.—but it wasn't worth losing their friendship.

As she picked up the toddler—who'd been busy messily feeding herself applesauce—the instinctive twining of Belle's arms around her neck filled her with unwanted emotion. When the doorbell rang, her heart lurched. Had the door locked? Did C.D. want back inside?

"No," she quickly murmured, blinking back tears. "I bet it's your dad, Belle." Glad for the distraction, she quickly straightened her face, slipped into the robe that matched her gown, then put Belle down to slip on her coat.

"That's a good girl," she said, pressing her lips to Belle's temple. Belle had been so frightened and lonely without her father, but now she was clinging to Eloise, her small chubby fingers flexing, grasping fistfuls of the robe. Sighing, training her mind off of C.D., which was next to impossible, Eloise hugged Belle close, the powdery baby scent reminding her that C.D. was right. She did want a child of her own. Desperately.

The only thing C.D. had been wrong about was his own feelings. Claiming to love her, she was sure, was just his way of grappling with their overstepping the bounds of friendship. But even if he apologized, she couldn't forgive the things he'd said. Or stand to be so close to what she could never have. Dammit, he was wrong about her not wanting to accept love. If C.D. was really offering it, she would…

Wouldn't she?

Fighting the tears pressing at her eyes, she lifted Belle's car seat from the table and started down the hallway, the toddler following beside her. Eloise noted that C.D. had left the diaper bags beside the front door. The show of thoughtfulness disarmed her, and she was still trying to swallow the lump in her throat when she swung open the door. "Annie?" Eloise squinted. What was her friend doing with Tom Cornell?

"'Morning, Eloise.'' With a toss of her blond hair, Annie grinned, hugging an arm around Tom's waist. Looking relieved, Tom leaned to pick up his daughter and give her a hug, murmuring a loving greeting.

"Are you two together? Where's your car?" Eloise asked Annie, staring into the yard as Annie's three boys tumbled from Tom's car and ran into the snow, packing snowballs.

"Hey, Eloise!" they shouted.

She managed a wave.

"We just dropped the other car at Tom's house," said Annie. "You wouldn't believe what all happened. It's a long story."

"Care to come in and tell it?" Eloise's eyes darted between Annie and Tom, lingering on the man who had caused her such distress, although what happened with C.D. gave new meaning to the word.

"You don't need to look at him like that," Annie assured her. "I'll explain everything, although we can't stay. I've got to get the boys to the sitter, then go to the hospital. Really, I would have called—"

"And I would have told you more yesterday," Tom interjected quickly, his concerned gaze flickering to Belle. "Believe me, I had no idea I'd be gone all night, Eloise. I knew Belle was in good hands, of course, but I was—"

"In love," piped in Annie with a sweet, girlish giggle. "That's what Tom said. He drove up to Braxton County, just to tell me that. All night, we tried to call, but the phones never came back on. I told him not to worry about Belle, especially since as of this morning you hadn't left a message on his machine at home."

"I figured if I told you who I was," Tom

continued, "you'd call Annie and warn her..."
He glanced down, his brown eyes warming as
they fixed on Annie's. "Since it was Valentine's
Day, I had to tell her how I felt." Chuckling, he
related the story of his ill-fated drive to Annie's
cabin, then he finished by saying, "I can't thank
you enough. Like I said, we started to call this
morning, but it was so early when we left."

"And we were sure you'd be asleep," Annie
added.

"The boys were acting up in Annie's car,"
Tom continued, "so we drove straight through."

Annie added, "We were following each other
on the interstate."

Eloise was struck by the easy way they finished each other's sentences. Smiles lit their
eyes, their cheeks were ruddy with the cold, and
their excited voices tumbled over each other
while their mingled breath fogged the crisp air.
No two people could have been more in love.
Her heart wrenched inside her. Last night, she'd
had such a taste of this.

"Belle was a sweetheart," she managed to assure.

Suddenly she felt as if her heart was being
torn in two because deep down she wanted what
Annie and Tom shared. C.D.'s voice sounded in
her head. *I've waited all my life for something*

like last night to happen. Why did he have to be so delusional? Why couldn't he have meant it? *What makes you so sure he didn't?*

"What?" she suddenly said, realizing Annie had spoken.

"I hope watching Belle didn't interfere with any plans last night."

Eloise shook her head. "C.D. came over."

Annie frowned. "C.D. Valentine?"

As if there was another. "He took me to the hospital, and we figured out that Belle belonged to Tom." Fighting the quiver of her chin, she tried to forget what happened afterward. She glanced at Tom. "I saw the sticker on your bumper when you dropped her off."

Tom rushed into another long apology. When he finished, he said, "This really was a first for me. Belle's never been anywhere overnight, and I was sure I'd only be gone a few hours. I did want to surprise Annie."

"You said." Suddenly feeling as if she might start crying in front of Tom and Annie, she forced an even brighter smile. "Actually I thought Annie might be harboring secret feelings for you."

Annie laughed. "You did? How did you guess?"

"The strength of your denial. You fixed him

up with every woman we know except yourself.''

Annie couldn't have looked more delighted.
''I suppose I did! The boys said I've been crazy
about him for months.''

''Well, Annie,'' Tom said, smiling. ''Next
time they tell you you're crazy about me, I want
you to listen. Meantime, I guess it's time to take
home my favorite little hellion, Eloise. To tell
you the truth, I can't believe you said she's been
a sweetheart.''

''She wasn't at first,'' Eloise admitted, reaching out to stroke Belle's soft cheek. ''Bye-bye,
little one.''

At her words, Belle's lower lip trembled. She
drew in a shaky breath and released a loud, gulping sob, her dark eyes injured and sulky, dark-
ening with betrayal.

Tom bounced his daughter on his hip and
slipped off Eloise's necklace. ''She's about to
blow. Here. This must be yours.''

''Let her keep it. I haven't worn it for years.''

''Thanks, but...'' Tom pressed the necklace
into Eloise's hand, ''it's yours.''

''There now, Belle,'' Annie cooed in soft, assuring tones as she reached inside the front door
and lifted Belle's diaper bags. ''We'll be seeing
Eloise again.''

"No doubt about it, Belle," Eloise rejoined. As Tom and Annie went down the porch steps, Eloise looped the necklace through her fingers, the beads feeling as comforting as an old-fashioned rosary. Annie called to the boys and, despite their shouted protests, they ran for the car, spilling inside while Annie and Tom situated Belle. One really could find love overnight, Eloise supposed. Annie's boys were peering curiously at Belle, probably contemplating how it might feel to be big brothers, and right before Annie offered a jaunty wave, Tom gave her a smacking kiss.

Eloise waved back, and when she realized Annie wasn't even watching, her hand stilled in the air. She became conscious of the cold wind whispering against her palms and of the snow flurries melting on her fingertips. Watching the car pull away, she felt a familiar, bone-deep sadness mix with her happiness for Annie, the same sadness that always came when she found herself abruptly left alone. It was a feeling every bit as old as her mother's death. "Sad but true," she whispered to herself.

Realizing she was freezing, Eloise turned and went inside, and with the jocular cries of Annie's boys still ringing in her ears, the house seemed eerily quiet. C.D.'s laughter was here, too, and pushing away another fit of threatening temper, she headed for the jewelry box. Just as she dropped the necklace inside, she glanced into the bureau mirror. Behind her, the bed was still unmade, as was the one in the guest room.

Trying to forget how good C.D. had looked, sprawled across the quilt, she glanced down again and, seeing her father's cuff links, recalled how hard she'd tried to win his love. By the age of five, her heart had broken at least a thousand times when Terrance Hunter had waved goodbye, or when she'd eaten alone after being served by housekeepers who never stayed very long.

The monogrammed letters TH were etched on the square gold links in masculine double-lined print. The night he'd given them to her, she'd disobeyed the housekeeper, snuck from bed, gone downstairs to wait for him, and promptly fallen asleep on the steps. She remembered him shaking her, how her eyes had opened to his, tired from a hard day's work.

"Aren't you supposed to be in bed?"

She'd shaken her head. "I wanted to see you, Daddy."

Rising, he'd shrugged from a wool coat and draped it casually over a chair. "You'd better get back upstairs, pumpkin. Why don't you put these away?''

Pumpkin. The endearment was such a small thing, but more than Eloise had come to expect, and in her hands, the gold links he handed her were like special stones or good luck charms, magical talismans that held real power. Just like Belle, she'd always secretly thought they'd bring her father back. But they never did. C.D. was right. She'd lost Terrance Hunter the day her mother died.

But had his selfishness made her unable to recognize another man's giving spirit? Was Eloise so accustomed to being unloved that she couldn't even recognize affection?

''What if I'm wrong about C.D.?'' She couldn't quite believe it, but what if...?

Opening a drawer, she took the first pair of jeans from the stack, thrust her legs into them, then pulled off her gown and tossed it to the armchair. Tugging on a sweater, she tried to ignore the hammering of her heart. ''Whatever you do, don't stop and think.'' Maybe C.D. was assuaging guilt. Or maybe they'd have a love affair that wouldn't last. Maybe Eloise had already lost his friendship. But at least she was going to find out.

''Really,'' she whispered, fiercely trying to

convince herself she was doing the right thing as she jammed bare feet into moccasins and curled her fingers over the cuff links once more. "Maybe I'm wrong about him."

And for the first time in her life, the man she was talking about wasn't her father.

HE WAS WAITING FOR HER.

C.D. hadn't realized it, but when he saw Eloise fling open her side door, he became conscious that he was staring through the window in the top portion of his Dutch kitchen door, across the expanse of their joined side yards, his angry eyes narrowed as if his gaze could melt the snow.

Things'll be fine, he'd been thinking. Someone else could water the plants when he went out of town. He wouldn't have to mow her grass anymore, and Annie could pick her up at the airport when she visited her father. Sure, for a while things would be awkward, but maybe C.D. would make it easy on himself and simply sell his house. He wanted a bigger one, anyway. He was sick of this neighborhood. At least that's what he told himself.

Biting back a curse, he watched her come down the porch steps, and he wondered which would be worse—living next door and never speaking, or never even seeing her again. At best, he imagined their relationship evolving into a choreographed system of strained smiles and halfhearted waves across the lawn. Whatever she intended to say now was only going to make things worse, he was sure of it.

"Well, are you coming over or not?" he muttered, wishing he hadn't seen Annie and Tom Cornell pick up Belle. C.D. didn't know why those two were together, but watching Annie's boys roughhousing in the yard only reminded C.D. of his brothers, and of how much he wanted boys of his own.

Eloise wasn't wearing a coat, just jeans and a sweater, and strong gusts of wind were lifting hair she hadn't bothered to comb. Still disheveled from their lovemaking, it whipped around her face. Bracing himself, he stepped onto the porch, feeling cold wind rushing through the chambray shirt he'd worn yesterday, and when he stared at Eloise, he was actually encouraged to see the determined gleam in her eyes.

Fighting with her, he suddenly decided, was better than nothing. In fact, the closer she got, the more repentant C.D. felt. While he didn't much care for Terrance Hunter, the man was Eloise's father; Eloise loved him, and maybe that's all that should count. With a start, C.D.

realized the gleam in her eyes was tears, and so, by the time she came charging up his steps, his emotions had done a three-sixty and his heart was thudding with hope.

She didn't say a word, only opened a palm, her slender, pink-tipped fingers uncurling, exposing some cuff links. Squinting, C.D. plucked them, his thumb smoothing the gold surface of one, his eyes registering her father's initials. And without a word being spoken, C.D. suddenly understood. By giving up these objects to him, she was signifying her decision to exchange the false hope she'd always held for her father's love for something more real with C.D. Even if she couldn't say it, her eyes were begging him for what her father never offered: love and the promise that C.D. would never abandon her.

It was a promise he knew he could make.

"I don't know," she whispered. "They were in the jewelry box, and I just..." She drew in a sudden, sharp breath. "Oh, C.D.," she said quickly. "You were right about my father—it just hurts to hear it. And you know how I feel about you, don't you? But I..." Her voice caught. "After last night, I was afraid of losing you, and if we..."

Pocketing the cuff links, he glided his hands around her waist. "We can't go back to the way things were," he said gently, leaning down, his cheek brushing hers.

"No," she agreed nervously. "We can't."

"Are you ready to say you'll marry me, Eloise? I meant what I said."

Her eyes communicated that she was, but she said, "I don't know if I can. Let's take it slow, C.D."

The only thing slow was the smile that spread across his face. "You're scared," he said, wrapping his strong arms more tightly around her, "but I can convince you to want more from me."

She glanced up, pain flooding her eyes. "C.D., I don't know if I..."

He knew she was talking about giving herself to him on a deeper level. "I know you can."

"How?"

He thought of the blanket she'd made for his sister. "Because you're a perfectionist. You always get things right. C'mon, come inside where it's warmer," he urged, pulling her across the threshold into the kitchen. "I'll start convincing you."

"It *is* warmer," she said, her voice catching with emotion.

"Eloise," he promised, "you're going to be amazed by what we can do together. It can get so much warmer than anything you've ever felt." He wanted to say that his loving family would accept her as one of their own, and that he could teach her whatever he knew about love, but instead C.D.'s lips found hers. Her small, firm mouth yielded, imparting heartfelt need that no other woman had ever come close to expressing with him, and he suddenly realized it was Eloise, not him, who'd teach the lessons of loving. "Never thought I'd wind up with the girl next door."

Leaning back a fraction, he was glad to see her tear-filled eyes sparkling, making her look like the same old Eloise he knew, and now realized he loved.

"I haven't said yes to anything, C.D.," she warned.

"Oh, really?"

"Really."

But as he closed the kitchen door on the bitter cold winter morning, her arms wrapped around his waist, feeling warmer than anything C.D. had ever encountered, and he knew what Eloise did—that their fate was sealed.

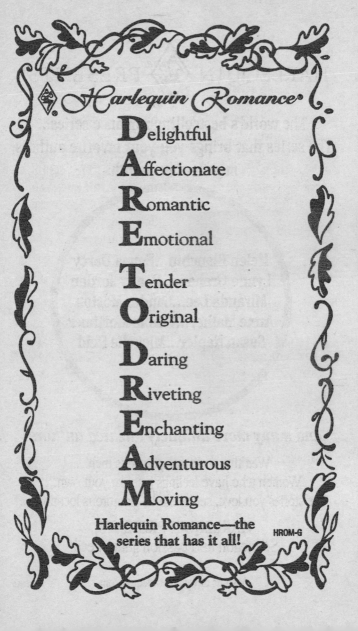

Harlequin Romance®

Delightful
Affectionate
Romantic
Emotional

Tender
Original

Daring
Riveting
Enchanting
Adventurous
Moving

Harlequin Romance—the
series that has it all!

HROM-G

Harlequin®
Historical

From rugged lawmen and
valiant knights to defiant heiresses
and spirited frontierswomen,
Harlequin Historicals will
capture your imagination with
their dramatic scope, passion
and adventure.

Harlequin Historicals…
they're too good to miss!